The SECRET *of* ST. CHRISTOPHER'S GIRLS SCHOOL

DAVID CROWLEY

First Edition

NEWMAN SPRINGS PUBLISHING
320 Broad Street
Red Bank, NJ 07701

First originally published by Newman Springs Publishing 2021

ISBN 978-1-63881-100-8 (Paperback)
ISBN 978-1-63881-101-5 (Digital)

Printed in the United States of America

Prologue

In 1967, St. Christopher's Girls School was a highly respected private school. Its widely recognized high academic standards had caused it to be regarded as one of the best boarding schools in the Midwest. Soon after its founding in 1897, it was already attracting students from across the country.

Most of its students came from well-to-do families who were quick to help the school financially whenever asked. As a result, the school expanded and prospered, replacing some of the original older buildings, including the wooden school itself and the girls' living quarters, while maintaining the sandstone church and convent. It purchased some of the surrounding land and built a wall to give the girls a private outdoor space.

At present, it seemed the perfect place for a family to send their daughters to receive a quality education in a disciplined environment. But all was not as it seemed. Inside those well-regarded walls, there was a secret, passed on through the years. But secrets have a way of being brought out into the light, and when Sister Margaret Mary was found stabbed to death in her room, the secret was in danger. Once exposed, could the forces that protected it be discovered and stopped before more bodies were found?

Chapter 1

The lights came on at 6:30 as they did every morning, controlled by Sister Willibald's hand in the main office. Off at 10:00 p.m., on at 6:30 a.m. Only on Saturday were the girls allowed to sleep until 8:00.

Marjorie wiped the sleep out of her eyes, stretched, and heaved a long sigh.

After allowing herself a few moments to steel herself for the day, she pulled the covers aside and swung her feet over the side of the bed and stood up. There was no time for more than a few moments. Mass was at 6:45, and she couldn't be late.

Her room was a typical dormitory room. A closet just inside the door along the right wall held the few clothes she needed. A few uniform skirts and blouses and her uniform jacket and gym clothes, which were also all the same uniform style. The girls were permitted only three sets of street clothes plus, of course, sufficient underwear and socks. A small dresser inside the closet held those smaller items.

Her bed was further along the right wall with the headboard against the outer wall, which contained a small window. A desk and chair were against the left wall as was a three-shelf bookcase. A small sink was in the left corner of the outer wall. The girls showered in a community shower at the end of the hall.

She washed her face quickly at the small sink then brushed her teeth. The same routine every morning. As she turned to go to the closet to get her uniform, she glanced at the clock to make sure she was on schedule.

"What?" she thought. *"Five thirty-seven? That can't be right. The power must have gone out."*

"Damn it!" she muttered, "Now I don't know if I'm on time or not."

As she hurriedly threw off her nightgown and started dressing, she realized what she had said. She closed her eyes, clasped her hands together and quickly whispered, "Father, forgive me for my language," then continued dressing.

She brushed her hair at the small mirror above the sink. As she put the brush down, she kept her eyes on the mirror.

"Why wasn't I born with blonde hair—or even black?" she asked out loud. "This mousy brown is so lifeless. And my eyes. They're too small and too close together. Guys want girls with huge eyes and big, long lashes."

She was about to start in on her pale complexion when there was a knock on her door.

"Marge, it's Sarah. Can I come in?"

Sarah had the room next to Marjorie's.

"Yeah, sure."

As the door opened, Marjorie felt a twinge of jealousy. Sarah Collins was the most beautiful girl in the school. Everyone agreed on that, everyone except Sarah herself. She was blonde with those big eyes and lashes, and every other feature on her face was perfectly proportioned. Her body was lithe and perfectly proportioned as well. She was the envy of all the girls, yet when anyone complimented her she always seemed embarrassed and uncomfortable.

"What do you think's going on?" she asked, clearly excited. "Why did they get us up so early?"

"Must have been a power outage. The clocks are just wrong."

"No, they're not. The word's being passed that Sister Mary Joseph said we're supposed to report to the assembly right away. It's gotta be something serious."

"Well, you know more than I do. I haven't been out of my room. I guess we'd better get to the assembly."

They hurried into the hall. Marjorie's curiosity was causing her to almost run, but the crowded hall kept her from going as fast as she wanted to go. She was still able to make her way past several girls while Sarah fell behind and was lost in the sea of uniforms.

The Assembly Room was also the school study hall. It was a large room with a high ceiling, at least twenty feet high. There were twenty rows of twelve desks per row facing a stage at the front of the room with a wide aisle in the middle. A set of double doors at the back led to the girls' quarters. Another set at the front to the right of the stage led to the school. The large windows on both side walls were covered by dark curtains, meant to keep the girls from being distracted by the world outside while they studied. Each of the girls was assigned a desk where they could keep their books and school supplies.

As the flow of girls entered the assembly and each went to her desk, Marjorie noticed something unusual. Only Mother Superior, Sister Mary Joseph, who was widely recognized as Mother's second in command, and Father Jerome, the school's priest-in-residence and pastor of the adjoining St. Christopher's church, were on the stage. When there was an assembly, all the nuns were always on the stage. The assemblies had, in fact, come to be referred to over the years by the girls as "penguin gatherings".

Something else unusual caught her eye as she looked around the room. Off to the left side of the stage was a man, clearly not a priest, standing in the corner almost as if he wanted to not be noticed. Something about him gave her the impression that he was a detective. Maybe it was the suit, maybe the way he stood watching them, but there was definitely the look of a detective.

She looked over her shoulder toward the door at the back of the room. The last few girls were trickling in.

OK, let's get this started, she thought, her curiosity now risen to an almost unendurable level by the unusual things she had noticed.

"Thanks for leaving me in the dust."

She turned to find Sarah seating herself at the desk next to her.

"I'm sorry. I just wanted to get here and find out what's going on. It's something big, I know it is."

Sarah was about to reply when the rap of a gavel brought the murmuring in the room to an immediate silence. As the girls turned their attention to the stage, they could see that something was wrong. Mother Superior was always a tower of strength, always in control, always calm. Now she looked tired and almost lifeless. As she began to speak, it was clear that it was taking every bit of strength that she had.

"What I am about to tell you is both deeply saddening and deeply frightening. I have tried to find a way to tell you this that would ease the sadness and lessen the fear, but there is no way other than to tell you the facts."

As Mother Superior paused, the silence was unbearable. Marjorie looked around the room at the other girls. They were all looking at each other with a question in their eyes, a question they were all fearful to have answered. Mother Superior's voice turned them back to the stage.

"I have the most dreadful task of telling you that Sister Margaret Mary was found dead early this morning."

The room burst into a loud collective gasp followed by cries of "Oh, no!" "It can't be!" then the clamor of girls all talking at once. The gavel brought silence again, broken only by the sound of soft crying. Sister Margaret Mary was one of the oldest nuns, so her death may not have been unexpected, but she was also the favorite of many of the girls. That fact was apparent from the number of girls who were quietly sobbing. Marjorie noticed that Sarah seemed to be crying harder than any of the other girls. Wondering why, she tried to get her attention without success. As Mother Superior continued, she turned back to the stage.

"The other thing I must tell you is the most difficult, not only to tell you, but to face, but it must be told as you must be prepared for what will happen here in the next several days. There are many questions that will be asked and many answers that will hopefully be found."

She paused. Clearly what she had to say next was difficult for her.

"I must regretfully tell you that Sister Margaret Mary was murdered."

This time, the gasp was followed by a silence as the shock made the girls unable to comprehend what they had just heard. One voice broke the silence.

"How, Mother?"

All eyes turned toward Marjorie standing next to her desk.

Mother Superior stood at the podium, looking uneasy, not really sure what to say. She looked over toward the man in the corner, who then moved to the side of the stage as Mother Superior walked over to meet him. After a short conversation, during which the girls all watched in silence, looking now and then at Marjorie who had remained standing, Mother Superior returned to the podium with the man closely behind her. She looked at Marjorie as she spoke.

"You may sit down, Marjorie."

Marjorie sat, suddenly feeling somewhat uncomfortable as she became aware of the many eyes that were focused on her. Mother Superior indicated the man next to her. She seemed to have regained her strength and was now in control of the situation.

"This is Detective Steven McLean. He was called here after Sister's body was found. He has advised me that any other information about Sister's death should be held in confidence. His investigation will require a certain amount of secrecy if it is to be successful in finding the heinous person who committed this despicable crime." She was fighting now to maintain her self-control. "I will now turn the podium over to Detective McLean. You will give him your undivided attention now and your full cooperation during his investigation."

Detective McLean moved to the podium, thanking Mother Superior as she stepped away. Now that he was more clearly in view, Marjorie was able to observe him more closely. He was tall and, she thought, good-looking, also much younger than she would have expected a police detective to be. His hair was a little long, too, for a man in his position. It made him look unprofessional, but she had to admit to herself that it made him look a little sexy. After all, the Beatles had all the girls wanting to run their fingers through their hair.

What are you doing? she thought. *Sister Margaret Mary's been murdered and you're checking out the detective? Get a grip, girl.* She shook her head and looked back toward the stage. The detective was looking over the room as if he was searching their faces, waiting to see a sign of guilt in one of them. He seemed to pause when his gaze fell on Marjorie, and she shifted uncomfortably in her seat. She felt like he was staring at her and that all the girls could see that he was. As he moved on past her, she wondered what he might be thinking. Did she look guilty to him? Did she make herself look guilty because she didn't just sit still? Why did he seem to look longer at her than the others? What were the others thinking? As the questions raced through her mind, she heard him begin to speak.

She listened, trying to quiet the questions as she did, but they kept coming until she questioned every move she made. Were her hands in the right position on the desk? Should she put them in her lap? Could the others around her see that she was starting to tremble? Could he see it as he looked back and forth around the room as he spoke?

Caught up in her questions, she could hear him talking but really didn't hear much of what he was saying. There was something about feeling sure that none of them were in any danger and something about staying in their rooms.

She knew whatever he was saying was important, and she tried harder to listen. As she concentrated on listening, a sound in her right ear made her turn to find Sarah still crying, looking down at her desk with a blank expression on her face and whispering something so inaudibly that Marjorie could only see her lips moving. She was about to reach across the aisle to ask what was wrong when Mother Superior's voice brought her attention back to the stage once more.

The detective had finished, and Mother Superior had again taken her place at the podium. The familiarity of her voice caused Marjorie to forget all the questions for a while.

"Thank you, Detective McLean. I'm sure the girls will all follow your instructions and cooperate in every way. Now, girls, you will return to your rooms as the detective instructed and stay there until breakfast, which will be served at 7:45 as usual. You will not talk about this while moving through the halls or during breakfast. A Mass for Sister Margaret Mary will be said later today and you will be informed of the time. Classes are suspended for today, and you are to stay in your rooms except during breakfast and the Mass or if otherwise notified. I suggest that you spend your time praying for Sister and for the perpetrator of this terrible crime to be found quickly. It would also be good to reflect on the fragility of our lives and the need to live them so as to be prepared to be called by God without warning. You are now dismissed to return quietly to your rooms. Marjorie Johnson, you will please remain in the assembly."

Marjorie felt the blood rush to her face as embarrassment and fear engulfed her whole body. The questions were back, whirling furiously through her mind. She looked down at her desk, knowing every girl who passed was looking at her as they did, wondering what she had done to be singled out like this, thinking it must be something terrible, even maybe that she was the one who did it.

Finally, the room was empty. She was still looking down, but she knew from the silence that everyone was gone. She raised her head slowly, wondering what horrible fate awaited her. She hadn't done anything wrong—she knew she hadn't—yet she felt like a criminal. It was the worst feeling she had ever felt. Her earlier concern for Sarah had been crushed beneath her fear and forgotten.

As she looked up, she saw Mother Superior and the detective standing at the front of the row of desks that hers was in. Mother Superior motioned for her to come forward.

"Come here, Marjorie. The detective would like to talk to you."

Marjorie swallowed hard. Whatever was going to happen, she had to face it. She forced herself to her feet then walked slowly toward the front of the room, steadying herself on the desks as she went.

Mother Superior watched her with a puzzled look.

"Marjorie, what's wrong? Don't you feel well?"

"Oh, Mother, I didn't do anything wrong, I swear it!"

She had reached the first desk in line and she dropped into the seat.

"Oh, Marjorie, no one thinks you did."

It took a few seconds for that to sink in. Suddenly she felt better.

"Really! I thought..."

"Thought what? That we thought you did it? This is one time you shouldn't have done so much thinking."

"Then why...?"

"Detective McLean said he wanted to meet you. He was intrigued by your question."

Marjorie felt confused. All she did was ask a question she thought was a perfectly logical one.

"Intrigued?"

The detective stepped forward and held out his hand.

"I'm Detective McLean. Yes, intrigued. You were the only one who seemed to want to know more about what happened. You asked how she was killed. Why?"

Marjorie didn't know what to make of all this. The fear was slowly draining out of her now that she knew she wasn't in trouble, but why was a simple question so important to this detective? As she tried to figure it out, Mother Superior broke into her thoughts.

"Marjorie, the detective asked you a question. Don't you think you should answer him?"

"Yes, Mother. It's just that I don't know what to say. It just seemed like the logical thing to ask. I thought everyone would know that."

Mother Superior stiffened.

"Marjorie, don't be impertinent! That's no way to speak to an adult!"

The detective chuckled.

"It's all right, Mother Superior. It's actually the answer I was hoping to get."

His remark took them both by surprise. Now they both wondered what this was all about.

He sat at the desk next to Marjorie and smiled. It was a friendly smile, and she felt that whatever he wanted it wasn't anything to be afraid of.

"You're a curious girl, aren't you?" he asked.

"Yes, sir. I guess so."

"If I'm right, you're the kind of girl who notices things, who remembers things she hears, and who tries to figure out what it all means. You ask questions other girls your age don't even think about, like today. You ask important questions, either out loud or sometimes, I think, just in your mind. I think you may be just the girl I need to help me."

"Help you? How?"

Mother Superior felt the need to cut in.

"Detective, you didn't mention anything like this. You should have discussed this with me first. I'm not about to put one of my girls in a situation that could endanger her."

"I'm sorry, Mother Superior. I probably should have said something, but there's no danger involved. I just need someone in among the girls who can listen and pay attention when she does. Someone may have seen something unusual but doesn't think it has anything to do with the murder or is maybe afraid to come forward for some reason. These girls talk among themselves, I know they do. All she has to do is keep her eyes and ears open. If she comes across something she thinks is important, she can let me know."

"Well, you may be right. I don't really like the idea, but if you can assure me that no danger is involved, I'll allow her to help you... It's her decision."

She stood directly in front of the desk and looked down at Marjorie.

"So it's up to you, Marjorie. You can say no if you want to. It's a great responsibility, so if you say yes remember that responsibility can be a burden at times. Detective McLean says there's no danger, and I hope he's right, but even among young girls, there are secrets, and where there are secrets, there may be danger. Think this over carefully before you decide."

Marjorie sat quietly, gathering her thoughts. Mother Superior was right. Girls do have secrets. She already knew many of them. None of them was dangerous, only embarrassing to the girls who had them. A few might get a girl in trouble but nothing more than a detention or a shift in the kitchen. The murder could change things, but it was unlikely that any of the girls would know anything that was connected to it. The dormitory was on one end of the school and the convent was on the other end. A girl would have to be crazy enough to break a lot of rules to be anywhere near the murder. She was certain she'd come up with nothing, but the idea of helping the police, undercover at that, made her feel important, even if no one else would ever know.

"I'll do it. I probably won't find anything important, but I'll do my best."

Mother Superior drew in a deep breath.

"You're certain about this, Marjorie?"

"Yes, Mother. Don't worry. I'll be careful. Even if I do hear something, no one will ever know who told."

Detective McLean reached his hand across the aisle.

"Okay, partner, let's shake on the deal."

He shook her hand, then his tone became serious.

"I don't know if you'll find out anything, but I wouldn't have you do this if I didn't think that there's a possibility you might. Make sure you don't let on to anyone what you're doing. I don't think it would put you in danger, but if the girls know that you're listening for me, someone who might know something would clam up when you were around."

"I won't let you down, Detective."

"Hey, we're partners. Just call me Steve. But not when anyone else is around."

"Okay, Steve."

Mother Superior shook her head.

"I'm still not comfortable with this, but you seem to know what you're doing, Detective. Marjorie, you may return to your room now."

"Yes, Mother."

She headed into the hall and walked slowly back to her room, reveling in her newfound status. Some of the girls had left their doors open, and she hurried past them looking straight ahead, trying to avoid being asked why she had been made to stay. It all went well until she passed Paula Harris's room, where Paula was standing in the doorway talking across the hall to Brenda Michaels, who was almost completely out in the hall. There was no way she could get past them before they stopped her.

"So," Paula asked, "what's going on?"

"What do you mean?"

Brenda stood in the middle of the hall with her arms crossed, blocking her way.

"You know what we're talking about. Why'd you have to stay? Was it because of that stupid question you asked?"

That was it! Her excuse. Her way out.

"Yeah. Mother Superior thought it was impertinent and inappropriate. Thankfully, all I got was a lecture, and I had to apologize to that cop for giving him a bad impression of the school."

Paula shook her head.

"Why'd you ask such a dumb question anyway? The old bag's dead. Who cares how it happened?"

"Look, Paula, I don't want to get in an argument. She was a nice old lady, and she died horribly. I don't know how you can be so unfeeling."

Paula's voice was rising along with her anger.

"Oh, everybody knows she had her favorites. You had to kiss up to her to get a good grade. She never gave me more than a C on my English papers."

A voice came down the hall from another room.

"Maybe that's because you're such a crappy writer!"

"Nobody asked for your opinion!"

Marjorie just wanted to get back to her room. She had to stop this before it got out of hand.

"Stop it!" she shouted. "We're not even supposed to be doing this. We're supposed to be in our rooms, and we're not supposed to talk about it. I want to follow the rules even if you don't. Get out of my way so I can get back to my room."

Brenda relaxed and stepped aside.

"Sure, go on. We've got better things to talk about anyway."

Marjorie walked past and went to her room.

Thank God, she thought as she reached her door, *I can finally be alone. I need time to think.*

She opened the door and went in, only to find Sarah sitting on the bed.

"Sarah, what are you doing here? We're supposed to be in our own rooms. You're going to get us both in trouble."

As Sarah stood up and turned toward her, Marjorie saw tears streaming down her cheek.

"Oh, Marge, I've gotta talk to someone. I don't know what to do."

She looked like she was about to faint. Marjorie put her arms around her to steady her.

"Sarah, what's wrong? Tell me what's going on."

"I've got to tell someone. I just can't keep it in any longer."

Chapter 2

Mother Superior's office was a large room, fifteen by twenty-five feet or so. Detective McLean made a quick scan of the room as he entered. The furniture was quite old but in excellent condition. Every piece would probably bring a good price at auction if the sisters were ever in need of money, he thought.

The center of the room was occupied by a large conference table with six chairs on each side and a somewhat larger chair at the near end. Beneath it lay a large Arabian print area rug. Beyond the table in front of the far wall was what was obviously Mother Superior's desk, Queen Anne he thought, with a comfortably padded leather chair behind it. The wall to the right contained a large window, which he estimated to be eight feet wide and twelve feet high. It was covered by a beige lace curtain with a pattern that let light in while keeping prying eyes out. A sofa sat in front of the window with matching wingback chairs to the right and left. A coffee table was set in front of the sofa with a small area rug, whose pattern matched that of the large rug, beneath it. The wall to the left was filled mostly by two bookcases and three filing cabinets, which looked quite out of place among the other furnishings.

Mother Superior had let him in and told him to make himself comfortable while she went to arrange for tea. He had politely told her he was a coffee drinker, and she had said she'd have both brought in.

He was standing near the end of the conference table observing the room when she returned.

"Please sit down, Detective. Your coffee will be here soon."

She indicated the chair to the left of the sofa and seated herself on the sofa in the center.

"Thank you, Mother Superior."

As he sat, a knock on the door was followed by the entrance of a young nun with a tray of coffee and tea and all the required accessories, including a small plate of cookies. The nun poured a cup of coffee.

"Cream and sugar?" she asked.

He shook his head, and she handed him the cup then poured tea and gave the cup to Mother Superior. With a slight bow, she left the room as quietly as she had come.

Detective McLean thought for a moment as he sipped his coffee, trying to find the right words to start the conversation. When he felt he had found them, he spoke.

"Mother Superior, I know this is an unpleasant thing..."

She raised her hand to stop him.

"I'd like to start, Detective, by asking you to address me merely as Mother. The whole thing can get to be a mouthful when you have to say it often and frankly it makes me uncomfortable. I am in charge of this convent and the school and therefore have been given the title, but I don't consider myself to be superior to any of the other sisters, or to anyone else for that matter. It has its place in certain situations, but as you may have noticed, even the girls address me only as Mother."

"Thank you, Mother, and while we're on the subject of names, as you heard me tell Marjorie, I prefer Steve. One syllable instead of three makes everything easier."

"I'll do that. However, in introductions to the staff and girls, I will use your title. I think it's only proper."

"Of course. Now as I was saying, this is an unpleasant thing in itself, but I fear there will be a lot of unpleasantness to come. Having attended a Catholic school I know something about nuns. I'm aware of your need for privacy and I know that my investigation, in order to be complete, will intrude on your privacy. I'll do everything I can to minimize the intrusion, but there will be some. There's just no way to avoid it. I hope you'll understand and cooperate as much as possible."

"In light of the current situation, I understand fully. Whatever consideration you're able to give us will be appreciated."

He thought carefully about his next words.

"There will be a need to search the sisters' living quarters. I know some of them may be uncomfortable with that. I have two very trustworthy and discreet female officers who can perform the search with little disruption to the sisters' privacy."

"Thank you. We're not a cloistered order, so your officers will be allowed in the quarters. I'll speak to the sisters beforehand and reassure them. There will be some grumbling, but nothing I can't handle."

"Well, that's taken care of then. Now to my next concern. I will, of course, have to interview all the sisters. I'll need a list of their names and whatever other information about them that you may be able to give me. It would also be helpful if I could get a drawing of the layout of the sisters' quarters showing who is in each room."

"I think that can be arranged. Sister Martha is our art teacher. I'll have her get to work on it. You should have it by later this afternoon."

"Really, Mother, it doesn't have to be fancy. Just a rough sketch will do."

"I'll tell her that...but you'll still get the equivalent of a blueprint. Sister Martha is very particular about her work."

"All right. I'll have to leave to get things started at the station. When I return, I'll start my interviews."

He stopped to choose his words again.

"Before I do—I hope you won't be offended by this—but is there anything I should know about any of the sisters?"

"Don't worry, I'm not offended. It's a perfectly logical thing to ask. People will always have the impression that women who all dress alike and shut themselves off from the world have something to hide. They picture a convent as something like a madhouse, full of troubled women, hiding some secret from their past, wandering the halls, tearing their hair. That's why we wear our wimples and veils you know."

"That's not what I was thinking, really."

Mother Superior laughed.

"Oh, I know that. I apologize for going off the rails a bit. I think I just need to let things out. It's not easy you know, being the one who has to keep everything together at a time like this."

She sat quietly for a moment. Steve didn't dare to break the silence. Finally, she took a deep breath and got back to business.

"I believe what you'd like to know is whether any of the sisters have any eccentricities that you need to be aware of. The answer to that is, of course, yes. The older ones especially tend to be set in their ways. I mean, we are human. But if you're asking about homicidal tendencies, I can't say that I've ever witnessed anything like that in any of them."

"I was actually thinking along the lines of quick tempers, trouble controlling their anger, things like that. Of course if you do know of any secrets any of them might be hiding I'd want to know that as well."

"Well, Sister Mary Claire can be a pistol at times, but it's normally with the girls. She gets frustrated when they act up in class, and that sets her off. I think the girls do it purposely so they can watch her tirades. I've never known her to get angry with any of the sisters, though."

"Well, it's good to know anyway. If it's possible, I'd like to also get a list of the sisters' names before they became sisters. And if you have any information as to where they came from, their home towns, things like that, it would be helpful."

"In what way? We usually put our old names behind us when we take our vows."

"Well, Mother, since the murder occurred in the sisters' part of the building, the first consideration is that the murderer is one of them. Information about their lives before they became nuns could shed some light on a motive."

"Yes. I see what you mean."

"Good. I think that's all I'll need at this time."

He started to rise, but her next words caused him to sit back down.

"You did mention secrets also."

She paused, then rose and stepped around the coffee table. There was hesitation in her manner and her voice. She walked slowly toward the other side of the room, keeping her back to him, obviously unsure of what his reaction might be to what she was about to say.

"I've been reluctant to tell you this, as it hasn't been mentioned in years, and I hate to bring it up after all this time because I really don't know if it's even relevant to what's happened. The more I've thought about it though, the more I've come to feel you should know."

She turned back to face him, more certain that she had made the right decision.

"Twenty-seven years ago a girl committed suicide here. She hung herself in the church. It had a terrible effect on everyone. The pastor and the Superior were both transferred to positions in other states. From what I understand, though, it was kept quiet in the town. The story that I've heard is that the girl was an orphan, here on a scholarship paid by one of our benefactors. That's about as close to the truth as anyone can get. There have been rumors, but you know how rumors go. Fiction becomes fact and fact becomes fiction until you can't tell one from the other."

"Well, fact or fiction, I'm glad you told me, Mother. It could very well have some connection to all this. Are there any sisters still here who were here then?"

Mother Superior thought for a moment.

"I'm pretty sure Sister Agatha was, and...oh, dear Blessed Mother! I just realized, Sister Margaret Mary was too! She mentioned not long ago that she remembered when Agatha came here thirty years ago."

The importance of what she just said left them both stunned for a moment. Was it possible that the suicide of a girl years ago could somehow be tied to Sister Margaret Mary's murder, or was it just a coincidence that she was at the school when it happened? Either way, it couldn't be overlooked.

Mother Superior moved back to the sofa and sat down.

"Do you think it means anything, Steve?"

"It could. Then again...it might be nothing. One thing I know, though, is that I need to talk to Sister Agatha as soon as possible."

Mother Superior rose and moved to her desk. She lifted the telephone receiver and dialed.

"Sister Mary Joseph, please have Sister Agatha come to my office. Yes, Sister, right away. Thank you."

She hung up the phone and returned to the sofa.

"She'll be here momentarily."

Steve sat back in the chair, considering the possible importance of what he had just been told.

"You know, Mother, this could complicate my investigation considerably. The prospect of trying to get information about something that happened twenty-seven years ago is daunting. It means there may be a number of possible suspects who we may never be able to identify, much less locate. Is it even possible, though, that someone could carry a grudge for something that happened that long ago?"

He became thoughtful again. Mother Superior felt it would be better to not interrupt him. He sat forward and shook his head.

"Mother, can you think of anything that could connect Sister Margaret Mary to this girl?"

"Well, Margaret has been the English teacher all these years, and all the girls are required to take at least three years of English. There are others who teach it as well, but I'm sure the girl would have been in Margaret's class at some point. Other than that, I'm afraid I could only speculate as to possible other contacts."

There was a soft knock on the door. Sister Agatha stepped into the room and nodded in Mother Superior's direction. Mother Superior rose and nodded in return.

"You wanted to see me, Mother."

"Yes, Agatha, please sit down."

She indicated the chair to the right of the sofa. Sister Agatha waited for her to sit then took her seat.

Sister Agatha was, Steve guessed, in her early sixties. She had been good-looking in her younger days, he thought, someone who would have had a lot of interested admirers. Even now, without her habit, she might still be attractive. He couldn't help but wonder what would make a good-looking young woman choose to live her life as a nun. That thought was replaced by something he noticed about her demeanor. She seemed tense as she sat uneasily in the chair. It made him wonder if she may have had an idea why she had been summoned. He was now eager to question her, but aware of the proper protocol, he allowed Mother Superior to take the lead.

"The detective and I have been talking, and something has come up that we feel we need more information about. Since you've been here the longest, we're hoping that you may be able to provide some of that information."

Sister Agatha shifted uneasily in the chair.

"Well, I'll try to help if I can, Mother."

"Excellent. I know you will. The information we're looking for concerns the girl who committed suicide here twenty-seven years ago. You were here then, I believe."

Steve was watching closely. He thought he saw a slight pause in her breathing when Mother Superior mentioned the girl.

"Yes, Mother, I was. I had just completed my novitiate and was assigned here. I was new and not really a part of the inner circle. I was usually left out of any discussions about the matter, so I really don't know how much I can tell you. Father Henry was here at the time. He found her. The poor man was beside himself for days. Well, I suppose I'd have been the same if I had found her. The school had to pay for her burial since her family had no money to speak of."

Mother Superior cut in.

"I thought I heard at one time that she was an orphan."

"She may have been. I thought someone mentioned back then about a poor family and that she had been paid for by a benefactor, but I might be wrong. It's been a long time since I thought about any of that. It's not something I want to think about."

Steve felt they weren't getting anywhere.

"Mother Superior, if I may?"

"Of course, Detective."

He stood and looked directly at Sister Agatha.

"Sister, what we're trying to find out is whether Sister Margaret Mary had any connection to the girl. You were both here at that time and we hoped you might know if Sister Margaret Mary might have been in a position to know something about what happened back then. I know that young girls can sometimes look for an older confidante. In a boarding school environment like this, I'm sure that some girls might find a sister who they look up to and may confide in. Perhaps this girl felt that way about Sister Margaret Mary."

He could see she was uncomfortable. Her hands were gripping the skirt of her habit, and her eyes were averting his.

"I really can't say. If that were the case, she didn't confide in me about it. We know all the girls to some extent every year of course."

She turned to Mother Superior.

"May I go, Mother? I really don't know anything else that I could tell you. I'd just like to forget it all."

She had become like a little girl pleading for her mother's permission to leave. Steve looked at Mother Superior and nodded his okay.

"Yes, Sister, you may leave."

Sister Agatha rose, nodded to Mother Superior, and hurried out of the room.

Steve watched her go and returned to his chair.

"She's hiding something, something that really scares her."

"Yes, I could see that. So what do we do now?"

"I guess we proceed to look for other leads. We need to find the weapon. That stab wound didn't look like it was made with a knife. I'll know more when I see the coroner's report. I'll head back to the station and bring back the people I'm going to need here. I shouldn't be gone for more than an hour or so."

They both rose and started to the door. Mother Superior stopped and turned to Steve.

"Forgive me, Steve, but my curiosity has gotten the best of me. You seem rather young to be a police detective. Are your looks deceiving, or are you just very smart?"

"I don't know about being smart, but I had a very good teacher when I started with the force. When my mentor retired he suggested they put me in his position. They apparently trusted his judgment, and here I am. I haven't encountered anything like this so far, so I hope I'm up to the task."

"From what I've seen so far, I believe you are."

"Thank you, Mother. I'll do my best."

"I feel certain that you will."

He continued to the door and turned back when he reached it.

"Thanks for the coffee."

He opened the door and turned back again in the hall.

"And it might be a good idea to keep an eye on Sister Agatha."

"I was thinking that myself. Goodbye, Steve."

"Goodbye."

Mother Superior closed the door and sat in the chair at the end of the conference table. She closed her eyes, trying to make sense of the situation. Why would someone kill a harmless old woman like Margaret Mary? And what did Agatha know? Was it something that could answer the first question?

"Oh, Agatha, what are you hiding?" she whispered to herself. "What is it you're afraid of?"

Chapter 3

Marjorie helped Sarah onto the bed and sat holding her as she sobbed. She waited until the sobbing subsided a little before she spoke.

"Sarah, please tell me what's going on. Why are you so upset? You're shaking like crazy."

"Oh, it's awful, Marge, just awful! I don't know what I'm gonna do now!"

"What are you going to do about what? What's so bad that it's made you like this?"

Sarah took some deep breaths, trying to stop the sobbing and to work up the courage to tell Marjorie what she had thought no one else would ever know. She bit her bottom lip and clenched her hands tightly, trying to control herself enough to get the words out. With her body as stiff as she could make it, she blurted it out as quickly as she could then broke down again, burying her face in Marjorie's shoulder.

"I'm pregnant, Marge! I'm pregnant! What am I gonna do?"

Marjorie sat stunned, unable to move, unable to even think for a while. Then the thoughts came rushing in, tumbling over one another. She sat silently trying to sort them out, put them in some kind of order. They were thoughts she'd never had before, feelings she didn't understand.

She felt guilty. Why guilty? She didn't do anything wrong. Slowly the answer crept in. It was her jealousy. She liked Sarah, she really did, but there were times now and then when she had been jealous of her. Jealous of her perfect face, her perfect body, her perfect life. But she didn't have a perfect life, did she?

Looking back, how often had she seemed unsure of herself, even when people complimented her? How many times did she seem to shy away when they did? Marjorie had seen those things, but she hadn't realized what they meant.

Now something even worse reared its ugly head. Shame. How many times had her jealousy caused her to wish things weren't so perfect for Sarah? Just some little thing to make her a little more human. Now she realized that what she had wished for had been there all along. She just didn't see it. And now something more terrible than she would have ever wished for had happened. Sarah's life was far from perfect now, and it could never be again.

This girl of whom she had been jealous so many times was now huddled in her arms, trusting her with a secret she felt unworthy to know. She felt unworthy to even be trusted.

She stroked Sarah's hair as she searched for something to say, something that could make it all seem OK. But something else had made its way into her mind. Something she hadn't felt since she was a little girl. It somehow snuck past all the walls she had put up to keep it out. She felt helpless. This girl who was bold enough to stand in the middle of the assembly and ask a question no one else would have dared to ask felt helpless.

"Say something, Marge, please."

Sarah pulled her away from her thoughts, but the helpless feeling wouldn't let go.

"I don't know what to say. I don't even know what to think. This is something I could have never imagined in a million years."

Sarah wiped the last of the tears from her eyes. She had cried herself out and now wanted to talk. Her secret was out, and now she wanted to let it all out. She leaned back out of Marjorie's arms.

"Are you mad at me?"

"Mad? Why would I be mad?"

"Because I'm bad. I'm dirty."

Marjorie pulled her back into her arms.

"You're not bad. And you're not dirty! Don't you ever say that again!"

The force in her voice made Sarah pull away a little, and she realized she had frightened her.

"It's okay. I'm not mad."

"You sure?"

"Well, I am a little, but not because you're in trouble. I'm mad at what you said about being dirty. Doing what you did doesn't make you dirty."

"That's not what the sisters would say."

"Well, the sisters have to say things like that. It's their job."

"But it's still wrong. I can't believe I ever let it happen."

Marjorie realized she hadn't asked the question that had flashed briefly through her mind with all her other thoughts.

"Well, who did you let it happen with?"

Sarah stiffened, stood, and turned away.

"I can't tell you."

Marjorie jumped up from the bed.

"What!? You just trusted me with the biggest secret of your life. Now you won't trust me with the second biggest?"

"It's not like that. I just can't."

"You can't? Or you won't?"

"I don't know. Both I guess."

She started to cry again. Marjorie could see her shoulders shaking. She took her gently by the shoulders and sat her back on the bed.

"It's okay. I won't keep asking."

Sarah was looking down at the floor. She lifted her head just a little and turned partway toward Marjorie.

"Thank you. I'm sorry I can't tell you. I really can't."

She started to cry even more. That and something in the way she said it made Marjorie uneasy. She sensed fear.

"You're afraid of him, aren't you?"

Sarah shook her head, but her crying increased.

"Sarah, please, why are you so afraid? What did he do? Did he rape you? Is that why you're afraid?"

She was shaking her head back and forth, punctuating each swing with "No, no, no, no, no!" her voice rising until she was almost screaming.

She jumped off the bed and turned away again.

"Please, just forget about it, okay!"

"Okay. Okay. I'm sorry. I'm just worried about you. At least he didn't rape you. I couldn't stand to think about that happening to you."

Sarah sat back down. She sighed a heavy sigh. There was a sound of resignation in her voice as she spoke.

"No, he didn't rape me. I wanted it to happen. At least I thought I did. He made me feel good all the time. He'd always say nice things, and I liked being around him. It just felt right at the time. After a while, though, it started to feel wrong. Then when I figured out that I was pregnant, I knew it was wrong and God was punishing me for it."

"God's not punishing you, Sarah. You made a mistake. We all do. More than once. If God punished us for every mistake we made, none of us would survive. But I won't have to ask who it is anymore. I think I figured it out."

"What do you mean?'

"What you said, about how you liked being around him. There's only one guy you've ever had a chance to be around enough to say something like that. It's the gardener's son. The one who comes to help him sometimes. Jack. That's his name, right?"

The color drained from Sarah's face. She jumped up.

"Oh, God, Marge, don't even say that. You're wrong. You're way off."

She was walking in a circle like an animal trapped by hunters, trying to find a way to escape.

"C'mon, Sarah. It couldn't be anyone else. I should have known right away. He's the only guy you've had any contact with since school started. He's the only guy, other than his father and the priests, who any of us see with any regularity. And you're always out in the garden. Some of the girls even call you 'the gardener'. I've seen you out there when he's been around. There's no use denying it."

Sarah stopped circling.

"I should have never told you anything."

She started toward the door, but Marjorie blocked her way.

"You can trust me, Sarah. I won't say a word. He'll never know I know. Please don't go. I can't help you if you don't let me."

Sarah turned and went back to the bed. She sat for a while, her head down, her feet tapping nervously on the floor. Marjorie stayed by the door just in case.

After a long silence, broken only by the sound of her foot tapping, Sarah looked up.

"You can sit down. I'm not gonna leave. You're right—about everything. He's the one. And I do need someone to help me. But you have to swear that you'll never, ever tell anyone."

Marjorie sat down next to her.

"Okay. I swear. But you're afraid. I can tell. And it's not just because you're pregnant. Did he really not rape you?"

"Yes."

There was a hesitation in the way she said it that Marjorie didn't like.

"Are you absolutely certain?"

Hesitation again. There was confusion on her face and in her voice.

"Yes…I'm pretty sure…I mean…I don't think he did. It was my first time. How am I supposed to know what it's supposed to be like?"

The tears came rushing back. Marjorie put her arm around her and held her again.

"I'm sorry, Sarah. I'm not trying to be mean. I just think we need to know for sure. If he raped you, it changes a lot of things."

"How?"

"Well, for one thing, nobody can be mad at you. And you don't have to be ashamed because it wasn't your fault."

"How do I know that? I didn't stop him, did I?"

"Did you want to?"

"Sometimes…but every time I thought about it, I just couldn't."

"Why not?"

"I don't know. I'd be thinking I should tell him to stop, but just before I said it, he'd do something that felt good, and I couldn't say it."

"Are you sure you didn't?"

"Pretty sure…I guess. Everything was moving so fast I don't remember all of it. I've been trying to forget the whole thing."

"Well, maybe you've forgotten something important."

"Oh, what's the difference? Even if I told him to stop, it doesn't change anything. I'm pregnant, and I've got to figure out what to do. And even if he did rape me, I can't tell anyone."

"Why not? If he raped you, he'll go to jail."

"What if he killed me first?"

"Killed you?"

"He said he would if I ever told anyone."

"What? When did he tell you that?"

"A couple weeks ago."

"A couple weeks? Does he know…?"

"About the baby? That's when I told him. He said it wasn't his. He said I must have slept with some other guy. That's not really how he said it, but I can't repeat the word he used. That's when I realized that that was all it was to him. That's all I was. He made me feel so cheap. I told him I was going to tell everyone about it. I didn't really mean it, but I was so mad I wanted to make him as scared as I was."

"It didn't work, though. He told me that if I ever told anyone, he'd fix it so I could never tell anyone anything. He grabbed a garden shears off the table and told me they'd find me with that shears in my throat."

She was shaking uncontrollably now.

"Marge, you've got to promise me you'll never let anyone know I told you. Please!"

Marjorie sat where she was, unable to move. Now she was afraid. This guy seemed really dangerous. She wished she had made Sarah go back to her room as soon as she found her in hers. She wanted to tell her that. She wanted to tell her that she wished she never met her. This wasn't fair. She didn't do anything wrong. She didn't let some guy seduce her. Of course it had to be Sarah, the beautiful one, the one all the guys wanted who had that happen. Even if she ended up pregnant, she at least had experienced something that Marjorie had yet to learn about. All the girls talked about it and wondered about it, but Sarah had felt it. The consequences should be hers and hers alone.

Her face felt hot, and she went to the sink to splash some cold water on it. As she wiped it dry, she caught sight of herself in the mirror. The face with all the defects. But her eyes didn't look the same. There was something in them, something that made her want to look away. She knew what it was. The shame had returned, or maybe it never left. Sitting on the bed was a girl who was not only pregnant with no idea of what to do about it, she was also in fear of her life. How could she be jealous of her? How could she have thought the things she had just been thinking? How could she judge her so harshly and still call herself her friend?

Sarah had watched her nervously, wondering why she seemed to have forgotten that she was in the room.

"Say something, Marge, please."

Marjorie swallowed hard and turned away from the mirror. She looked down at the floor as she passed Sarah and went to the closet, talking as she did. She took off her uniform jacket and hung it up, all the while keeping her back to Sarah. She didn't want her to see the tears that had welled up in her eyes.

"I'm sorry. There's just so much to think about. We've got to figure out what we're going to do about all this. And then there's this business about Sister Margaret Mary that's going to have everyone talking and asking questions."

Sarah started crying again. Marjorie remembered how she was crying in the assembly.

"Sarah, what's going on? I mention Sister Margaret Mary and you start crying like she was your mother or something. You did the same thing in the assembly when Mother Superior said she was dead."

"I don't know if I should tell you. It's probably better if you don't know."

Marjorie sat down next to her, trying to keep calm. She had made up her mind to let go of her jealousy and fear and help her but now there was another secret. What else was she hiding?

"Sarah, I can't help you if you're not going to tell me everything. You either trust me or you don't, and if you don't, you'll have to find someone else to help you."

"That's just it, I did. Now she can't."

Marjorie was about to ask who when she suddenly knew.

"You mean Sister Margaret Mary?"

Sarah nodded.

"How could a nun help you? And why did you even tell her in the first place?"

"When I told Jack, he told me I'd better get rid of it. He said that if I didn't do it soon I'd start to show and then people would know, and they'd figure out it was him. He told me he had heard stories that one of the sisters had helped other girls before. He said I'd better find her right away because he didn't want to have to take care of it himself. He told me to talk to Sister Margaret Mary."

"Sister Margaret Mary! If you're telling me what I think you are, I don't believe it. A nun, especially an old one like her, would never be a part of something like that."

"Marge, I'm sorry. It's true. I told her I needed help, and she said she could take care of it. She said she knew how I could get an abortion and no one would know."

Marjorie stormed across the room to the door, leaned against it, and sank to the floor, crying like she hadn't cried in years.

"You're lying! You have to be! A nun would never help anyone like that. It's against the law! It's against God's law!"

"Hey, Marjorie, are you okay?" a voice from the hall asked.

Marjorie hadn't realized she was sitting next to the door yelling as loud as she was. She regained her composure and thought quickly.

"Yes. I was just reading a book out loud, and I guess I got carried away during a really intense part."

"Okay. Sounds like a pretty wild story."

"Well, I tend to overact when I read like that. Sorry."

"No problem. I'm glad it's almost time for breakfast. I'm starved. See you there."

"All right."

She pulled herself up and moved away from the door. She didn't want anyone else to hear them talking. She felt drained, like all her energy had been sucked out of her.

"Sarah, are you really telling me the truth?"

Sarah nodded sadly. She had been so consumed by her problem that she hadn't given any thought to how wrong it really was considering who was involved. Marjorie found enough strength to move to the bed and sit.

"How could she tell us about obeying God's law, obeying the Ten Commandments, and then do something like that? Are they all like that? Is it all just a big show they put on?"

"I don't think so, Marge. I think most of them really believe it. Maybe she did too. Maybe she just felt sorry for girls in trouble."

"Yeah, I guess that might be it. I guess we're all human, even nuns. It just doesn't feel right, though. I mean, I'll never be able to think of her the same way I did. That makes me feel bad because I liked her."

They both sat quietly, thinking it all over, scrutinizing their long-held beliefs. Suddenly, Marjorie jumped to her feet, her energy renewed.

"Oh my gosh! I just realized something!"

Sarah had almost fallen asleep in the quiet. Marjorie's outburst jolted her awake.

"What?"

"This could be important! I've gotta tell Steve!"

"Steve? Who's Steve?"

"The detective. I'm not supposed to tell anyone, but I guess I can tell you. He asked me to help him."

"Help him? What do you mean?"

"He told me to listen and watch to see if any of the girls knew something that might be important, you know, maybe someone saw something but didn't realize it meant anything. Or maybe someone knew something but was afraid to tell him but they might tell other girls and I might hear them talking."

Sarah stiffened as she listened. None of it sounded like a good idea to her.

"Marge, what are you gonna do? You're not going to tell him. You can't. You promised."

"I know I did. But this changes everything. What if she was killed because of what she's been doing?"

"But what about Jack? He said he'd kill me. We can't tell anyone!"

"What if Jack killed her?"

"Why would he do that? He wanted her to take care of it."

"I don't know. All I know is that Steve has to know about this. If we tell him everything, he'll protect you."

"How?"

"He'll have someone guard you, or he'll send you somewhere Jack can't find you. You'll be all right, I promise."

"You promised you'd never tell."

"This is different. It could be the key to finding the murderer."

"And what about me? What about the baby? My parents will find out. The other girls will find out. This will ruin my whole life."

"It won't ruin your life. Your parents will understand, and who cares what the girls think?"

"You obviously don't know my parents."

"Look, we'll be called for breakfast any minute now. I have to tell Steve. If you don't want to come with me I'll do it alone, but you'll be much better off if we do this together. You're gonna be all right, really you are."

A thought occurred to her. It could be a way to get Sarah to be more willing to go with her. She was a little surprised by the way her mind was working.

"If Sister's murder does have something to do with what she's been doing, how do you know that the murderer doesn't know that she was helping you? What if you're one of those 'loose ends' people talk about that has to be taken care of?"

It worked. Sarah was definitely running that around in her head. Marjorie let her think for a moment.

A bell signaled that breakfast was ready.

"There's the bell. Are you coming, or should I go alone?"

"I'm coming. I don't like this, and I'm scared out of my mind, but if you're right, it's probably the best option. I guess I knew when they told us she was dead that I'd have to face the music eventually. I just kept hoping I could find another way, but the more I've thought about it, the more I've realized that I got myself into this and the only one who can get me out is me. I felt so helpless I couldn't see any other way. You're a good friend. I'm sorry I dropped all this on you. But without you, I don't know what I would have done."

She hugged Marjorie, moved to the door, and turned back.

"Will we do it after breakfast?"

"Yeah, I think we better. The sooner Steve knows, the safer you'll be. I know it's going to be hard for you. I feel like I'm betraying you, and I'm sorry, but I know it's really the best thing to do."

"Don't be sorry. A while ago I would have hated you for saying you were going to tell, but after all we've talked about and knowing that you're going to be with me, I think I'll be glad to finally get it off my shoulders. It's really been a heavy weight."

"I'm glad, then, that you feel that way. You looked so sad when I first walked in, and you were so scared it scared me." She looked at the clock.

"We'd better get going."

As Sarah went into the hall, Marjorie went to the sink, looked at her face in the mirror and smiled. *I guess it's not so bad*, she thought and headed off to breakfast.

Chapter 4

The dining hall was already crowded when they arrived. It had, as the Assembly Room did, a high ceiling but was only a little over half the size. It was bright and airy, with large windows on either side that matched the ones in the Assembly. Several rows of square tables for four filled the room.

By the time Marjorie and Sarah arrived there, most of the tables were fully occupied or had only a single seat left. Marjorie made a quick scan of the room and found one in the far-right corner with two openings. The girls hurried over and took their seats. Jan Parker and Peggy Williams greeted them as they sat down, and the two returned to the conversation they had been having.

"Do you really think Sister Mary Claire did it?" Jan asked.

"Sure," Peggy responded. "She's got a terrible temper. They probably had an argument about something and she got mad and strangled her."

Jan shook her head.

"Nuns don't have arguments. They're not allowed to. It's one of their rules. Besides, I think Sister Camillus did it. She's got the face of a murderer."

"Oh, don't be so stupid. Murderers don't look like murderers."

Marjorie had heard enough.

"You know, we're not supposed to be talking about it. That detective said not to. And it's silly anyway. All they said was that she was murdered. We don't know how, we don't know where, we don't know when. All anybody can do is guess, and you can do that all day and you still won't know any more than you did when you started."

"Well, what are we supposed to talk about?" Peggy asked. "It's the only interesting thing that's happened here in years. Look around—*everyone's* talking about it. You may as well get used to it. It's probably going to be the only thing we talk about for a long time."

The ringing of a bell interrupted the conversation just in time. As she stood for prayer, Marjorie realized that Peggy's remark had upset her to a point where she had been just about to say something about how there might soon be other things to talk about.

I've got to be more careful. I can't let things like that slip out, she thought as Sister Willibald said grace, ending with a prayer for Sister Margaret Mary's soul.

The girls sat and waited for their food. The freshmen were required to take turns serving the others. It was, the sisters said, a way to learn humility and service to others. Marjorie's recollection of it was that all it taught her was how to be a waitress.

The four ate in silence, barely looking at each other as they did. When Peggy was finished, she stood and shot an icy glance at Marjorie.

"Come on, Jan. Let's go find someplace where we can talk without getting a lecture from Sister Marjorie."

Marjorie watched them go, stifling a laugh as she did.

"Well, I guess I'll have to find someone else to sit with at lunch," she said under her breath as they walked away.

Sarah didn't seem to see the humor.

"Marge, you can't do that."

"Do what?"

"Tell everybody else what to do. You're not Mother Superior."

"I don't think I am. It's just that Steve said…"

"Steve said. Where do you get off calling him Steve?"

"He told me to."

Marjorie suddenly realized that there were still girls at some of the nearby tables. She leaned closer to Sarah and whispered, "I have to call him Detective around the other girls so I don't give myself away. I just figured since you know I'm helping, I don't have to do that around you."

Sarah understood the need to whisper and did so as well.

"It just doesn't seem right to me. I mean, he's a police detective, and he's old. You should show him more respect."

"He told me to do it. And anyway, he's not that old. Didn't you get a good look at him? He can't be over thirty, and he's actually pretty good-looking."

Sarah pulled away, horrified.

"Marge, really! I hope you don't have any crazy ideas about him!"

"You're kidding, aren't you? I just noticed that he's good-looking. I'm not in love with him or anything."

"Well, I still don't like this whole thing about you calling him Steve and 'working' with him. I don't think it's a good idea. After we talk to him, I think you should just go back to being yourself and not his spy."

Marjorie noticed that the girls at a table a row away were staring at them. She straightened up in her chair.

"I think we should find something else to talk about, like how bad breakfast was."

Sarah looked around the room as she sat back in her chair. The girls at the other table went quickly back to their breakfast.

"I see what you mean. Let's finish up and get out of here. I want to get this over with."

"Yeah, I'll feel better when Steve—I mean 'the detective'—knows about Sister Margaret Mary."

Sarah shook her head.

"You're impossible."

The dining room was at the far end of the school near the sisters' convent. A short hallway led from the dining room to the convent. At the end of the hallway to the right was a door leading outside. It was the sisters' private entrance, used only by them and any visitors. The girls were strictly prohibited from using the door either coming or going. On the left was a large heavy wooden door with a large intricately carved cross on its face. The convent was the original living quarters of the sisters, which was built in 1897. It was constructed of sandstone in the fashion of the great cathedrals of the East, and the door reflected that style.

An imposing-looking desk was positioned about ten feet in front of the door, and at the desk was seated an imposing-looking nun, Sister Agnes, who was known to the girls as "the Gatekeeper". Other than the sisters, no one got past Sister Agnes without her permission.

The girls had managed to enter the hall from the dining room without being stopped and asked where they were going. They were relieved, since a reply of wanting to see Mother Superior would have been met with questions they didn't want to answer. Their purpose and the information they were bringing to Steve had to be kept secret. It was going to be bad enough dealing with Sister Agnes.

They approached the desk slowly, as if prisoners going to their execution. Neither of them had ever encountered Sister Agnes other than seeing her around the school at times, but they had heard stories from girls who had, girls who had been summoned to Mother Superior's office.

They reached the desk and stood like statues, afraid to make a wrong move of any kind. Sister Agnes was reading a newspaper. She became aware of their presence and looked up, holding them in a cold stare.

"Yes," she said bluntly. "What do you want?"

Marjorie swallowed hard.

"We need to see Mother Superior, please. It's really important."

Sister Agnes continued her stare.

"Mother Superior is very busy. You should know that. She hasn't time for girlish emergencies. You were told to stay in your rooms. That's where you should be."

Sarah turned to leave, but Marjorie stopped her. If they left now, she knew, they'd never have another chance. They had to get in. She turned back to Sister Agnes and shouted, hoping it would make her realize that it really was important.

"Sister, it's not some girlish emergency. I have to see Detective McLean. He asked me to help him, and I found something out that he needs to know about."

Sister Agnes stood up and leaned forward over the desk.

"Don't you raise your voice to me, young lady. Who do you think you are? And why would Detective McLean ask you to help him? This is no time to be making up stories."

"It's not a story, Sister, it's really true! Just ask Mother Superior! She'll tell you!"

Sister Agnes came out from behind the desk. She was clearly not going to be swayed by anything Marjorie said.

"I will not bother Mother Superior with such nonsense! Go back to your rooms and wait there as you were told."

Sister Agnes was indeed a large woman. With her teeth clenched and anger flashing in her eyes, she would have frightened the most battle-hardened soldier. Marjorie and Sarah stepped back away, terrified. They were about to turn and run back down the hall when the outside door opened and several people filed in.

Two women in police uniforms were first, followed by three men in uniform. Behind them were two men in dark suits. One of them was Steve.

Marjorie saw him and turned back to Sister Agnes.

"There's Detective McLean. Ask him! He'll tell you!"

"That is enough, young lady! I won't bother him with your foolishness! Do as I tell you!"

Steve moved up through the group of officers.

"Is there a problem, Sister?"

Sister Agnes shot an angry look toward the girls then turned to Steve. She immediately became the "Gatekeeper", dealing with visitors as a nun should properly do. Her tone and demeanor were apologetic as she explained the situation.

"I'm sorry about this, Detective. We don't usually have an unseemly commotion like this. These girls asked to see Mother Superior. When I told them she had much more important matters to attend to, that one (she added extra emphasis on the words as she pointed to Marjorie) came up with a ridiculous story that you had asked her to help you. She became unruly when I told them to leave. I was just sending them away when you came in. I'll see to that now then I'll notify Mother Superior that you're here."

"Please, Sister," Steve began to explain, "I think I'm the one who owes you—and Marjorie as well—an apology. I realize now that I neglected to tell you that I had asked her to help me and that I would want to see her if she came looking for me."

Sister Agnes shot another glance in the girls' direction. Her expression had turned to one that seemed to shout "Why!?" She looked around cautiously as she turned to Steve.

"It's not my place, and I hope you'll forgive my impertinence, but what help can a girl like that be in this matter?"

Steve moved closer to her and spoke in a confidential tone.

"Tell me, Sister, if you were a teenage girl, who would you be more likely to talk freely with, a policeman or another girl?"

He stepped back and winked at the girls. Sister Agnes turned and walked around the desk to her chair, giving the girls a look of combined suspicion and disapproval as she passed. She dialed the phone and informed Mother Superior that Detective McLean and his officers had arrived. She listened to the reply and hung up the phone. With a slight bow, she told Steve that he could go in.

Steve talked to the group of officers, telling them to wait for instructions which he would give them after a short meeting with Mother Superior. He motioned for the girls to follow him as he moved toward the door to the office, which was on the wall to the right of the large door, behind the desk. Sister Agnes fixed her eyes on them as they passed her desk. She clearly did not approve of the situation.

As they approached the office door, Marjorie felt a combination of relief and apprehension. They had overcome the hurdle of Sister Agnes and would be safe with Steve and Mother Superior, but for how long? What if Steve didn't think what Sarah had told her meant anything? They'd have taken this chance for nothing, and Mother Superior would know about Sarah's pregnancy. What if he did, and he questioned Jack, then decided there wasn't a connection? He'd be gone after he finished the investigation, but Jack would still be here. She had felt so sure that this was the right thing to do. Now she couldn't help but wonder if she was putting Sarah in danger for nothing.

Steve opened the office door and motioned for them to go in ahead of him. It was too late now to change her mind.

Neither of the girls had ever been to Mother Superior's office. That honor was usually reserved for the girls who got in trouble, and big trouble at that. Sister Mary Joseph normally handled the run-of-the-mill kind of trouble. So they looked it over slowly, filled with a sense of wonder.

So this is how nuns live, Marjorie thought. *Pretty nice.*

Mother Superior was at her desk as they entered. She rose and approached them. The formality of the room and the way she looked as she walked toward them gave both girls a sudden feeling of trepidation, a feeling of being in over their heads in a situation they really didn't belong in. Sarah felt a strong urge to bolt and run out of the room, but Marjorie held her hand tightly, seeming to sense what Sarah was thinking. They both looked down at the floor, almost instinctively feeling that it was the proper way to stand in Mother Superior's office.

The skirt of her habit appeared in front of them.

"Sit down, girls."

They looked up to find her indicating that they should sit on the sofa. They moved around the coffee table and sat stiffly on the edge of the seat cushion. Mother Superior sat in the chair to the left. Steve waited for her to sit and then took a seat in the chair to the right. He nodded to Mother Superior, who again took the lead in the conversation.

"I understand you gave Sister Agnes quite a time in the hall."

Marjorie quickly blurted out a defense.

"Oh, Mother, we didn't mean to, it was just that—"

She was stopped by the raising of Mother Superior's hand.

"I understand that you feel that whatever you have to tell is important, but that is not the kind of behavior we expect from our girls. However, since I believe you felt strongly about your need to be seen, I will do my best to smooth things over with Sister. It may require me to hand down some form of discipline, but I will do so as fairly as possible. I only hope that what you have to tell us is worth all this excitement."

At last! They could tell their story. Marjorie began, knowing Sarah was dreading having anyone else, especially Mother Superior, know what she had done. She couldn't hold back the excitement as she spoke, the words tumbling out almost on top of each other.

"It is, Mother, it really is. I didn't think I'd find out much of anything, especially something like this, and I'd have never in a million years thought—"

She was stopped again by Mother Superior's hand.

"Yes. Well, I am curious about what you could have found out so quickly this morning that you feel is so important. It seems hard to believe that any of the girls would actually have any knowledge about this terrible crime, not something that could be as important as to make you so excitable."

Marjorie felt Sarah shifting uncomfortably next to her. She knew she had to calm down and get it all out before Sarah had second thoughts. She was about to begin again more slowly when Steve spoke.

"Mother Superior is right, Marjorie. I asked you to help because I thought you were someone who could handle the responsibility without getting flustered. I hope I haven't put too much on you."

Marjorie felt her face redden. This was awful. She was embarrassing herself in front of him. Acting like a child when he expected her to be more mature. She took a deep breath and started in as calmly as she could.

"I'm sorry. I never imagined I'd find anything like this, and it's really just a coincidence, I guess, but Sarah was in my room when I got back, and we started talking, and I realized that what she told me was really big, at least I'm pretty sure it is."

She felt Sarah shifting even more.

"This is Sarah. Well, you know who she is, Mother, but Steve doesn't. She's really scared because she doesn't want anyone to know about this. And she's really worried about anyone finding out that we were the ones who told—"

Mother Superior cut in.

"All right, Marjorie. We can tell you're both nervous. Just come out and tell us what you know."

"Not nervous, Mother. Scared to death. Well, she is, not me as much, but she's got more reasons."

This time, it was Steve.

"Marjorie, we understand you're scared, but there's no reason to be. Whatever you're afraid of, I'll make sure you're protected from it, but we need to hear what this is all about."

"Okay. I told Sarah you would. I guess I am talking and not saying much."

She collected her thoughts and turned to Sarah.

"You ready? You should probably start since you've got the most to tell."

Tears welled up in Sarah's eyes as she looked at Mother Superior then back to Marjorie.

"You tell her, Marge. I can't. I just want to leave."

Her tears were flowing freely now.

"We can't. It's too late. You have to tell."

Mother Superior was now deeply concerned. Whatever this was about it was definitely more serious than she had expected it to be. She moved onto the sofa next to Sarah and put her arm around her.

"Sarah, dear. Don't be afraid. Whatever you're frightened of will be easier to deal with if you tell me."

"But, Mother, I'm so ashamed." Sarah sobbed. "You'll think I'm a terrible person."

"Nonsense. I could never think that of you. Please tell me. Just say it and it will all be over. You really will feel better once you do."

Something in Mother Superior's voice and the feel of her arm around her made Sarah feel less afraid. She held her breath and summoned every bit of courage she could find in herself.

"Oh, Mother, I'm pregnant!"

She buried her face in Mother Superior's shoulder and wept uncontrollably.

There was a long painful silence before Mother Superior spoke.

"Does anyone else know?'

Marjorie spoke for Sarah, who was still crying too hard to speak.

"No, Mother. Not anymore at least...now that Sister Margaret Mary's dead. That's what we came to tell you."

"We'll talk about whatever it is you have to tell later. Right now we need to take care of Sarah."

She pulled a handkerchief out of her sleeve and handed it to Sarah.

"It's clean. Go ahead and wipe your eyes."

As Sarah wiped her eyes, Mother Superior continued.

"What about the father, does he know?"

Sarah was still unable to talk, so Marjorie answered.

"Yes, Mother, but he told her if she told anyone he was the father, he'd kill her. He threatened her, and she's really scared."

Steve had been listening, trying to be as unintrusive as possible, but this was his department.

"Threatened her?"

"Uh-uh. That's why she didn't want to tell you. He really scared her."

"Well, I'll need to know. After I have a little talk with him she won't have to be afraid."

Sarah pulled her face away from Mother Superior's shoulder.

"No, you can't do that! Even if people know I'm pregnant, as long as no one knows who the father is I'll be safe. Please, just forget about him."

She returned her face to the safety of the shoulder. Mother Superior put her finger to her lips just as Steve was about to say more. She gently drew back from Sarah, holding her by her shoulders.

"Sarah, look at me."

Sarah reluctantly lifted her face toward her.

"My dear, you don't have to tell me. I think I already know."

"Oh, Mother, no! You can't!"

"Under the circumstances, once the secret of your pregnancy is known, it won't be difficult for others to figure out the rest."

Sarah's eyes widened in horror.

"I knew this was a bad idea! Now everyone will know! I should have never told anyone! I just should have…"

"Should have what?"

Mother Superior's question stopped her and made her ask it herself. What should she have done? What *could* she have done?

Nothing. Except... But that was something she would have never been able to do...unless she had no other choice.

A feeling of clarity swept over her as she realized that she had thought about just that choice when she heard about Sister Margaret Mary. It was that thought that had made her go to Marjorie's room because she was afraid to be alone in her own room. If Marjorie had turned her away, was it possible that she could have actually gone through with it?

This wasn't a bad idea. There really were only two possible solutions, this, and what she had been considering as she sat on Marjorie's bed. She turned to Marjorie and threw her arms around her, tears streaming down her cheeks.

"Thank you! Thank you! Thank you!" she cried, hugging her tighter and tighter with each "Thank you."

Marjorie was confused and finding it hard to breathe.

"Sarah," she gasped, "I'm glad you're happy about something, but could you let me breathe?"

Sarah relaxed her hold and sat back a little.

"I'm sorry. I just had to thank you!"

"For what? I thought you were mad at me."

"I thought so too, until I realized that you saved my life."

"What do you mean?"

"I quit thinking about it after you said you'd help me because that made me feel better, but before you got there I was thinking there was only one way to solve my problems. In fact, I was just about to go back to my room when you came in."

Marjorie was crying now. The shame had returned. All those things she had been thinking back in her room seemed cruel now that she knew how desperate Sarah had been. She didn't deserve her thanks. It was her turn to hug Sarah.

"Oh, Sarah, I'm really glad that I got there in time, and I'm glad you let me talk you into doing this even though you didn't want to. But I don't deserve to be thanked. I pushed you to do this because I wanted to be able to say I actually found something important. I could have helped you find some other solution to your problem without anyone else knowing."

"No, you couldn't have. It took me a while, and a question from Mother Superior, before I finally realized there were only two choices. You saved me from making the wrong one."

She turned to Mother Superior.

"I'm ready to tell you everything, Mother."

A new sense of confidence had replaced her uncertainty. She looked over her shoulder at Marjorie and smiled, turned back, and continued.

"And I can do it myself."

She began to relate the story of everything that happened with Jack. It was a little uncomfortable with Steve there, especially when he pressed her for details that she felt were too intimate to tell a man. He assured her that it was information he would need when he talked to Jack. If he was to make a determination as to whether it could be a case of rape or not, he needed all the facts.

It all seemed to happen so quickly, she said, that she couldn't be sure if she had tried to make him stop. Her confidence seemed to waver as she relived the moment, and her uncertainty about the details heightened her nervousness. When she reached the point at which Jack started to unbutton her blouse Mother Superior could see that she was reluctant to go further in front of Steve. She asked him to leave the room, telling him she would inform him of anything she felt was important.

As Steve started toward the door, Marjorie stood and said something about maybe she should go too.

"No, Marjorie," Mother Superior replied, "I think you should stay. It might be good to learn something about the manipulations young men use on young girls."

Sarah looked up at her.

"Please stay, Marge. It'll be easier if I can feel like I'm telling you and not Mother Superior."

She paused, suddenly feeling that she had said the wrong thing.

"I don't mean anything bad about you, Mother. It's just that..."

"I understand, Sarah. At your age I'd have felt the same way I'm sure."

Marjorie sat down and Sarah began to relate the most intimate, and therefore the most embarrassing in her mind, details. When she mentioned being led to the bed Mother Superior stopped her.

"What bed? I thought you said this happened in the gardener's shed."

"Yes, Mother, there's a small room with a bed there."

"In the gardener's shed? Whatever for?"

"Jack said that the first gardener was an old man who had no family. The sisters back then felt sorry for him, I guess, so when they built the shed, they put a little room on it where he could live."

"I was in that shed when I looked around the property to see where everything was when I first came here. I didn't see another room."

"Well, there's a big board with hooks on it where they hang tools. It covers the doorway, but Jack said it moves pretty easily."

Mother Superior thought this new information over.

"A bed in a hidden room on the grounds of a girls' school. I don't think that's a good idea. I'll have to make sure it's taken care of quickly. Now I think you've been through enough. I don't think there's any reason to continue. What I've heard up to now is plenty damning to that young man."

She turned to Marjorie.

"Marjorie, please ask Detective McLean to come back in. I want to hear how you think this has a connection to Sister Margaret Mary's death."

Marjorie went to the door feeling a sense of relief. She really didn't want to hear any more of Sarah's story, especially when it concerned something she had only been given a basic explanation of by her mother. She wasn't ready for an actual description.

Steve returned and settled back in his chair.

"That actually worked out well," he said as he sat down. "I was able to give my instructions to the others. Sister Agnes protested a bit when I said the female officers would be checking the sisters' rooms. Sister Mary Joseph came by just in time to verify that you had given your permission."

Mother Superior smiled.

"Yes, Joseph is indispensable. She seems to be in the right place at the right time as if she knows beforehand that she'll be needed. Speaking of Joseph, I need to find out what time the Mass for Margaret Mary will be held. Joseph takes care of those matters, and I've been so preoccupied that I haven't checked with her about it. If you'll excuse me for a moment."

She rose and moved to the desk, dialed the phone, waited for an answer, and began her instructions.

"Please ask Sister Mary Joseph to let me know the time of the Mass today… Yes, Sister Agnes, I did give my permission… I understand that, but this is an unusual situation… Well under the circumstances we're all under suspicion… No, Agnes, of course I don't think you're a murderer, but someone is… I have other matters to take care of. We'll talk about this later. Thank you."

She hung up and returned to her chair.

"Well, you certainly have Agnes riled up. I'll calm her down later. Let her enjoy her indignation for a while."

She noticed the girls were looking at her curiously.

"Yes, we nuns are human. We even have a sense of humor!"

She laughed and then continued.

"As I said, it's time to find out what you think you know about Sister Margaret Mary."

Sarah looked at Marjorie.

"You should tell. You're the one who thought it's important."

Marjorie suddenly felt nervous. What if she was about to embarrass herself in front of Steve again. What if he ended up saying this was just a waste of time? *Well, here goes nothing*, she thought.

"Well, what we didn't get to tell you was what happened after Sarah found out she was pregnant. It blew me away when she told me, and I think it's going to be a big shock to you too, Mother."

"I'm not sure you girls can shock me any more than you already have."

Marjorie took a deep breath and blew it out slowly.

"Okay. Here goes. When Sarah told Jack she was pregnant, he told her she'd better get rid of it before she started to show because once she did everyone would know. When she asked him how she was supposed to do that, he told her one of the sisters had helped some other girls in the past and—"

She stopped when she heard Mother Superior gasp loudly, almost cry out. She looked at her, and her face had a look of horror on it. She was leaning on the arm of the chair as if she was going to fall to the floor at any moment.

"Mother, are you all right?" Marjorie shouted.

Steve had risen and come over to Mother's chair, ready to catch her if she fell.

Mother Superior raised her hand and signaled him that she wouldn't need his help. She sat back in her chair, her face a pale gray. She closed her eyes and spoke softly, weakly.

"Are you telling me that Sister Margaret Mary has helped girls to get abortions? That can't be true, it can't be."

Marjorie looked down at the floor as she spoke, not wanting to be the one to have to confirm it.

"I'm sorry, Mother. It is true."

Sarah reached over and held Marjorie's hand. She squeezed it tightly. They sat watching Mother Superior through tear-filled eyes. She seemed to age at least ten years as they did.

Steve sat, not knowing what to say or do. He considered going to get Sister Agnes, but he realized that would require an explanation and this was something that had to go no further than the walls of the office. Asking Mother Superior if she was all right or if there was anything he could do seemed ridiculous. She obviously wasn't all right, and there was nothing he could do.

The silence had reached a point where it was almost unbearable. Marjorie wanted to scream, "Please, Mother, say something," but she knew they had to wait. Finally, Mother Superior spoke. There was an air of defeat in her voice, like she had lost something precious that she knew she would never be able to replace or find again.

"If you'll excuse me, I think I need to be alone for a while. Please tell Sister Agnes that I'm not to be disturbed until I call her."

Steve rose and signaled to the girls to come with him.

"Yes, Mother. I'll take care of it."

They started for the door. Marjorie turned and looked back, feeling that she had to say something. She felt Steve's hand on her shoulder, and he shook his head. They left as quietly as they could, and Steve closed the door slowly, easing it into place without a sound. He kept his voice low as he talked to the girls.

"You girls go back to your rooms. Be sure not to talk about any of this. No one knows what happened in there so you'll be safe as long as you keep it to yourselves. I'll send for you when you're needed so just wait. Don't come back here or people will wonder what's going on. Just blend in with the girls as if it's a regular day."

Neither of them wanted to go back.

"Can't we just stay with you?" Marjorie asked.

"No. I have things to do, and you have to give everyone the impression that nothing about you is different. If you attract attention, people will ask questions."

He looked at Sarah.

"You don't want anyone to get suspicious that you might have told someone, do you?"

Sarah's whole body stiffened, and she quickly shook her head.

"Good. Get going. I'll need to see you later."

The girls hurried away, turning their heads away from the desk as they passed, not wanting to meet the gaze of Sister Agnes.

Steve watched them go then went to the desk to give Sister Agnes Mother Superior's directions.

"But, Detective, Mother Superior asked me to notify her of the time of the Mass for Sister Margaret Mary."

"Write it on a piece of paper and slip it under the door."

"What!? Detective, we don't do things that way here!"

"Mother Superior is extremely tired. This has been a very trying day for her. She needs some privacy and rest. It would be best to follow her orders."

Sister Agnes threw up her hands, frustrated beyond her limit.

"All right, if you say so! I don't understand what's happening here! Murder! Police rummaging through our rooms! Girls being completely disrespectful! Mother Superior sending me orders through a police detective who has the gall to think he can tell me how to do my job! What's next? Boys in the girls' rooms?"

Steve was able to contain his laughter until he got outside. He found her outburst funny and couldn't help but laugh, but he knew there wasn't going to be much more to laugh at. If he was right, there was more than just a simple murder here. What he had expected to be a case of a couple of nuns arguing had taken an ominous turn. If Sister Margaret Mary's activities had caused her murder, there were many more questions to be answered. On top of that, there was a dangerous young man still on the grounds of the school and two girls who could be in danger, both from the young man and from the murderer.

He couldn't shake the feeling that the answers to the questions lay somewhere in the past. He started his car and headed to see the one man he felt could help him unravel some of this tangle of secrets. Harry Larson. The man who taught him everything he knew.

Chapter 5

As they passed through the rear door of the dining room, Sarah looked up at the clock on the wall above the door.

"It's only a little after ten. I thought it was later. I'm starving and lunch isn't till noon."

"You're hungry?" Marjorie asked. "I'm not. Even breakfast was hard to finish. This whole thing has my stomach in knots."

"I should probably feel the same way with all that's been happening. Maybe I react differently to stress than you do. Or maybe it's because...well, you know."

"I guess it could be either way, but it doesn't really matter, does it? And we should probably stop talking about anything. We're almost to our hall. Let's just walk as quickly and quietly as we can. Will you be okay alone? I think we should do like Steve said and do everything the way we're supposed to. Hopefully we won't run into anyone before we get to our rooms."

"Yeah. I'll be fine. What are we gonna say if somebody asks us where we've been?"

"I'm just gonna say 'None of your business' and keep walking."

"Really? Okay. I guess I'll just let you do the talking then."

Marjorie bumped her shoulder against Sarah's playfully.

"Chicken!"

Sarah bumped her in return.

"I'd rather be chicken than you!"

It started with a snort from Marjorie and quickly turned into both of them laughing as they made their way through the school.

They were still laughing when they walked through the arch that led into the dormitory. They tried to stifle their laughter as much as possible, but it was difficult to do. They needed some laughter after what they'd just been through.

"What's so funny?" came out of one of the rooms as they passed.

"None of your business!" shouted Marjorie.

It was just too much. They burst into loud, boisterous laughter and ran the rest of the way to their rooms. When they reached their doors, they looked back up the hall. It was filled with girls standing outside their rooms watching them.

Marjorie couldn't help herself.

"Move along," she called out. "Nothing to see here."

She and Sarah looked at each other, burst out laughing again, and went into their rooms. Marjorie closed the door and leaned back against it, letting her laughter subside gradually. She hung up her uniform jacket and laid on the bed. She felt good. Her fear of Steve telling her that what she found out about Sister Margaret Mary wasn't important was gone. She had done something important and she had impressed him. The early morning wake up was catching up to her, and she started to drift off to sleep. It was a good feeling, so she didn't fight it. In just a few minutes, she was fast asleep.

In her dream, she heard someone knocking and calling her name. She rolled over toward the wall and murmured, 'Go away.' A second louder knock caused her to roll onto her back and open her eyes. She looked at the clock. A few minutes before 11:15.

Great! she thought.

As she fell asleep, she had been hoping to sleep until lunch. Now she'd have to find some other way to pass the time.

"Who is it?" she called out as she swung herself out of bed.

"It's Ginny."

Ginny Davison was Sister Mary Joseph's student assistant. Sister would tell Ginny things she wanted the girls to know, and Ginny would come around and pass the information or directives to the rest of the girls. She was nice and didn't act like the position had gone to her head, so Marjorie liked her. It was the general opinion that she was going to end up becoming a nun herself.

"Just a minute."

Marjorie smoothed some of the wrinkles out of her blouse and skirt and straightened her hair before she opened the door.

"What is it?" she asked.

"The Mass for Sister Margaret Mary will be held at eleven-thirty. Lunch will be delayed until twelve-thirty."

"Really? They couldn't let us eat and then have the Mass?"

"Marjorie, you know we have to fast before receiving Holy Communion."

"Oh, yeah. Well, okay, I'll be there."

She started to close the door, but Ginny stepped further into the room.

"Marjorie, what's going on?"

"What do you mean?"

"Where did you and Sarah go after breakfast? Everybody's talking about it."

Marjorie stiffened. Now what? They had done just the opposite of what Steve had told them to do. Her mind was racing. She couldn't just say "None of your business." That would just cause more curiosity. There was no lie that anyone would believe, but she couldn't tell them the truth…or could she?

Just in time, an idea popped into her head. Maybe not the whole truth but part of the truth.

"We were being questioned by that detective."

"Questioned?"

"Yeah. We were the last ones in the dining room after breakfast. We were just leaving to come back here when that detective came in and saw us. He said they're probably going to question all of us, and since we were right there, he'd start with us."

"They're going to question all of us? Why?"

"Well, maybe. I think it all depends on if they find the killer before they get around to everybody."

"What did he ask you?"

"Just whether we saw anything unusual around the school yesterday. I told him nothing unusual ever happens around here. And

I also told him that since we're not allowed in the sisters' quarters, if anything unusual happened there, none of us would have seen it."

"Why were you gone so long? What else did he ask you?'

Marjorie was stumped. There weren't any other believable answers she could make up. All she could do was tell a little more of the truth.

"Well, he brought us to Mother Superior's office to question us and—"

"Mother Superior's office! You got to see Mother Superior's office? What's it like?"

This was good. She'd managed to change the subject.

"It's nice. The furniture is all really old and pretty. There's a table that's twice as big as our dining room table back home."

"Gee, I hope I get questioned so I can see her office too. Was she there? I can't imagine being questioned by the police with her right there."

"Yeah, she was there."

Marjorie remembered seeing the tea and coffee things on the coffee table.

"She even had some tea and cookies brought in. That's what took us so long."

"Tea and cookies! Now I really hope I get questioned!"

It was time to get her out of there before the half-truths ran out. Marjorie looked at the clock.

"It's getting late. You better get going."

Ginny looked at the time.

"Oh, gee. I still have the rest of the hall to notify."

As she started out the door, Marjorie stopped her.

"You can skip Sarah. I'll tell her."

"Okay. Thanks. That'll save me a little time."

Ginny hurried up the hall to the next door. Marjorie went to Sarah's door and knocked. She was glad she had thought to tell Ginny to skip Sarah. She had to get with her and tell her what she had told Ginny before anyone else talked to Sarah. What she had told Ginny would be known by the entire student body before the end of Mass.

She was certain of that. And if they didn't tell the same story, they'd be caught in a lie. That would ruin everything.

There was no reply to her first knock so she knocked again. An irritated voice answered.

"What do you want?"

"It's me, Sarah."

"Oh. Well, come on in."

Sarah was on the bed still half asleep. She opened her eyes just enough to make sure it was Marjorie then closed them again and covered her head with her blanket.

"Just let me sleep till lunch."

"You can't. We have to go to church first."

"What do you mean?"

"I mean the Mass for Sister Margaret Mary is at eleven-thirty. We only have a few minutes to get over there."

Sarah's head poked out from under the blanket.

"Huh? What about lunch?"

"It's gonna be after Mass. C'mon. Everyone else is already heading over there, and I need to talk to you before we go."

"After Mass? That's not fair. It's cruel and inhumane, that's what it is."

Marjorie pulled the blanket off Sarah.

"Well, like Sister Mary Grace always says, 'Offer up your suffering for the poor souls in purgatory.'"

Sarah sat up and tried to wake herself up enough to stand and straighten her uniform. Her head was a little clearer now.

"What do you need to talk to me about?"

"We have to get our stories straight. I had to do a little fibbing to get Ginny off my back."

"Ginny? What about her?"

"She asked me where we were for so long. She said all the girls are talking. I had to tell her something, so I made something up."

"So what do I need to know?"

"I mostly told the truth. I just left a lot of it out. I said Steve saw us in the dining room and said since he was planning to talk to all the girls, he'd start with us. Then he took us to Mother Superior's office and asked us if we saw anything unusual yesterday and we just said no. Then Mother Superior had some tea and cookies brought in, and we talked a while. I think that covers it all."

"I like the tea idea. I wish she had. I wouldn't be so hungry now."

"Okay. Just make sure you remember it all."

She looked at the clock.

"Oh my gosh! We gotta hurry!"

All the other girls were gone, and the hall was empty. They ran until they had almost caught up to the last stragglers, keeping some distance between them, hoping to avoid being asked any questions.

The church was connected to the school by an enclosed walkway that ran from the side of the church to the hallway outside the dining room. As they passed the door to the dining room, Sarah stopped and looked longingly in. When Marjorie grabbed her arm to keep her moving, she grudgingly complied.

As they moved into a pew in the girls' section of the church, Marjorie saw that all the sisters were in their pews at the front across the center aisle from the girls' side. As she knelt and bowed her head, it hit her, just as it had earlier in the assembly, that something wasn't right, though. She knelt up as straight as she could and stretched her neck to look over there again. She was right. One of the sisters wasn't there. Mother Superior wasn't in her usual place, alone in the first pew.

She felt Sarah nudge her.

"Marge," she whispered, "what are you doing? Everyone behind us can see you. You look like an ostrich."

Marjorie put her head back down, but she wasn't praying. The questions left no room in her mind for prayers. How could Mother Superior not be there? This wasn't something she would miss. Marjorie was sure everyone else must have noticed. Suddenly another thought rushed in. What if something had happened to her? What if the killer murdered her while everyone else was on the way to Mass?

She resisted the urge to jump up and run to check to make sure nothing was wrong. She'd only get in trouble if nothing was. And the sisters must have noticed that she wasn't there. They'd have checked;

she was certain of that. The bell rang, and everyone stood as the choir began the processional hymn.

She tried her best to keep her mind on the Mass, but she had to keep pushing her concern out of the way to do it. It was mostly an ordinary Mass like the one they had every morning except that Father Jerome used Sister's sudden death to remind them in his sermon that "We must all remember that God may call us at any time," "We know not the day nor the hour," and "We must all live our lives so that we will be ready when the time comes."

At the end of the Mass the girls filed out of their pews and moved to the walkway. Only the shuffling of feet was heard as they went. Once inside the walkway, it was a different story. The chattering began, and the volume rose as more and more girls entered and joined in.

Marjorie and Sarah were among the first into the walkway. Sarah walked quickly, determined to get a table close to the kitchen where the freshmen servers would see them first when they brought the food out. Sarah's hunger had seemed to make her forget the earlier events of the day, but Marjorie couldn't stop wondering about Mother Superior. She wished Steve hadn't told them to wait until he sent for them. Her worries only increased when Paula and Brenda sat at the table with them.

This isn't going to be a pleasant meal, she thought.

Paula didn't waste any time.

"So when did you two get to be so pal-zy well-zy with Mother Superior?"

Marjorie told herself to stay calm then answered as matter-of-factly as she could.

"It's not like that. She was just nice while the detective was asking us some questions. Maybe you'll get tea and cookies if he questions you."

"He better not try to question me. There's no reason to. I haven't done anything wrong."

"Neither have we, but he questioned us."

"Well, that makes sense. You two look like you're guilty of something."

Marjorie noticed that Sarah was getting nervous.

"C'mon, Sarah. Let's find some better company."

She stood up, and Sarah followed her lead. As they did, Paula and Brenda stood. Marjorie held her breath, not knowing what to expect.

"Aw, sit down," Paula said. "We don't want to eat with any teacher's pets anyway."

As she and Brenda started to walk away, she stopped and turned around.

"I guess we'll have to be careful what we talk about from now on when you're around. We don't need any snitches."

Marjorie and Sarah sat back down. By now, Sarah was visibly shaking.

"I don't feel so hungry anymore," she said. "I thought she was going to punch you."

"I know. Something's not right about those two. There's something they're hiding, something they don't want anyone to know about. I hope Steve gets back soon. He needs to know about this."

Their food came, and they ate in silence, trying to watch the other girls without being too obvious about it. How many others might be hiding something, and if they were, how far might they go to keep it hidden?

Chapter 6

Steve turned off the highway onto a narrow dirt road. About a hundred yards later, he pulled up in front of a small rustic-looking cabin. The front door opened as he was getting out of the car, and he was greeted by his friend's familiar voice.

"What the hell are you doing here?"

Harry Larson was tall, 6'4" or so. He still had his crew cut, cut so close in fact that from his early thirties, no one had been sure what color his hair actually was. He had replaced his detective suit and tie with a brown flannel shirt and khaki work pants. Steve thought he looked younger than he did when he retired.

As he walked to the porch where Harry waited, he loosened his tie.

"I just thought I'd come and see what the good life looks like."

"Well, this is it. It ain't fancy, but it's quiet."

As he went up the two steps and onto the porch, Harry put out his hand.

"It's good to see you, Steve. You better not be coming to tell me you can't handle the job and you want me to go back."

Steve put his hand in Harry's and shook it.

"No, I can handle it. I just might need a little historical information that I hope you may be able to provide."

"Historical information, hey. Well come on in and we'll talk."

The cabin was basically two rooms, a bedroom and a large living room with a kitchen in one corner. They sat at the kitchen table while Steve told Harry about Sister Margaret Mary and what he had been told by Mother Superior and the girls. When he finished, he asked the question he had come to ask.

"You were around when that happened back in '40. Anything you remember about it, anything more than what I've been told so far?"

"You know, I've been thinking while you were talking, and it all seems to make a little more sense. I was fairly new back then, so I wasn't directly involved, but we all talked about it at the station. There was no reason that anyone could come up with for her to do that. But if it turns out that one of the nuns was helping some of the girls to get abortions and the kid had one, she could have felt guilty. There's usually a lot of guilt in a place like that."

"Can you remember anything the investigation might have turned up other than the rumors I've heard?"

Harry thought again.

"Not really. But I know someone who may be able to help. Got time to take a about a twenty-minute drive?"

"Sure. Who are we going to see?"

"Bernie Bernstein. He broke me in years ago. It was his case. He's eighty-nine, but he's still pretty sharp. You never know what he might be able to remember."

Harry drove as he filled Steve in on how his three kids were doing. He was especially excited about his new twin granddaughters. In fact, he told Steve, if he had come a day later, he'd have missed him because he was flying out in the morning to go to Los Angeles to see them for the first time.

He told Steve a little more about Bernie too. How he fought in the Spanish-American War and came home with a couple of medals. That he had been a beat cop in Chicago in the mid twenties and decided in '28 that he wanted a little less action than what he was dealing with in the city.

"He came here and was the best cop on the force, probably the best cop for miles around. I owe him a lot. If he knows anything, he'll tell you."

They turned into a driveway where a sign on the left informed Steve that they had arrived at Green Meadows Retirement Home.

Harry parked the car in front of an elegant-looking two-story building that Steve would have thought was an old but well-kept-up mansion if not for the sign by the road. Two large white two-story columns stood on either side of an impressive double front door. Each door had an eight-by-ten beveled glass window and a brass handle that Steve felt were bigger than they needed to be.

Somebody wanted to show off when they built this place, he thought as he followed Harry toward the door.

Harry seemed to read his mind.

"This place was built by a farmer around 1910, I think. He owned pretty much all the land you can see from here in all directions. A dozen years ago, he decided to retire. He sold off all the land except for the house, had it partially remodeled into a retirement home. Then he donated it to the county. Said this place was good to him, so he wanted to give something back. Probably didn't hurt his taxes either."

He opened the door and Steve followed him in. The entry was at one time, Steve felt, a very large grand entry hall. What remained of the original space was two stories high with a large staircase on the left leading to a balcony that ran across the width of the room. From his vantage point, Steve could see that a hallway extended in either direction from each end of the balcony. A wall at the back side of the balcony held two doors, looking and spaced much like hotel room doors.

In the center of the wall below the balcony was a set of French doors. They were closed, so Steve couldn't tell where they led. Both the upper and lower walls were obviously part of the renovation. Steve felt that the area behind them was once a part of the grand entry hall.

On the right was the equivalent of a hotel registration desk. With its modern style, it looked out of place, he thought. To the left of the desk along the right wall was a small sitting area with a few comfortable-looking chairs and small tables. Apparently a place for visitors to meet with residents.

Harry talked to the woman at the desk and motioned for Steve to follow him. They turned right down a hall, which also had the appearance of a hotel. They passed three doors and stopped at the fourth. Harry knocked on the door on the left side of the hall.

"Come on in," came a voice from inside.

Harry opened the door and went in. As soon as he was in the room, Steve heard the voice again.

"Harry! It's about time you showed up again. I hope ya got your money with ya."

Steve went in and closed the door. In the middle of the room was a wheelchair where a man, almost bald with just a few wisps of thin white hair, sat chewing on an unlit cigar. He was dressed in a robe and slippers, and a pair of wire-rimmed glasses sat near the tip of his nose.

"Who ya got with ya, Harry?" the man asked. "I hope ya told him to bring money."

'Bernie, this is Steve McLean, the kid who took my place. I told you about him."

"Oh yeah, the whiz kid. Nice to meet you. Sit down."

"It's an honor to meet you, sir," Steve said as he and Harry sat in the only two chairs in the room.

"Sir? Don't call me 'sir.' I ain't old enough for that yet, kid."

Steve was about to apologize when Harry spoke up.

"Don't let him kid you, Steve—he's old enough to be called a lot worse things than old, and he's been called a lot of them over the years."

"Yeah, and you called me most of 'em. Ya wanna get the cards out of the drawer?"

"Actually, we're not here to play. I'm helping Steve with a case, and I'm thinking you might be able to help too."

"Me? I've been cooped up here for the last eight years. How would I know anything that could help you?"

"It's about St. Christopher's."

Steve felt there was an ominous sound in the way Harry said it. Bernie's voice had the same sound when he spoke.

"St. Christopher's. You're up against it if you have a case there, kid. Those sisters know how to keep a secret. What happened?"

Steve's spirits sank. He had been hoping Bernie would be able to give him at least a small piece of information about what had happened in 1940. It didn't seem now like there was much hope of that, but he'd give it a try anyway.

"One of the nuns was murdered last night."

"Murdered? A nun? Well, that tops anything I ever dealt with there."

"We think it might have some connection to the girl who killed herself years ago. Harry said you worked the case, and I was hoping you might remember something more than what the sisters have told us."

"The girl who killed herself. Yeah, that was really something. You'd think they'd want to know why. You'd think they'd want us to help them find out. Instead, they had the body cut down and at the undertaker's before we even heard about it. I told them there had to be an autopsy and we needed to examine the scene, but they refused to let us in. When I went to the chief to get a court order to get the body, he told me to forget it. He said it was their business, and we should just leave them alone."

Steve couldn't believe what he had just heard.

"Why would he tell you that? It makes no sense. Just because they're nuns they shouldn't have been able to ignore the law."

"Well, the order didn't come from him. Somebody higher up told him to back off. Who or why we'll never know. They just buried her the next day, and that was it."

Steve shook his head.

"Wow. I was hoping I might get something to help me sort this out, but now I have even more questions. What were they so secretive about? For all we know, she didn't even kill herself. Maybe she was killed, and they covered it up. Maybe…"

Harry stopped him.

"Don't do this, Steve. Don't get caught up in trying to solve a twenty-seven-year-old case. If it wasn't solved then, it won't be solved now. It'll just distract you from this case."

Bernie nodded in agreement.

"Yeah, kid. Just like that other girl when she disappeared. We never found out what happened to her either."

Harry and Steve looked at each other, stunned. Other girl? No one had said anything about another girl. Steve needed to hear more.

"What other girl?"

"The one who they said ran away. It was in 1930. I had just come here a couple years before that."

"So what happened?"

"Gimme a second. I wanna make sure I don't forget anything."

He closed his eyes and thought for a minute or so, Steve waiting anxiously to hear the story. It was so long ago that it probably had nothing to do with the murder, but then again, there were so many secrets piling up that there was certainly something not quite right about the school. He had to find out everything he could about its past.

Bernie opened his eyes.

"Okay. I think I got it. We got a call in the middle of the night from the school. A sister had done a bed check and found one empty. She was apparently new and panicked. From what we eventually learned, she didn't want to wake the other sisters in the middle of the night, so she looked around herself. She didn't find the girl anywhere, so she thought if she had left the school, she should get us out to look for her."

He turned to Harry.

"Ya wanna get me a beer? Get yourself one too. Want one, kid?"

"No thanks. I'm still on duty."

"That never stopped us back in the day."

Harry returned with the beer and handed one to Bernie.

"Times have changed, Bernie. They got rules now."

"Yeah, rules. I'm glad I'm where I am."

He took a drink and went back to his story.

"Anyway…Joe Harris and I were on the night shift. We took a ride out there to get a little more information. The sister who answered the door acted like we were crazy. Told us no one had called and nobody was missing. I told her we had the call registered in the log at the station. She said someone must have been playing a joke.

The sister who called had given us her name because we always got a name when someone called in, so I asked to see Sister whatever. I don't remember the name anymore. That one tells me there was no one there with that name. I wasn't gonna call a nun a liar, so we went back to the station. I just didn't like the feel of the whole thing, though.

"The next day, I get a call at home from the mayor himself telling me to go back to the school. He said he'd been called and asked to send me back. When I asked why, he told me to just go and not tell anyone else about it. Well, I wasn't about to say no to the mayor.

"The same sister answered the door. She was a whole different person, all friendly and apologizing for her mistake last night. She brought me in to see the head nun, the Mother Supreme or whatever."

Steve resisted the urge to correct him.

"She sits me down and tells me that a girl had indeed run away, but for the sake of the school and her family, they wanted to keep it as quiet as possible. I guess her old man was some big shot who didn't want a scandal to sully his reputation. She tells me the girl had been seen talking to some drifter a couple of days before. There were a lot of drifters around in those days, going from town to town looking for work. Their theory was that he turned her head and convinced her to run off with him. She reminded me that it would be greatly appreciated by both the school and the girl's family if nothing more was said about it, then she hands me an envelope and says it was a token of the family's appreciation, shows me to the door, says she enjoyed our talk, and closes the door. I looked in the envelope and found twenty crisp hundred-dollar bills inside. I put the money in my pocket and went home.

"That night, when I went in for my shift, I took Harris outside, told him the story, and gave him half of the money. We swore we'd never speak of it again. This is the first time I've told the story to anyone. But the thing haunted me for years."

"Why?" Steve asked. "It seems pretty cut and dried to me."

"It just didn't wash. I kept asking myself why a girl from a family that obviously had a lot of money would run off with an outta-work bum. Why give up the good life for a life of cold beans and sleeping on the ground? Something else happened, and I don't know what, but I wouldn't be surprised if I found out she's buried out in the woods behind the school."

That thought piqued Steve's interest.

"What makes you think that?"

"Just makes sense. She was never seen or heard from again. If she didn't run away, and I don't think she did, something else must have happened to her. I'm convinced she died—accidentally or on purpose, it doesn't matter. But the sisters definitely didn't want anyone to know about it. The only way to keep a secret like that would be to bury the body, and the only place they could do that without any risk of being seen is on the property."

Steve was intrigued.

"So if you're right, we have two mysterious deaths and now a murder which may or may not be connected to one or both of those deaths. The trouble is, what we know so far doesn't necessarily show any connection. I have a feeling someone knows more than they're willing to admit, but if I can't get them to come forward, Sister Margaret Mary's murder may very well become just one more mystery that stays hidden in those walls."

Bernie froze in the middle of taking a drink. He put the bottle down on the table. "What did you say?"

"I said this could become..."

"No. Not that. The name. What was the sister's name?"

"Margaret Mary. Why?"

Bernie's whole manner became that of a cop who knew he had just discovered something important.

"It's been so long I didn't remember, not until you said it, but that's the name. The name of the sister who called in that night."

Every good detective can feel when they've made a breakthrough. All three had that feeling now.

Steve tried to imagine how it all might fit. If Sister Margaret Mary knew the truth about what happened the night the girl disappeared, who might, after all these years, want to kill her because of it? There was only one person, he thought, who would know the answer.

"Harry," he said, "I've got to get back. You don't mind taking off so soon, I hope."

"If I was in your shoes, I'd want to get back there as soon as possible. I see this old buzzard every couple weeks or so. He always gets me into a card game. If we go now, I'll at least leave with money in my pocket."

He looked at Bernie.

"Speaking of money, what'd you do with that thousand bucks? That was a lot of money in those days."

"I bought bonds. Every time they came due, I bought more. It added up pretty good. Do you think I could afford to live in a place like this on what I get from my retirement?"

"You cagey old man. Kept that secret from me all those years we worked together."

"I kept a lot more secrets than that. Maybe some day I'll tell you a few more."

"I don't know. Maybe it would be better if I don't know."

"You're probably right," Bernie agreed.

He turned to Steve.

"I expect you to come out and tell me everything after you solve this thing."

"I'll make sure I do, if I solve it."

"It's not a question of if. You're going to do it. I'm sure of that. Of course, if you are, you got to get back to that school. So what are you standing around here for?"

"You're right! Thanks for your help. I really appreciate it."

He and Harry said their goodbyes and headed back to Harry's place. Steve tried to figure out how everything might be connected, asking Harry for his thoughts now and then. He knew that if there was a connection, he needed to find the missing link that would tie everything together. If there was one, there was only one person who could help him find it.

He had to talk to Sister Agatha, the sooner the better. If he was right, she could be in danger too.

CHAPTER 7

Marjorie and Sarah had finished eating, but they waited for most of the girls to leave the dining room. After their encounter with Paula and Brenda, they weren't sure they'd be safe in their rooms. It seemed crazy to think that they might have been involved in the murder, but if they weren't, what were they hiding?

They talked as quietly as they could, trying to think of a reason for Paula and Brenda to act the way they had. There were only a couple of possibilities as far as they could see. Maybe they had cheated on a test, or they might have somehow managed to sneak out to meet some guys. Things like that had happened in the past, so they were legitimate possibilities. But even if they were afraid that Sister Margaret Mary may have found out, that didn't seem like a reason to kill her. A little detention sure didn't seem worth taking a chance on ending up in prison for the rest of your life.

Marjorie looked around and saw that there were only three girls left in the room, and they looked like they were ready to go back to their rooms.

"I sure wish Steve didn't tell us to wait for him to send for us. I don't want to get him mad but I don't want to go back to my room. Paula and Brenda will probably be in the hall again, and I don't want to meet up with them. We can't just sit here forever. That'll attract more attention. I think we should go to Mother Superior's office. Maybe Steve is back and we can tell him what Paula said."

"And face Sister Agnes again? I don't know."

"Sister Agnes or Paula and Brenda?"

Sarah mulled the choice over for a few seconds.

"Okay, let's go. But I'm gonna stand back and let you do the talking."

They watched the three girls go out the back doorway and moved cautiously toward the front of the room. Two freshmen servers came out of the kitchen and looked at them suspiciously then began to remove the last few dishes from the tables. When their backs were turned, Marjorie and Sarah slipped out the front and into the hall.

They hurried down the hall, watching over their shoulders to make sure no one had seen them. When they got to Sister Agnes's desk, Sarah stopped a few feet away. Marjorie approached the desk slowly, watching for Sister Agnes to notice her. Her heart skipped a little when she saw Sister turn toward her.

"You again! What is it now?"

Marjorie swallowed hard and summoned her courage.

"We need to see Mother Superior right away."

"You can't. She's in with that detective. You'll have to wait."

"But it's important. If Steve's in there, it's something he needs to know about."

Sister Agnes eyed her reproachfully.

"Steve? If you mean the detective, you're a little young to be that familiar with him."

Marjorie was getting a little impatient.

"He told me to call him that. Mother Superior said it was okay. Please, just let them know we're here. I'll bet they'll tell you to let us in. Tell them we've got some important information."

"Well, you've certainly got some gall, I'll tell you that. Go wait over by your friend."

Marjorie moved back to stand by Sarah. Sister Agnes picked up the phone and dialed then turned her back to the girls. She spoke softly, turned around, and replaced the receiver on the phone. There was definite displeasure in her expression.

"You may go in," she said, almost as if she only said it because she had no choice.

The girls entered the office, somewhat fearfully knowing they had gone against Steve's instructions. Marjorie quickly blurted out an apology and explanation as she came through the door, hoping to avoid a reprimand from Steve.

"We're sorry, Steve! We just couldn't wait! We had to tell you this right away!"

"Besides," Sarah chimed in, "we're too scared to go back to our rooms."

Her remark took Mother Superior and Steve off guard. Steve had his lecture about not following his instructions all prepared and ready to go. Now that would have to wait until he found out what had made the girls so afraid.

Mother Superior sat the girls on the sofa, and she and Steve sat in what by now were their usual chairs. Her face showed concern, but her voice was calm and reassuring.

"You're safe here. Now tell us as calmly as you can what's happened."

The girls looked at each other, waiting to see who would start first. Marjorie already knew what she was going to say. She looked at Steve.

"You've got to question Paula Harris and Brenda Michaels right away! They're hiding something, I just know they are. They even threatened us and called us snitches."

Mother Superior looked at Steve with a worried look then turned back to the girls.

"Threatened you? How?"

"Well, they didn't actually say anything about hurting us or anything, but Paula said, 'We don't need any snitches.' The way she said it was scary, like she was thinking about beating us up. She said they'd have to be careful about talking when we were around."

"Why would she say that?" Steve asked.

Marjorie knew she had to tell them about what she told Ginny and why she felt she had to come up with some explanation for where they had been. When she finished, Steve nodded his agreement with her reason.

"I guess I didn't realize the other girls would notice how long you were gone and wonder why. Apparently, I have some things to learn about teenage girls."

"Don't worry, Steve," Mother Superior said with a smile. "We're with them all the time and we keep learning new things almost every day."

She turned to the girls.

"I'll have Paula and Brenda brought here, so we can try to find out what they may be hiding. I think, however, that you shouldn't be here when we do. It may not be a good idea to send you back to your rooms, though."

She went to the phone and gave Sister Agnes some instructions. She explained as she returned to her chair.

"I've sent for Sister Joan. Most of the older sisters are grieving and would, I think, feel put upon by having an additional duty. Sister Joan hasn't been here very long, and while she's sad about Margaret Mary, I don't think she'll mind taking you girls under her wing."

The girls looked a little confused.

"What do you mean, Mother?" Marjorie asked.

"You'll go with her. She'll take you to the recreation room, and you can wait there while we talk to Paula and Brenda."

The girls looked at each other, the same question in both their minds.

Recreation room? What do nuns need a recreation room for? They just work and pray, don't they?

Mother Superior seemed to read their thoughts.

"You're surprised that we have a recreation room, I see. As I've said, we're human. Just like you, we like to relax when we have the chance. There are books and magazines there as well as some board games and playing cards. There's a television also, but we don't use it very much. We mainly watch *The Lawrence Welk Show* and, of course, Ed Sullivan. Some of the sisters do enjoy the Saturday morning cartoons once in a while. I'm sure you'll find something there to help you pass the time."

There was a knock on the door, and Sister Joan entered.

"You sent for me, Mother," she said as she bowed slightly.

"Yes, Sister. Please take these girls to the recreation room and stay with them till I send for you to bring them back here. Detective McLean and I have other girls to talk to, and we don't need them all here at once."

Sister Joan looked conflicted for a moment then spoke.

"But, Mother, the sisters are in the recreation room praying a rosary for Sister Margaret Mary."

"Why are they praying in there and not in the church? I thought that's what had been planned."

"Well, you know how the church roof has been leaking. Father Jerome had scheduled it to be repaired today. The sisters felt the noise would be too much of a distraction."

"Oh, yes. Now I remember. Father had mentioned it to me. It seems with all that's happened, I forgot. We'll have to find somewhere else."

She paused just a few seconds.

"It seems the best solution is for you to take them back to their rooms and stay with them there. Take them there now. I'll send Mary Joseph to get the other girls in a moment."

Sister Joan nodded.

"Yes, Mother. Come along, girls."

Steve stepped forward quickly.

"Sister, before you go, I'd like to talk to you for a moment."

He looked toward Mother Superior.

"If you don't mind, that is, Mother."

"No, certainly."

Steve turned back to Sister Joan.

"I'll have to question all of you eventually, so while you're here, I can take care of my questions for you now. I really only have one question, actually. Did you hear or notice anything out of the ordinary last night?"

"Well, sir, I did think I heard someone in the hall quite late. It was well after lights out. I'm a very light sleeper, and sometimes a little noise can wake me easily. I didn't think too much of it at the time. Some of the older sisters do need to use the bathroom during the night now and then."

"I'm going to get a drawing of the layout of your rooms later, but while you're here, can you tell me where your room is in relation to Sister Margaret Mary's?"

"Yes, sir. My room is one down and across the hall from hers."

"So you're fairly close. Are you sure you didn't hear anything else?"

"No, sir. I'm sorry I can't be more help than that."

"Well, I do have one more question. Would someone going to use the bathroom pass your room as they went?"

"It would depend on where their room was in relation to the bathroom, but now that you mention it, sir, it did seem like someone was going toward the stairs."

"Thank you. You have been a help."

"Thank you, sir."

She made another slight nod to Mother Superior and led the girls out of the room and back to the girls' quarters. As they moved down the hall, as Marjorie had feared, Paula and Brenda were outside their doors. She held her breath as they neared them. She could see their surprise when they saw Sister Joan. Paula recovered quickly though and smiled. It was an evil smile, Marjorie thought.

"Sister," Paula said ever so sweetly, "why are you with them? Are they in trouble?"

Sister Joan replied calmly.

"No. They're not. But some others here may be."

It was almost as if she knew which girls Mother Superior meant when she said they were going to talk to other girls, Marjorie thought.

When they got to their rooms, Sister Joan suggested they all stay in Marjorie's room so they could keep each other company. The girls sat on the bed, and Sister Joan sat in the desk chair. Sister Joan tried to keep the conversation going, asking them about their classes, which one they liked best and which they didn't like.

She asked them about their families, if they had brothers and sisters, what kind of music they liked. Anything to pass the time.

"What's your family like, Sister?" Marjorie asked.

"My family? Well, I have two older brothers and a younger sister. I haven't seen them for quite a while. None of them nor my parents live near here. We exchange letters and once in a great while we talk on the phone. Long distance is expensive, so we have to keep the calls short and infrequent."

"Yeah," Marjorie agreed, "my parents only call about every two months or so. I wish it could be more often."

She heard a sniffle next to her and turned to see Sarah beginning to cry.

"What's the matter?" she asked.

Sarah shook her head.

"It's nothing really."

"Oh, c'mon, Sarah. Did I say something wrong? If I did, I want to know what it was."

Sarah went to the desk and grabbed a Kleenex then sat back down and wiped her nose.

"It's just what you said about talking to your parents. It made me think of what's going to happen the next time I talk to mine. I never like talking to them as it is. All my dad does is ask me about my grades and tell me I'm not doing good enough. I can have As and Bs, and he tells me the Bs should be As. I don't even want to think about what he's going to say when I tell him…"

Her voice trailed off as she realized that Sister Joan was in the room with them.

"Tell him what?" Sister Joan asked. "You seem troubled. Maybe I can help."

"It's nothing, Sister," Marjorie said quickly.

Sarah got up and walked over to the window.

"Oh, what's the use, Marge? Everyone's gonna know soon anyway. I'm pregnant, Sister."

She didn't cry when she said it this time. There was only a sound of resignation in her voice. She stood quietly looking out the window.

Sister Joan rose and went over to her. She put her hand on Sarah's shoulder. "I'm sorry, my dear. If you ever need someone to talk to, you can come to me anytime."

"Thank you, Sister."

Suddenly, Sarah turned away from the window and rushed over to sit next to Marjorie.

"What's wrong?" Marjorie asked her.

"I thought I saw him in the courtyard."

"Who did you see?" Sister Joan asked

"It's nothing, Sister," Sarah answered. "I think it was just my imagination."

Sister Joan could see that this was something that should be better left alone. She was fairly sure she already knew the answer anyway.

Suddenly, they heard an angry voice from the hall.

"Marjorie, you bitch! I knew you couldn't be trusted!"

They hurried out and looked up the hall. Sister Mary Joseph was there with Paula and Brenda. Sister was clearly not happy with Paula. She was giving her a piece of her mind, and everyone knew if there was any sister you didn't want to get a lecture from, it was Sister Mary Joseph.

"Paula, that is not the kind of language a young lady uses! After you meet with Mother Superior, you and I will meet to discuss your use of that word. We don't have time now, but you will apologize to Marjorie later."

Paula was defiant.

"I will not apologize to her! I only called her what she is!"

The shock showed unmistakably on Sister Mary Joseph's face.

"Paula, I'm surprised at you! This disrespect is intolerable! I'll report it to Mother Superior when we get to her office! Now come along. We can't waste her time."

Paula and Brenda turned and grudgingly started through the now full hallway, Paula angrily pushing girls out of her way. Brenda moved slowly with her head bowed, following behind Paula. Sister Mary Joseph walked behind, directing the girls to go back to their rooms. As the hall started to empty, Sister Joan motioned for the girls to go back into the room.

"I wondered," she said as they sat down, the girls back on the bed and Sister Joan again in the desk chair, "if those were the girls Mother Superior meant."

"Why did you think that?" Marjorie asked.

"I just noticed that they've been acting differently lately. Secretive."

"Yeah," Sarah said, "we thought they were hiding something too."

"We were wondering," Marjorie added, "if they knew something about Sister Margaret Mary's murder."

Sister Joan sat back in the chair and considered that possibility.

"I rather doubt it. Considering the distance between here and the convent, it seems pretty unlikely that any of you girls could know anything. The only way I can think of that happening is if one of you overheard someone saying something incriminating, and that would be highly improbable. I think if they are hiding something it's a lot less important than that."

Marjorie looked disappointed.

"I suppose you're right. Now, though, I'm kinda curious about what it could be."

There was a soft knock on the door. Marjorie answered it and found Rachel Williams standing nervously on the other side. Rachel had the room across the hall. She looked like she was trying to decide if she should say something or just turn and run. Finally, she spoke, softly and hesitantly.

"Can I talk to you, Marjorie?"

"Sure. Come in."

Marjorie started to open the door, but Rachel grabbed the handle to stop her.

"Could we talk alone?'

There was an almost pleading sound to her voice.

"Yeah. I'll come out there."

She looked over her shoulder.

"I'll be right back."

"Don't go too far," Sister Joan warned.

"No. I'll just be out in the hall."

She went into the hall and closed the door behind her.

"Rachel, what's going on?"

"I think I'm in trouble. I didn't know who else I could talk to, but you seem to know something about why Paula and Brenda had to go to Mother Superior's office, so I thought I'd ask you if you know why."

"Well, I don't know if I'm allowed to say anything."

"Please, Marge. It's really important!"

The pleading sound was even stronger.

"Okay. All I can tell you is that the way they've been acting so secretively lately they're being questioned if they know anything about the murder."

Rachel seemed to relax a little.

"Oh...well, if that's all it is...maybe it'll be okay. Thanks, Marge."

She turned to leave but her last remark made Marjorie wonder why she was so interested in why Paula and Brenda were being questioned. She obviously didn't think it was about the murder, so what made her so frightened and what did it have to do with the other girls?

"Wait, Rachel."

"Why?"

"Because I can tell you're afraid of something, something Paula and Brenda know that you don't want them to tell anyone about."

The nervousness had returned but she was trying to control it.

"No, really, there's nothing. It's not important. If they're just asking them about the murder, then it's okay."

"Rachel, it isn't just Mother Superior who's going to be questioning them. There's a detective there too. If they're not hiding something about the murder, the detective will find out what they are hiding."

The nervousness was gone. In its place was terror. She was shaking and pacing, tears flowing from her terrified eyes.

"No, no! This can't be happening! What am I gonna do? What am I gonna tell my parents?"

Marjorie grabbed her shoulders to stop her pacing. She held her in place as she tried to break away.

"Rachel! What are you talking about? What is it that's so terrible? Tell me!"

"I can't, I just can't! I don't want anyone to know! But if they tell...oh God, oh God, what am I gonna do?"

They had been talking in hushed tones, but now her voice was getting louder. She'll be shouting any minute, Marjorie thought.

"Come on," she said as she held onto Rachel as tightly as she could, opened the door, and pulled her into the room. Sister Joan and Sarah jumped to their feet.

"Help her sit down," Marjorie told them as she went back to the door, opened it and looked both ways down the hall. No one was there.

Good, she thought, *nobody else heard us.*

She closed the door and went to check on Rachel. She was on the bed with Sarah sitting on her right and Sister Joan on her left. Sister Joan was trying to calm her down as she sat murmuring "What am I gonna do?" over and over. She was clearly frightened of something, but what?

Marjorie knelt in front of Rachel and held her hands.

"Rachel, you've got to tell us what you're so afraid of. You're making yourself sick holding it in. I know you want to tell us."

"I do, but I just can't. I can't bring myself to say it."

Sister Joan tried to help.

"Come now, Rachel, surely it's not that bad."

Sarah reached out and turned Rachel's face toward her.

"Rachel, just this morning, I sat where you are now and told Marge something I thought I could never tell anyone. I thought it was too shameful to admit to anyone. But I told her, and now I'm glad I did. It feels so much better to not feel so alone."

Rachel looked from Sarah to Marjorie then down at the floor. She turned to sister Joan.

"I think I can tell, Sister, but not to you."

Sister Joan smiled and nodded.

"I think I understand. I'll wait in the hall."

She stood and went to the door. As she went out, she stopped and looked back at Rachel.

"God give you courage," she said, and closed the door.

Marjorie took Sister Joan's place next to Rachel.

"She's gone. You can tell us now."

Rachel still seemed hesitant. Sarah felt she knew what to do.

"I told you I told Marge something this morning, but I didn't tell you what it was. It was something I didn't want anyone to ever know. I was so ashamed. I thought if anyone found out I couldn't bear it. But I'm so glad now that I told her. You'll feel that way too. I know you will. What I told her is that I'm pregnant."

Rachel raised her head and looked at Sarah.

"Pregnant? Really?"

Sarah nodded.

Rachel looked back down at the floor.

"Are you scared?'

"Yeah. But not as much as I was when I was keeping it all inside and feeling like I had no one to help me."

Rachel kept looking at the floor as she choked out the words through her tears.

"I let Paula and Brenda take pictures of me."

Neither of the girls fully understood.

"Pictures? Why?" Marjorie asked.

As soon as she did, she suddenly felt she knew.

"What kind of pictures?"

"Pictures of me...without any clothes on."

Rachel's tears gushed out as she put her hands to her face and sat shaking and rocking back and forth.

"I can't believe I let this happen. I should have never listened to them."

The girls let her get it all out before asking any more questions. She slowly began to calm down and wiped her eyes. Marjorie asked the only question she could think of.

"Why did you let them do that?"

"Money."

"Money? They paid you so they could have naked pictures of you? That's kinda weird."

"No, they didn't pay me. There's a man who's going to. He paid them for pictures they took of each other, and they said I could get paid too. I feel so stupid."

Sarah put her arm around her.

"I know. I felt the same way. I still do a little. But you don't have to be stupid to make a mistake. People make mistakes every day, and that's all you did.'

"But they don't make mistakes like this."

"Some of us do. Mine's gonna change my life forever."

Marjorie had been lost in her own thoughts while they talked. Now she had another question.

"Why do you need money? I could have given you some if you were short."

"That's just it. I'm always short. You wouldn't understand because your families have money. Mine doesn't. I'm only here because there are people who give the school money to pay for kids like me to come here. Sometimes I feel like I shouldn't even be here with the rest of you."

Marjorie suddenly felt uncomfortable about her family's money. She had grown up with other kids just like her. She could tell Rachel was embarrassed to admit that her family didn't have money and it made her feel embarrassed that hers did. She struggled with what to say next.

"Gee…I'm sorry. I heard there were girls like that, but I didn't know you were one of them."

"Yeah. There are about twenty of us. We all try to hide it so the rest of you won't look down on us or feel sorry for us."

Marjorie immediately regretted what she had just said.

"Oh, well…I don't mean I feel sorry for you. I mean I feel sorry that you feel like you shouldn't be here. You belong here as much as any of us. How much money you have doesn't make a difference."

"Yes it does. Why do you think I hardly ever go into town on shopping days? I see you all buying things I can't afford, and sometimes I want to cry. I remember the time you bought that transistor radio. You came back and showed it to everybody. I went back in my room and cried. I would have given anything to be able to have something like that."

Marjorie's conscience was burning.

"Rachel, I didn't know. I'm so sorry. If I had known, I would have…"

"I know you didn't know. I didn't want you or anyone else to know. It was easier to cry in private than to wonder if everyone was feeling sorry for me."

Sarah was now struggling with her conscience. She wondered if she had done something in the past to hurt the other girls. She felt she had to apologize even if she hadn't.

"Rachel, I don't know if I ever made you sad, but I'm sorry if I did."

"You don't have to do that. Neither of you do. You've both always been nice to me, and that's all I really wanted. I think some of the girls knew, though. They acted different around me. Sometimes I felt like they were talking behind my back. I'd hear them laughing and wonder if they were talking about me."

"Like Paula and Brenda?" Marjorie asked.

Rachel nodded.

"They came to my room one day and said they noticed I seemed to hardly have any money, and they asked if I wanted to know how I could get some without doing any work. At first, when they told me, I was pretty shocked. I said I could never do something like that. They said it was easy and that they had done it and they each got a hundred dollars for it. I still said no."

"So what made you change your mind?" Sarah asked.

"After that, every time I'd see them, they'd stop me and talk about the things they were buying with the money. I started to feel jealous, and before long, I was thinking it wouldn't be that bad. It would just be them taking the pictures, and we've all seen each other in the showers, so that wouldn't be a big deal. I thought if I didn't think beyond that, I'd be okay."

Marjorie wanted to say something. She wanted to ask Rachel how she could be that dumb. But she knew that wouldn't be the right thing to do. She found what she thought was the right question.

"Rachel, didn't you think at all about what was going to happen to those pictures? I mean, if a guy's willing to pay a hundred dollars, he's probably not going to just keep them himself."

"What do you mean?"

"I'm not sure, but I think he's probably selling them to other people. There are a lot of guys looking for those kinds of pictures. You know there are magazines with pictures like that, don't you?"

"Magazines!? You mean my picture could end up all over the country? I'd die if that happened! What am I gonna do?"

Marjorie could see that she was getting panicky again.

"I think the only thing we can do is tell Mother Superior."

The thought of telling Mother Superior horrified Rachel.

"Oh God, no! I can't tell her. She'll expel me. My parents will find out. If that happens, I might as well be dead!"

Sarah tried to calm her.

"I told her about me. She was really nice. She didn't get mad or make me feel bad about what I did. She's not as scary as everybody thinks."

Rachel grew quiet. The girls let her think it over. Sarah, especially, knew what she was going through.

Finally, Rachel turned to Marjorie.

"Okay. I guess I can do it. I hope you're right about what she'll do."

"I am. You'll see. I can't wait to see the expression on Paula and Brenda's faces when you turn them in."

Rachel stiffened.

"I didn't think about that. They'll kill me. Maybe we should wait."

"They won't be able to do anything to you," Marjorie reassured her. "Mother Superior will see to that."

"You sure?"

"Of course. And Steve will probably make sure they don't either."

"Steve?"

"Yeah. The detective. I've been helping him with his investigation. I told him that Paula and Brenda were hiding something. I sure didn't think it was anything like this."

There was a knock on the door, and it opened slightly.

"May I come back in soon?" Sister Joan asked.

Marjorie jumped off the bed.

"Oh, Sister! I'm sorry! Yes, I think we're done."

"It must have been something very important you had to discuss."

"Oh, yes, it was. I'm really sorry. We forgot about you."

"That's all right. As long as you were able to find a solution to whatever has been bothering Rachel, that's all that matters."

"Yes, Sister, we did. But we need to see Mother Superior right away."

"Marjorie, Mother Superior is busy with Paula and Brenda right now. I don't think we should disturb them."

"But that's just it, Sister. This is about them. Rachel knows what they've been doing. If she tells Mother Superior, they won't be able to lie their way out of it, and I know they'll try."

Sister Joan turned to Rachel.

"Is it really that important, Rachel?"

Rachel nodded. Sister Joan smiled understandingly.

"All right. We'll go to Mother Superior."

They made their way through the school to the convent. After passing through the dining room, Sister Joan stopped just inside the doorway to the hall.

She looked at Rachel.

"Since you didn't want me to hear what you had to tell Marjorie and Sarah, I think I can assume you'd rather I didn't go in with you now."

Rachel nodded.

"Then I'll leave you here. I'd like to join the sisters in prayer for Sister Margaret Mary, and this will allow me to do that."

She turned and moved down the hall and through the large wooden door. The girls approached Sister Agnes's desk slowly, swallowing hard as they did.

Sister Agnes looked up, and they stopped where they were. Rachel, having never encountered Sister Agnes, stood between Marjorie and Sarah, who were holding her hands to prevent her from turning and making a run for it.

"You two again! And I see you've brought a friend. I suppose you want to see Mother Superior."

Marjorie replied respectfully, "Yes, Sister."

"And of course, it's important."

"Yes, Sister."

"You know she's busy with some other girls right now. I don't think she wants to be disturbed."

"We know, Sister. But Rachel knows something about those girls that Mother Superior needs to know right away."

Sister Agnes fixed a stern gaze directly on Rachel. The girls tightened their hold as they felt her try to pull her hands away.

Sister Agnes shook her head.

"Why don't you girls just bring your beds and set them up in the hall here? It'll save you a lot of walking back and forth."

She picked up the phone.

"I'm sorry to disturb you, Mother, but they're here again. There's three of them this time... Yes, they said it's important... They claim it has something to do with the girls you have in with you now. The new one apparently knows something they say you need to know... All right, Mother, as you wish."

She hung up and turned back to the girls.

"You can go in."

As the girls hurried past the desk to the door, they heard Sister Agnes muttering. They had to stop outside the door to stop giggling before they went in.

"They should just bring the whole school in there. It'd save a lot of time."

They knocked, and Mother Superior's voice told them to come in. As they did, they saw Mother Superior standing at the far end of the conference table. Paula and Brenda were seated on either side of that end of the table. Steve was seated, as had become his custom, in the chair by the sofa.

As Paula and Brenda turned to see who was coming in, Paula's expression changed from the genial one she was using on Mother Superior to one of seething anger when she saw Rachel. She jumped suddenly to her feet.

"What's she doing here?" she shouted. She turned to Mother Superior.

"They shouldn't be allowed in here! They shouldn't be allowed to listen in! We have a right to privacy!"

Mother Superior stood calmly at the end of the table.

"Please sit down, Paula. That outburst was uncalled for. I won't tolerate shouting in my office."

Paula clenched her fists and looked down at the table, fighting to bring her anger under control. She turned and glared at the girls as she slowly sat down.

Brenda had been following Paula's lead as Mother Superior asked questions about why they had threatened Marjorie and Sarah and what they had meant when they said they'd have to be careful about who was around when they talked. They denied threatening anyone and said they didn't remember ever saying anything about being careful.

Mother Superior had pressed them, though, about other things. Had they cheated on a test? Did they have cigarettes they were hiding? They were, of course, able to give honest answers since they hadn't done any of those things. Still, she felt there was definitely something they were hiding. Their evasiveness to the initial questions was evident. Her problem was that they seemed too hard to break, especially Paula.

She kept her eyes on the girls at the table as she asked the others to come forward and tell what they had come to tell. Paula sat defiant, a steely expression on her face, but Brenda looked worried. There was concern on her face, and she was clearly avoiding looking at Paula.

In Paula's presence, especially after her outburst, Rachel's resolve had been swept away. When Marjorie tried to get her to move further into the room she refused to move.

"I can't, Marge," she whispered. "She's gonna kill me as soon as she gets a chance."

Marjorie stood close to Rachel and whispered. Her voice was low, but her tone was forceful.

"It's too late to change your mind. You can't let her scare you. She knows that you told me and Sarah. If she gets away with this, she'll come after all of us."

Paula watched them whispering. She jumped on it immediately.

"Look, Mother, they're over there getting their story straight. They've got some lie to get us in trouble. They lied about us threatening them, and now they're gonna lie about something else."

Marjorie knew she had to act fast before Mother Superior got tired of waiting. She looked Rachel in the eye.

"If you won't tell, then I will!"

She stepped further into the room and blurted it out as fast as she could.

"They've been selling naked pictures of themselves to a man in town!"

Paula was on her feet, ready to rush at Marjorie, but Mother Superior put her hand on her shoulder to stop her. Steve was already up and moving quickly around the table to where Marjorie was standing. Sarah and Rachel stood near the door, frozen with fear. Paula made a half-hearted attempt to break free then sat back down.

There was a moment when time seemed to stand still, then Mother Superior turned to Marjorie.

"How do you know this, Marjorie?"

Suddenly, Marjorie felt she had no right to expose Rachel's secret. It wasn't her story to tell. But what else could she say? The only other thing she could do was to say that it was a lie. But if she did that, she'd be the one in trouble and Paula and Brenda would not only get away with what they were doing, they'd be free to come after her and Sarah and even Rachel. But she had no choice. She had to protect Rachel's secret.

She felt everyone's eyes on her as she closed her eyes and prepared to throw herself to the wolves. Just as she started to open her mouth, she heard a voice behind her.

"I told her, Mother."

It was Rachel. She turned to see Rachel walking slowly into the room, tears streaming down her cheeks.

"And how do you know this, Rachel?" Mother Superior asked.

"Because I did it too."

She blurted out the words and fell into Marjorie's arms, barely able to stand. Steve helped Marjorie get her to a chair. Mother

Superior turned and walked around the desk to her chair. She sat stunned and almost lifeless.

"You're not going to believe her, are you, Mother?"

Paula had gone to the desk and was leaning on it, trying to get Mother Superior's attention, oblivious to the fact that Mother Superior was in shock.

Brenda stood watching Paula and shaking her head.

"Give it up, Paula. We're caught. It's over."

Paula wheeled and glared at her.

"No, we're not! There's no proof. Just her word against ours!"

She sat down, a smug, confident smile on her face.

Marjorie remembered something Rachel had said in the room.

"Rachel, you said you were going to get paid, but you didn't get the money yet, did you?"

Rachel was still weak, and as she answered, she sounded dazed.

"No. Why?"

"When did they take the pictures?'

"A couple days ago."

Marjorie turned to Steve.

"We haven't gone into the city in over a week. That's probably why Rachel didn't get the money yet. They couldn't have given them to the guy because we haven't been to town."

Steve shot a quick look at Paula and Brenda.

"I guess I better send one of my men over to take a look in their rooms."

Paula was on her feet again.

"You can't do that! That's our private property! It's illegal!"

Mother Superior had recovered somewhat from her shock.

"That's not true, Paula. Anything within the walls of this school is controlled by the school. Detective McLean can look anywhere he feels the need to look."

"Well, he won't find any pictures."

Marjorie thought quickly. Of course there were no pictures. There was nowhere at the school to develop the film.

"Don't look for pictures, Steve. Look for a roll of film."

Steve walked over and stood next to Paula.

"There will be a roll of film, won't there?"

Paula glared at Rachel.

"We should've never tried to help you!"

"Why, girls?" Mother Superior asked. "What were you thinking?"

Brenda hung her head.

"We just wanted the money. He offered us a hundred dollars each. We thought if it wasn't gonna hurt anybody, it was no big deal."

Steve shook his head. It wasn't that long ago that he was a teenage boy, yet he had forgotten over those few years just how naive teenage girls could be. "Actually," he said, "it could hurt someone. It could hurt you."

Brenda raised her head.

"How?"

"Did you really think that guy was going to just keep those pictures for himself? If he paid you each a hundred dollars, he probably already sold them to a magazine for twice that."

The word *magazine* got Paula's attention.

"A magazine? You mean those pictures could end up in a magazine all over the country?"

"More than likely."

"Oh, God! What if someone who knows me sees them? If my parents found out…"

She turned to Mother Superior.

"Oh, Mother, I'm so sorry! We didn't think…"

"No, you didn't think, did you?"

Mother Superior was herself again.

"Now that you've finally told the truth and we know what the problem is, it would seem that the next thing we need to do is figure out what to do about it."

"I think I have an idea," Steve said. He looked at Rachel.

"How old are you, Rachel?"

"Fifteen."

"I thought so."

He turned back to Paula and Brenda.

"I don't know what Mother Superior may have in mind as discipline for you, but I can tell you that there are criminal charges I could bring. However, I'm more interested in this man you've been dealing with. If you're willing to help me catch him, I think I can let you off with a warning."

"What do we have to do?" Paula asked.

"When do you go into the city next?"

"We're supposed to go the day after tomorrow."

"That's when you were going to give him the film."

"Uh-huh."

"Well, that's what you'll do."

Before Rachel could protest, he turned to her.

"Don't worry. He won't get to keep it."

He went back to telling them his plan.

"We'll be watching from a distance, and as soon as he has the film and you have the money we'll grab him. Considering your age and the situation, I'll ask that you be allowed to give a deposition rather than having to testify in court. The judge should go along with that. Are you willing to do that?"

They both nodded.

"All right. We'll go over the details before you leave for town. They're all yours, Mother."

Steve took Marjorie, Sarah, and Rachel into the hall.

"You won't have to worry about them. They're harmless now. Will you be OK, Rachel, if you go back to your room on your own? I need Marjorie and Sarah to stay here a while longer."

"I think so. Are you sure you'll get the pictures back?"

"He won't get away, I promise."

"Okay."

She hugged each of the others, whispering "Thank you" as she did, then headed off down the hall.

"Why do you want us to stay here?" Marjorie asked.

"Because I haven't had a chance to talk to Jack yet, and I don't want either of you to be where he can find you after I do. I don't think he'll try anything, but I'd rather be safe than sorry. I've made arrangements with Mother Superior for you to stay in their visitors' guest room."

He motioned to one of the two female officers who were waiting in the hall. She came over to them, and he introduced her.

"This is Officer Gordon. She'll stay with you as long as I think she needs to."

A young nun who was also waiting in the hall approached and introduced herself.

"I'm Sister Juliette Marie. I'll take you to the guest room. Please come with me."

She turned and led them through the large door. Paula and Brenda came out of the office almost at the same time as the others were going. Steve called the other officer over.

"This is Officer Hansen. She'll accompany you to your rooms. You'll give her the film and the camera. She has permission to search your rooms to make sure you're not holding anything back. You will cooperate with her and assist her if needed. I can count on you to do that, right?"

They nodded solemnly. Paula's bravado was gone. Steve felt a little sorry for them as he watched them go down the hall. They had let themselves get talked into something without giving any thought to the possible consequences. Now they would have to face them. He wondered what Mother Superior had said to them, but he wasn't going to ask her.

Sister Mary Joseph approached the girls.

"I'll be accompanying you to your rooms. Mother Superior has given orders that all room doors in the girls' quarters are to be kept closed until further notice. There will be periodic checks to make sure that the order is not violated."

"Don't worry, Sister," Brenda told her. "I'm never gonna break another rule as long as I live!"

Sister Mary Joseph eyed her doubtfully.

"Don't make promises you can't keep, my dear," she said as she turned to head down the hall.

When Steve went back into the office, Mother Superior was still at her desk. Her face had the look of someone who had lost all hope.

He crossed to the end of the conference table, pulled out a chair, and sat.

"Well, that's one mystery solved," he said. "Unfortunately, it hasn't brought us any closer to solving the bigger mystery."

Mother Superior laid her head back against her chair.

"Yes. One mystery solved and one more secret to add to the list of secrets this school has been hiding for far too long. What does one do when one's faith has been shaken, when the good that held one's beliefs intact has been swallowed up by evil, an evil that was always there? Has it all been an illusion? Was the good just a facade and the evil the only reality all this time? And what, I fear, is still left to be discovered?"

Chapter 8

Sister Agatha was still at prayer with the sisters. Steve saw no point in disturbing her while she was with them. He didn't think she'd be in any danger while she was surrounded by nuns. Besides that, he did have other matters to attend to. The first was Jack.

He learned that Jack was on the grounds helping his father as he often was. Since Jack had told Sarah that Sister Margaret Mary could help her, he could very well have more to tell. From what he knew so far, though, Jack could be a tough nut to crack.

Mother Superior had decided to lie down for a while. She told Steve she thought he could handle Jack by himself. Besides, she wasn't sure she wanted to hear his description of what she had come to refer to as "the incident". As far as she was concerned, Sarah's story had been more than she really wanted to know.

Sister Agnes ushered Jack into the room, eyeing Steve with a look of disapproval. She clearly felt he had no business in Mother Superior's office when she wasn't there. He thanked her, and she went back to her post, giving Steve one more look over her shoulder as she did.

Steve was seated on the right side of the conference table. He told Jack to sit on the other side in the chair across from his. Jack made no pretense of the fact that he didn't want to be there. He was tall, and tan from working outdoors. His hair was dark brown and uncombed, and his shirt and jeans were marked by the places where he rubbed the dirt off when he was working in the garden. He walked with an air of self-importance and a cock-sure attitude that was intended, Steve thought, to give Steve the feeling that he was in over his head with such a cool character.

He sat down, leaned the chair back, and threw his feet on the table.

Steve wasn't impressed.

"Get your feet off the table!"

Steve wanted there to be no mistake in Jack's mind that he wasn't the least bit threatened by Jack's attitude.

Jack pulled his feet off the table.

"Sure. I wouldn't want to get the table dirty."

Steve felt the best approach was to get right to the point.

"I've got some questions I'd like to ask you."

"What, about the old nun's murder? You think I know anything about it?"

"Well, we'll get to that later. First, I've got some questions about a girl you know."

"Really? Which one? I know lots of girls."

His cockiness was already starting to irritate Steve.

"A girl named Sarah. Sarah Collins."

"Sarah, huh? What's she look like?"

"Look, kid. You wanna dance around, you can try, but I don't have time to dance. So if you're gonna waste my time now, I'll just send you down to the station and we can do this little dance there. I'll have a lot more time tomorrow."

Jack leaned back and crossed his arms.

"You don't scare me."

Steve was out of his chair and around the end of the table in the proverbial blink of an eye. He grabbed the back of Jack's chair with his left hand and pulled his gun out with his right. He pushed the chair back and leaned over Jack.

"You want to be scared? We can get you plenty scared when we get you alone at the station. Now you're either going to cooperate or you'll be out of here and on your way in less than a minute. I don't like punks with attitudes, and I especially don't like punks who take advantage of young girls. It would be a pleasure to get you down to the station."

He straightened up and looked down at Jack.

"Your choice."

Jack's cockiness receded, but he held on to enough of it to still be belligerent. "Fine. Sure, I know her. Like I said, I know a lot of girls here."

Steve went back around to the other side of the table and sat again.

"How many of the others have you gotten pregnant?"

"Pregnant? I didn't get her pregnant. I never did anything with her."

"Well, that's funny, because she says you did, and I know she's not lying. She also says you threatened to kill her if she told anyone."

Jack didn't realize it, but just the split-second movement of his eyes gave him away. Steve kept talking before Jack had a chance to deny it.

"She says you threatened her with a grass shears. You told her they'd find her with the shears in her throat."

He could see Jack's mind working feverishly, making up more lies. And he saw the anger in the way his jaw was set so firmly.

"And before I go any further, I'm going to tell you that if you go anywhere near her or try to hurt her in any way I'll make you regret it for the rest of your life."

"Look, I told you, I never did anything with her. You're not much of a detective if you can't tell the difference between a lie and the truth."

"That's just it, I can. That's why I know that she's telling the truth and you're lying. You may as well give it up. We may have to wait several months, but once she has the baby, we'll be able to tell who the father is."

"What do you mean, when she has the baby?"

Steve only had to look at Jack's face to see that he hadn't expected that.

He thought she already had the abortion! he thought.

"You look a little troubled, Jack. Wanna talk about it?"

Jack was pulling himself together again.

"There's nothing to talk about. If she's pregnant, the kid ain't mine."

"Well, if it is, you may have more trouble than just having a kid to support. You ever hear of statutory rape, Jack?"

"Aw, c'mon. Who's gonna rape a statue?"

"I don't know if you're just trying to be funny or if you really don't know what it is. I thought a smart guy like you would know. From the way you talk, it's probably something you should know about."

"Okay. So I don't know what it is. What's the big deal?"

"The big deal is, she's only seventeen."

"Yeah. So what? They all might have been for all I know. I don't ask them how old they are."

"Well, you should. You see, statutory rape is what they call having sex with a girl under eighteen. It's a crime. You go to prison when you do that."

Jack's outward appearance changed. The realization that he had just told a cop that he had probably been committing a crime made his body lose its big man persona. But in his head, he was still working on a way out.

"Well, OK," he said, holding on to as much confidence as he could, "but like I said, I don't know how old they were, and anyway, I doubt that you'll find any girls who'll admit to doing anything. They know their parents would find out, and they don't want that to happen. And as far as this other girl goes, I can't say for sure that it was me, and neither can you."

"You're right, I can't. Not right now at least. But that'll change in a few months. I guess Sister Margaret Mary's death was bad luck for you. You didn't know Sarah hadn't gotten the abortion yet, did you? Or did you think she did and figured you should knock off the sister to make sure nobody would find out?"

Jack was out of his chair, almost jumping onto the table.

"Oh, no! You're not gonna pin that on me!"

Steve had risen also, prepared to counter Jack if he tried to get across the table.

"Sit down. I could try, and make your life miserable in the process...or maybe you know something that might help me find another suspect. Maybe you know more about Sister Margaret Mary than I do."

Now Jack was rattled. The rape thing bothered him a little, but there was a way to beat that. He just needed time. But someone might have seen him talking to the nun, and if he denied it now, it could look bad later if the cop found out. He didn't have to tell him everything, just enough to make it seem like he was trying to help.

"OK. You're right. I knew about the nun. There was another girl about three years ago. When she told me she was pregnant, she said she was scared and didn't want the kid. She told me I had to help her. It scared me too. I asked my dad what I should do. He told me about the nun. She had taken care of the same problem for him a couple times when he was younger."

Steve had to stop him there.

"Wait a minute. Are you telling me your dad's been doing the same thing you've been doing?"

"Well, not now. But years ago, when he was my age, he was."

A whole new stack of questions was piling up in Steve's mind. Another secret. Another possibility. And an unexpected suspect.

"And Sister Margaret Mary has been helping girls get abortions all these years?"

"Not helping, doing them."

This was too much for Steve. The idea of a nun helping these girls was unbelievable as it was, but the thought that she was actually performing abortions was impossible to comprehend. His mind was spinning out of control.

"Well, that surprised ya, didn't it, Detective?"

Steve regained his composure. He was a trained cop who was supposed to be able to deal with things like this.

"I've got to admit that's something I never could have imagined. You're sure?"

"Oh, yeah. The girl, the one three years ago, told me about it. Well, she only told me that the nun did it. She was sworn to secrecy about the details. She did say it hurt pretty bad, but it turned out okay."

Steve was still trying to make himself believe what he just heard. But Jack wasn't making it up. This was one time he was telling the truth. He felt he had gotten everything out of Jack that he could. He just had to make sure he got to Jack's father before Jack did. He didn't want the guy to suddenly disappear.

"All right, Jack. I'm done with you…for now. Just wait here for a minute. I need to talk to Sister Agnes."

He went out to the hall and sent one of the officers to get Jack's father and returned to give one more little jab at Jack's cocky attitude.

"Before you go, I just want to remind you that if you go anywhere near Sarah, I'll come down on you so hard you'll wish you'd never been born. And you can expect a visit from me a few months from now. I'll either have good news or bad. I probably won't even have to tell you which it is when I show up because I think you already know. So enjoy what freedom you have left."

Jack tried to look like he wasn't worried, but Steve could see it in his eyes.

"Go on. Get outta here."

Jack kicked the chair as he left and tried his best to swagger out of the room. Steve sat down and started to plan for his next interview. He wondered how many more surprises he was going to encounter before he solved this murder.

Mother Superior was still resting when John Miller was shown into the office. Steve was seated as he had been for Jack's interview. He told Mr. Miller to sit where Jack had sat then gave Sister Agnes a big friendly smile as she turned to leave, obviously still not happy with the whole situation.

Steve felt a little like he had been transported twenty or so years into the future. John Miller was basically Jack, only older, and with a mustache. He didn't have the same cockiness as Jack, though. That difference made Steve think about the old saying, "older and wiser". Would it prove to be true with John Miller?

Steve started with an easy and nonthreatening question.

"You've been working here for quite a while, haven't you?"

"Yeah. My old man had the job before me. I used to help him when I was a kid, like Jack does with me. I took the job in '46 after the war when my old man dropped dead."

"So you've been around here since the '30s, I guess."

"Yeah. I was gone during the war. In France with Patton. I was with him when we took Bastogne. That was really something to remember."

"It must have been. My dad has some stories. He was at Normandy. He doesn't talk about that very much though."

"Yeah, those guys saw some terrible stuff."

"So when did you sign up?"

"January '42. After Pearl Harbor, all the guys around here wanted to go."

"Were you married?"

"No. Got married when I got back in '45. Some of the local girls sent letters to us. One of them sent a picture. We wrote back and forth and got to like each other. When I got home, it didn't take more than a few months and we got hitched."

"So you must have been here when that girl hung herself."

There was an immediate change in John's attitude. Steve's seemingly innocent questions had made him relaxed and comfortable. Now he was noticeably tense and eyeing Steve suspiciously. Steve knew he had hit on something, and he wanted to strike before John had time to realize fully where he was going with his questions.

"You know something about that, don't you? I can see it in your eyes, so there's no use denying it. Did you know her?"

"Uh, no. All I know is what I heard back then. Everything was all hush-hush. I just know they didn't want the police involved."

He was clearly avoiding making eye contact with Steve.

"I think you know a lot more than that. I think you knew the girl. You have sex with her? I was told you were having sex with some of the girls back then."

"That's a lie! Who the hell told you that?"

John was leaning forward, looking straight at Steve.

"Your son."

"My kid!? I'll kill that little son of a bitch! What else did he tell you?"

Steve had John where he wanted him. Angry, easily goaded into saying something without thinking. He pushed him farther.

"That you told him to go to Sister Margaret Mary because she could get one of his conquests out of trouble. That she had helped you with the same kind of problem when you were young. Looks like it's true when they say, 'Like father, like son'."

John was seething now. As he jumped up out of his chair, Steve put his hand on his gun just in case.

John was shouting loud enough to be heard in the hall.

"You shut your mouth! Where do you get off accusing me of crap like that? I know what you're trying to do! You're gonna say I killed the old broad! Well, I didn't! Why would I?"

"Maybe you were afraid she might say something someday about the times she helped you, and it would get back to your wife."

"So what if it did? That all happened before I was married!"

"I thought you said it never happened."

John knew he had made a mistake. He stood glaring at Steve for a moment then sat down.

"So what if I did? I was young and single, and the girls wanted it."

"Even the girl who hung herself?"

Steve could see him struggling with what his answer would be. It took him a while to make up his mind.

"Yeah, her too. I don't know why. She was fat and not all that good looking. But she told me one of the girls had told her about me. At first, I said no, but I couldn't stand her crying and saying she knew no one would ever want her. I guess I felt sorry for her. I should have said no."

"Why is that?'

John knew again that he had said too much. He took his time with his next answer.

"She got pregnant."

There it was! A connection between the girl and Sister Margaret Mary! Steve wasn't sure if it would lead anywhere but he at least had something more to ask Sister Agatha about. First, he wanted to know if John knew any more than what he had told so far.

"So you sent her to Sister Margaret Mary."

"I had to. She came to me all worked up, said it would ruin her life. Then she said something about getting married. There was no way I wanted to end up married to her. A few days later, I heard she was dead. I guess killing the baby was too much for her to live with."

"Any chance someone helped her do what she did?"

"Hey, don't look at me when you ask that! I told you the truth. The last time I saw her was when I told her to go to the nun."

"And that's all you know."

He was quiet again. There was more, Steve was sure of that. He waited for him to decide what to do.

John weighed his options. It was so long ago that whatever happened then shouldn't matter now. The cop already knew he had known about the nun back then. Nobody could think he killed her because of that. But if he said anything more, they could make it all add up somehow. Still, he didn't want to look like he was hiding something.

"All right. The nun came to see me the day after the girl died. I could tell she was nervous. She warned me to never say a word to anyone about anything I knew. She said if I did, my old man would lose his job. Then she said she could fix it so it would look like I killed the girl, so I better make sure I never let it slip."

"Had she ever done that before?"

"No. She had reminded me a couple times that when she helped a girl, she was helping me too so I'd better remember to keep my mouth shut, but she was never mean and threatening about it."

"Well, obviously she might have been worried about questions being asked because of what happened. But no one asked any questions anyway, did they?"

"No, they didn't. The cops weren't even allowed to talk to anyone. That's why it seemed so strange to me. I never saw a nun act like that before."

"It sure seems like she was afraid of something more than her abortion activity being discovered. Unfortunately, she may have been the only one who could tell us why."

"Well, I've been around here since I was a little kid, and these nuns got plenty to hide. I could tell you…"

John stopped short.

Damn it! he thought. *He's a smart one. He let me talk until I put my foot in it.*

He saw Steve watching him, waiting to hear more.

"I just mean, ya know, how they're so secretive and all."

He shifted in the chair then sat looking up toward the ceiling and around the room, trying to look as nonchalant as possible.

Steve recalled his conversation with Bernie. John would have been here when the girl disappeared. He just said that he'd been here since he was a kid and followed that by saying the nuns have plenty to hide and then cut himself off like he had more to say. Steve decided to play his card.

"So you were here in 1930 when a girl disappeared. The nuns said she ran off."

Steve could see that John was having a hard time holding something back. He looked angry, which didn't make sense. He knew he had hit a nerve, but he didn't know why. Suddenly John spoke, quietly but with an anger that he struggled to contain.

"Why the hell did you have to bring that up? It was long ago. It should have been forgotten by now. It took me years to forget, and now you brought it all back again. I should have never told you anything. I should have kept my mouth shut."

Steve could see tears welling up in his eyes. He obviously not only knew something about the girl, he had a close connection to her in some way. John stood up.

"I'm done with this," he said as he started toward the door.

Steve got up quickly and moved to stop him.

"If you leave now, I'll just have to find you later. You know something, and I'm going to keep after you until you tell me what it is."

"Why? Why does it matter? It was so long ago. The past should stay in the past."

"Not if it can help me learn something about the present."

"How can it help you? How can a dead girl help you?"

So it was true. She didn't run away. But what happened to her?

"How do you know she's dead? If she ran off, she could still be alive somewhere."

John gave up. He went back to the chair and sat down. Steve followed and sat in the chair next to him.

"Tell me what you know."

"I know she's dead because I saw her body."

He sat back in the chair and blew a long, slow breath of air out between his pursed lips. He was the picture of a man who had spent a long day doing heavy labor and was finally able to sit down to rest. He spoke quietly with a tired, emotionless voice.

"I may as well tell you all of it. I was nine. The phone rang in the middle of the night. I heard my old man ask, 'Right now?' then he said 'All right, I'll be there as soon as I can' and he hung up. He came to my room and told me to get dressed. He said he needed me to help him with something.

"We went to the school. Before we went in, the old man told me to keep my mouth shut and just do whatever he told me to do. He said I was never to tell a soul what I was going to see.

"We went in through the door in the wall that he used to come and go for work. It was the only door he had a key to. We went to the gardener's shed and got two spades, then I followed him into the woods in the far corner of the property. There were two nuns there and a wheelbarrow that had something in it. As we got closer, I could see that there were legs hanging over the edge of it. I wanted to say something about it, but I kept my mouth shut like I was told. When we got to where the nuns were, there was a sheet covering the rest of what was in the wheelbarrow, but I knew what it was, and I got scared.

"The nuns whispered to the old man and pointed to a spot about ten feet away.

"He said 'Follow me,' and we went to the spot and started digging. We dug for an hour at least until the hole was about four feet deep. My old man wheeled the wheelbarrow over and set it alongside the hole. He got into the hole, and the nuns gave him the sheet. He spread it out on the bottom, and then the nuns handed the girl to him and he laid her down. All she had on was a nightgown, and it was stained with blood. The nuns had her uniform, and they threw it in the hole."

The last few words came out haltingly, and he stopped. He swallowed hard, fighting back tears. As he continued, tears began to stream slowly down his cheeks.

"I wanted to look away, but I couldn't, and I later wished I had. I saw her face, and I wanted to cry, but I couldn't let my old man see me doing that so I held it in. She was beautiful. She looked to me like an angel sleeping. I may have only been nine, but I fell in love with her on the spot.

"The hardest part was throwing the dirt back in on top of her. As I watched her slowly disappear under the dirt, I wanted to jump in the hole and brush the dirt away from her face. I wanted to wake her up and shout, 'Stop. She's alive!' but I knew I couldn't."

He stopped and took a few long heavy breaths.

"My old man had been careful to take a layer of sod up when we started digging. When the dirt was all back in, he put the sod back down and stomped it into place.

"I felt bad about that. It didn't seem right to stomp on her like that. He talked to the nuns for a minute, then we put the shovels back in the shed and went home.

"The only thing he said on the way was, 'Forget what you saw and don't ever tell'. I cried myself to sleep every night for weeks with my face buried in my pillow so my old man wouldn't hear me."

The two men sat silently for a while, John feeling the effect of the memory and Steve thinking how sad it was for a nine-year-old boy to have experienced such a terrible thing. Finally, John put his hand out to Steve.

"I guess I should apologize for the way I acted. I've had that story inside of me for so long. It took me years to forget it, and when you brought it up, I couldn't stand the thought of reliving it again. Now I'm glad you forced me to. I know now that I never really did forget it. It might not have been on my mind all the time, but it was there somewhere. When I was in France, I saw dead girls, killed by the bombing or the Nazis. Their faces were always dirty. Every time I saw one, I'd see her face with the dirt falling on her.

"There's something else I remember now too. Those girls, when I got a little older, when I look back, I remember that every time I was with one of them, I pretended it was her. I'd always try to pick the prettiest ones I could find because I wanted them to look as close as possible to her. What the hell does that say about me?"

"I'm no psychiatrist, but I think it says you were a nine-year-old boy who experienced something you never should have experienced. When you got older, you dealt with it the best way you could."

"I've managed to not think about it for a long time but I realize now that the one thing I needed in order to really put it behind me was to do what my old man told me never to do. I had to tell it. Until I did just now, I didn't know how guilty I actually felt."

Steve shook his hand. He was still thinking about that nine-year-old boy.

"There was nothing to feel guilty about. You had to do what your father told you to do. It wasn't right for him to have made a nine-year-old help him like that, but I'm sure you only did because you were afraid of disobeying him."

"I don't know that I felt guilty for having helped him. You didn't argue with him or refuse to do whatever he told you to do. I know I had no choice in that. I felt guilty for not telling anyone. After my old man died, I could have. Maybe if I did the nun would be in jail instead of dead."

"Are you sure no one else knew about it?"

"Well, the two nuns did. One of them was pretty old at the time. I think she died in '38 or '39. The other one was Sister Margaret Mary. She was young then, just got here a few months before. Unless they told someone, I don't think anyone else could have found out."

There was a knock on the door, and Steve answered it. It was Officer Hansen.

"I have the film and the camera. I did a thorough search of both rooms, and there was nothing more to find."

"Thank you, Helen. Have the film and camera sent to the station and then wait in the hall. I'll have another job for you in a few minutes."

Steve returned to John with his next question.

"Do you remember where she's buried?"

John nodded.

"Yeah. What are you gonna do?"

"Well, I think if she has any family members who can be located, they might want to know the truth about what happened. Someone somewhere may have been waiting all this time, hoping to hear from her, wondering how her life turned out. I think if I were in that position, I'd want to know. They might even want to have her buried with the family."

"When do you want me to show you?"

"I think we should do it right away. Long-buried secrets can sometimes provide answers when they're brought out into the light. I'll call and have the coroner come out with a couple of street department workers to help with the digging."

He was almost to the door when it opened, and Mother Superior came in.

"Oh, Mother. I'm glad you're back. I have a quick phone call to make, and I'll be right with you. Mr. Miller is going to show me something, and I need to get some help to take care of it."

As he went out into the hall, Mother Superior went to her desk and sat down.

"Good afternoon, Mr. Miller," she said as she passed him.

John stood and nodded respectfully.

"Good afternoon, Mother Superior."

She was curious about what John had told Steve, but she didn't ask. It would be better to have Steve tell her. She noticed that John was still standing, looking quite uncomfortable.

"Please sit down, Mr. Miller."

"Thank you."

He sat but remained uncomfortable, shifting in the chair and looking around the room, everywhere except toward Mother Superior's desk.

A few minutes later, Steve returned and crossed to the desk. Mother Superior prepared herself to hear the latest news.

"So what have you discovered now, Steve?" she asked.

Steve hesitated.

"Is it that bad?"

"Yes, Mother, I'm afraid it is."

"Well, tell me and get it over with. I'm not sure anything can shock me anymore."

Steve walked back and stood next to John, searching for the best way to tell her the news.

"John told me a story of something that happened when he was nine. It concerns the girl who was reported to have run away."

Mother Superior interrupted. She sat forward in the chair and leaned forward on the desk.

"You've known this all this time, Mr. Miller?'

"Yes, Mother Superior."

She sat back and closed her eyes. She knew what Steve was going to say.

"Go on, Steve."

"I have a feeling you already know what I'm going to tell you. She didn't run away. She died…and she's buried in the woods out back. John was going to show me when you returned."

Mother Superior sat motionless. It was strange, she thought, that she wasn't surprised by what she just heard. Somehow it seemed almost to be expected. She stood and walked around the desk.

"Well, let's get started."

Steve was uncertain about this.

"Are you sure, Mother? This isn't going to be pleasant. It might be better if you let me handle this."

"No. I want to be there. This school is my responsibility, and I can't shirk from it. I'm prepared to see what I see."

"All right. Let's go."

Just as they got to the door, Steve stopped.

"Oh, Mother, I had been planning to talk to Sister Agatha before this came up. Do you know if the sisters are done with their prayers?"

"Yes. I passed the recreation room as I came down. They were just near the end and should be finished by now."

"I'm concerned about leaving Sister Agatha alone. Would it be all right if I had one of my female officers stay with her?"

"Certainly. They're all going back to their rooms. I'll have Sister Juliette Marie bring the officer to Agatha's room."

She went into the hall and through the large door to the convent. While he and John waited for her to return, he gave instructions to Officer Hansen. A few minutes later, Mother Superior returned with Sister Juliette Marie, who took Officer Hansen into the quarters.

"I looked in on the girls," Mother Superior told Steve. "I don't think they're very happy cooped up in that room. I told the officer she could bring them to the recreation room now that the sisters are gone. I hope you're all right with that."

"Oh, sure, as long as Isabelle stays with them."

The coroner arrived as they were talking, and John led them all out through the yard into the woods. When they arrived at the spot, he took Steve aside.

"I said I'd show you where she is, but I don't want to help with the digging. I don't even want to be here. If you don't mind, I'll go wait in the shed. Just have them fill it back in. I don't want to have to do that either."

"I understand. We can take care of it. I'll make sure it'll look like we were never here."

"Thanks."

"Thank you. I know this has been hard on you."

John walked off toward the other part of the yard near the school where the shed was located. Steve had the diggers remove a layer of sod and begin digging.

Mother Superior stood at a distance, watching silently. At about three feet, they began to dig more slowly and carefully. Pieces of a skeleton started to show through the dirt, and they put the shovels aside and started to brush the dirt away with whisk brooms and dustpans.

Finally, enough dirt had been removed to reveal the entire skeleton. Pieces of a uniform lay over her feet, and a few pieces of her nightgown still clung to the bones. The coroner came to the edge of the grave and took several pictures then was helped down into the hole to examine the skeleton more closely.

"Will you look at that," he said, obviously surprised by what he saw.

"What?" Steve asked from above.

The coroner pointed to an area in the center of her pelvis.

"Do you see that? There's a tiny skull there. This girl was pregnant when she died."

Steve heard Mother Superior take in a sharp breath behind him. She came to the edge and made the sign of the cross and bowed her head in a short prayer. The coroner continued describing what he saw.

"Her gown is pretty much rotted away, but there appears to be a large dark spot on what's left of it from the waist down. My guess is, the girl had a heavy vaginal bleed and bled to death. I can't be sure, but I don't think it was a miscarriage. It looks to me like a botched abortion."

Mother Superior turned quickly and hurried from the grave. Steve followed her.

"Mother, are you all right?"

She turned, her face filled with anger. The coroner and the workmen watched uncomfortably as she released her rage in a shout loud enough to echo off the wall that surrounded the property.

"How could someone do that? How could any nun do that? To let her die like that! To throw her so unfeelingly into a ditch to hide the crime! What kind of monsters have we been hiding inside these walls?"

She collapsed to the ground, kneeling and sobbing.

"This is too much! This is too much!"

Steve called the coroner over to help him. They helped Mother Superior to her feet and supported her as they walked back to the school. As they came into the hall outside the office, Sister Agnes rushed to them as they came through the doors from outside.

"What's wrong? What happened?" she asked loudly.

She took the coroner's place at Mother Superior's side and helped Steve get her into the office and onto the sofa. Steve explained as they walked.

"She had a spell. I think you should call Sister Mary Joseph to come and stay with her for a while."

"I'll do that, sir. Should I call the doctor?"

"I don't think so right now. She just had a shock that weakened her."

As soon as Mother Superior was safely on the sofa, Sister Agnes hurried out of the room to get Sister Mary Joseph. Steve sat to her left on the sofa, while the coroner waited near the door.

Sister Mary Joseph soon rushed into the room and sat on Mother Superior's right, putting her arm around her to support her. As she did, Steve rose to leave. He was stopped by Mother Superior grabbing his sleeve. Her eyes were those of a frightened child pleading for help. Her voice was tired and weak.

"Put an end to this, Steve. Stop these terrible things."

"I will, Mother. I promise," he replied reassuringly.

She released his sleeve, and he and the coroner left to go back to the grave. As they walked, the coroner questioned Steve.

"What's going on here, Steve? I've seen a lot over the years, but this tops it all."

"Well, by the time I'm through here, it's going to be impossible to keep this quiet, so I may as well tell you, but you've got to keep it under your hat until I finish it all up."

"Oh, sure. I'll do that."

"You're probably right about the girl. I wasn't surprised when you said it. It appears there's been a nun here who's been giving abortions to girls who've gotten themselves in trouble over the years."

"Abortions? A nun? I can't believe it!"

"Unfortunately, it's true. I'm pretty sure the nun who got killed here last night was the one doing it. She helped bury the girl."

"Who is the girl, anyway?"

"She disappeared in 1930. The sisters told her family they believed she had run off with a drifter who was passing through town. Like you said, apparently something went wrong during the procedure. They couldn't let anyone find out or they'd have too much explaining to do. They got the gardener to help bury her, and he brought his nine-year-old son to help him."

"A nine-year-old kid? Seeing something like that? Must have messed him up pretty good."

"He's the gardener now. I was questioning him about Sister Margaret Mary, the dead nun, and this came out. I'll tell you later about how I got a lead on it. I have to admit, I didn't care much for the guy when I first met him, but after hearing his story about that night, I feel a little sorry for him. That was a hell of a thing for his father to do to him. He said he was relieved, though, to get it all out finally."

"I'll bet he was. That why he didn't stick around while we were digging?"

"Yeah. He's got a nine-year-old boy's memory of a beautiful girl laying in that hole and having to throw dirt on her. I can understand his not wanting to see her now."

They were back at the grave. The coroner sent the men to get a gurney and a sheet from his station wagon. The sheet under the girl had rotted away too badly to be of any help in lifting her out, so the bones were brought up one at a time and laid on the sheet on the gurney. It was taking more time than Steve felt he had to spend there, so he gave instructions to the workmen about filling in the hole properly and went back to Mother Superior's office.

CHAPTER 9

When Steve returned, Mother Superior had regained much of her composure. She was still fighting to understand how anyone, especially a nun, could let something like that happen to a young girl and still function as if nothing had ever happened.

"I don't think it's possible to ever understand, Mother." Steve told her. "There are apparently some people who lose touch with their normal human feelings. No one has ever been able to figure it out completely."

"I just can't believe I knew Margaret Mary all these years and never saw a sign of what she was hiding."

"She did do a good job of covering everything up. I wonder if the plan to say that the girl had run away was hers or the other nun."

"The other nun?"

"John said there were two there, Sister Margaret Mary and an older sister. He said he thinks the older one died in '38 or '39."

"I'd have to check the records to see who that might have been. Agatha may know, though. She would have been here at that time."

"Speaking of Sister Agatha, I think I now need to talk to her. She has more to tell, I'm sure of that. But finding this girl has opened up another possible trail to follow. Is it possible that she has any living relatives who may not have believed the story?"

"And decided after all this time to take revenge? It hardly seems likely."

"But not impossible. The girl might have had younger siblings who would be in their mid to late forties now. Maybe she mentioned Sister Margaret Mary's name in a conversation or a letter. If they learned that she was the only one left who was here at the time, they could have contacted her by mail. They could have met with her. She's obviously been very good at coming and going without anyone's knowledge."

"Yes, that's true. We'll know soon enough, I hope. Mary Joseph is looking through the records to see if she can identify the girl. Our best hope is attendance records that may show one girl's name that suddenly stops in the middle of the year."

"That sounds like a reasonable approach."

He felt it was time to get back to the matter at hand.

"If you'll send for Sister Agatha now, we can hopefully get a few more answers."

"Certainly. I too am anxious to hear what else she may know. It's time to bring all the secrets out into the light."

She went to the phone and gave Sister Agnes instructions then went to her chair by the sofa and sat down.

"I think she'll be more comfortable here than at the table," she told Steve.

"You're probably right. I'll stand though if you don't mind."

"Of course."

After several minutes, a knock on the door was followed by Sister Agatha's entry into the room. Mother Superior indicated that she should sit in the chair that she had sat in earlier.

"Sit down, Sister. Detective McLean would like to ask you a few more questions."

Sister Agatha was noticeably worried. She eyed Steve suspiciously out of the corner of her eyes and then looked down at the floor. She not only knew something, Steve thought, she was ashamed of what she knew. That meant getting her to tell was going to be more difficult. He decided the best approach was to tell her what he knew and see how she reacted to it.

"I'll get right to the point, Sister. The body of a young girl was discovered this morning buried on the grounds of the school."

He saw her stiffen. She knew something.

"We know that Sister Margaret Mary was involved in the girl's death. Did she ever tell you anything about what happened in 1930?"

Sister Agatha's hands began to shake. She looked at Mother Superior.

"Please forgive me, Mother. I promised her I'd never tell anyone. I thought it was so long ago that it didn't matter, that it didn't have anything to do with what happened to Margaret Mary. I didn't think anyone else would ever know. Sister Theresa's been dead for so long, and Margaret Mary told me no one else knew."

"Sister Theresa?" Steve asked.

Sister Agatha was silent. She knew she had said too much. She looked back down at the floor.

Mother Superior moved from her chair to the end of the sofa near Sister Agatha.

"Agatha, we know about what Margaret Mary has been doing, but we don't know everything. We believe her murder may have been caused by something she did in the past. If you want to help us catch her killer, you have to tell us all you know."

It took a few minutes for Sister Agatha to speak. Steve was impatient and ready to come down hard on her with his best "bad cop" interrogation technique, but Mother Superior put her hand up as he started to step toward Sister Agatha. It was a subtle but clear signal to wait. Finally, Sister Agatha raised her head and sat up in the chair. She didn't look at Mother Superior or Steve. She looked straight ahead to the far wall. As she spoke, her voice was dull and lifeless, as if she was reading an entry in an encyclopedia. She was merely passing along information as she had been instructed to do.

"I can only tell you what Margaret Mary told me. Sister Theresa arrived here in 1901 or 1902—Margaret Mary wasn't sure of the exact time. She had taken her vows later in life than is usual. She had been a nurse in New York City. Her intent, as she told Margaret Mary, was to help in the poorer districts of the city.

"She found a position with a doctor who also wanted to help the poor. He opened a practice in the Bowery, hoping to help the many indigent people there.

"What Sister Theresa found there horrified her. Prostitution was widespread, and disease was everywhere. The thing that troubled her most were the abortions. The prostitutes would get pregnant, and they'd come in and say they wanted to take care of it. A few months later, the same girls would be back again. The doctor was so overwhelmed he taught Sister Theresa how to do it. She did for a while, but her conscience finally made her unable to continue. She left the place and looked for work elsewhere but found none.

"One day, she passed a church and decided to go in and pray, hoping for some help from God. There was a sister there, and when she saw that Sister Theresa was troubled, the sister asked her if she needed help and it was the sign Sister Theresa was looking for. She entered the convent and after taking her vows was assigned here. She told Margaret Mary that this was the place she wanted to come to, away from the city and all she had seen there. The girls here would be a welcome change from the prostitutes and what she had been made to do."

She stopped, and a sorrowful look came over her face.

"Some of us sometimes choose this life to escape from something in our past, thinking we can hide from the world. That doesn't always prove true though."

Mother Superior's face showed that she was bracing herself to learn yet another secret. Sister Agatha continued.

"Because of her training as a nurse, Sister Theresa was called upon to treat the usual minor illnesses or injuries. One day, several years after she had arrived, she found a girl crying in the woods. When she asked the girl why she was crying, the girl told her it was just a silly thing that had upset her. The next day, though, the girl stopped after class and asked Sister Theresa if she could help her with a medical problem. When she was told that if it was something other than what Sister Theresa normally took care of, the doctor in town would have to be called, the girl left without a further explanation.

"Later that night, Sister Theresa found the girl crying in the woods again. This time, she told the girl she would take her to Mother Superior if she didn't tell her what was wrong. When the girl told her she was pregnant and that she planned to kill herself, Sister Theresa tried to tell her that suicide wasn't the answer and that she could have the baby and give it up for adoption. The girl told her that her family would disown her if they found out. It would be better, she said, to be dead. At that point, Sister Theresa made what she told Margaret Mary was the hardest decision she ever made. A few nights later, she gave the girl an abortion."

Mother Superior had expected to hear what she had just heard so she was able to keep her composure, but there was a question she needed an answer to.

"Agatha, how could she have done something like that here in the school without anyone knowing? There isn't a place private enough to do it."

Sister Agatha grew quiet again for a moment.

"Yes there is, Mother. No one remembers it anymore because it hasn't been used for years, but in the early days, it was used quite regularly. It was the perfect place to do something like that. It was built with thick walls to make it soundproof. No one would have heard her if she screamed."

Mother Superior stopped her.

"Agatha, what are you talking about?"

"The discipline room, Mother."

Steve looked at Mother Superior.

"What's a discipline room?" he asked.

"I don't know. I've never heard of it."

Sister Agatha rose and began to walk aimlessly around the room, clearly uncomfortable with what she now had to explain.

"Years ago, corporal punishment was not only accepted, it was recommended. It wasn't unusual for a girl to be disciplined with a whip. That, of course, wasn't something that could be done quietly. So a room was built in the basement of the convent building with thick walls and a double set of doors so that no sound could escape during the punishment. Margaret Mary told me that she thought it was 1915 or maybe '16 when Sister Theresa helped that first girl. By then, the room wasn't used as regularly. Paddling had become a more humane punishment, the pain of the whip replaced by the combined pain of the paddle and the humiliation of being administered publicly in front of the student body."

"A public spanking," Steve interjected. "I suppose that would be a little embarrassing."

"Detective, a paddling was more than a spanking. A paddling required bare skin to be effective. Imagine how you'd feel bending over the back of a chair with your skirt flipped up over your back and your underwear pulled down with everyone watching."

Steve was now the uncomfortable one. Mother Superior felt she should save him from any more discomfort. She also wanted to continue before she allowed herself to laugh. Despite the seriousness of the situation, she couldn't help but find the humor in Sister Agatha's indignation and her mention of "your skirt" in regard to Steve.

"Agatha, please tell us more about this room. Where is it?"

"That I don't know, Mother. Margaret Mary wouldn't tell me. She said it was better if I didn't know."

She went back to the chair and sat down.

"I only know that that's where it was done. Sister Theresa had been here when it was being used, and she knew it would be the best place for what she was going to do. From the way Margaret Mary described it, it seems like it was. There was even a table there where the girls were made to lay for their punishment. It suited Sister Theresa's purposes quite well, apparently."

Steve hadn't wanted to interrupt, but there was something he couldn't figure out.

"Excuse me, Sister Agatha. There's something I don't quite understand. I'm not a doctor, but I do know that an abortion requires several medical instruments. It seems unlikely that things of that kind would be found in a girls' school."

"You're correct, Detective. Margaret Mary told me that Sister Theresa had brought her nurse's bag with her when she came here. It contained a number of small instruments. After that first girl came to her, Sister Theresa made an excuse to go into town to see a doctor.

"In those days, not all the girls lived at the school. A few local girls lived at home and attended classes during the week. The girl who Sister Theresa was going to help knew one of the local girls. She had confided in her about her 'trouble'. The girl told her about a doctor in town who secretly took care of problems for girls. At first, the girl had thought about going to him, but she realized she couldn't leave the school for as long as she would have needed to, and she also didn't have the money he wanted.

"Sister Theresa chose that doctor to go to. She told him that she knew about what he was doing. He denied it at first, but Sister Theresa told him she knew girls who could testify against him if she were to turn him in to the authorities. He confessed to what he was doing and asked her what she wanted in exchange for her silence. She took the instruments she felt she needed and hid them in her habit when she returned to the school."

Steve had to admit to himself that he was somewhat impressed by Sister Theresa.

"It appears that Sister Theresa was a woman who didn't let anything stand in her way."

"Oh, no, Detective. According to Margaret Mary, her experiences in New York had made her very tough and had taught her how to deal with difficult people."

"You've referred to the girl as the 'first girl' more than once. I'm correct then that there were others who Sister Theresa helped?"

"Yes, Detective. It seems every few years, girls here have found a way to get themselves in trouble. I don't know how they've been doing it lately, but there were stories back then about young men meeting the girls in the woods. There was no wall until 1917, so if a girl wanted to meet a boy badly enough, she could sneak out there and meet him. Even after the wall was built, there were stories of boys scaling it to meet the girls."

"So the girl in 1930 was also one of Sister Theresa's…I guess we could call them 'patients'."

Sister Agatha seemed conflicted about having to answer his question.

"Mother, must I really answer all these questions? Margaret Mary is dead, and I don't see how going over all this ancient history is going to help find her killer."

Mother Superior rose and went to the door.

"Could I talk to you in the hall for a moment, Steve?" she asked

"Certainly, Mother."

He followed Mother Superior into the hall, closing the door behind him.

"What is it, Mother?" he asked, keeping his voice as quiet as possible.

"Is it necessary to go on? We already know about Margaret Mary's activities. She and Agatha were close, and Agatha is grieving. This is very hard for her."

"I understand that, Mother. But there are still things we need to know, and I believe Sister Agatha has the answers. If we stop now, whoever did this may very well get away with it. Worse than that, though, I'm concerned that Sister Margaret Mary's death may not be the last."

"What? Why do you say that?"

"I just feel there's something more here. Something we don't know but which may be very dangerous. I'm sorry, but I need to find out what else Sister Agatha knows."

"Very well. I'll tell her we must continue."

They went back into the office. Mother Superior sat again on the sofa.

"I'm sorry, Agatha, Detective McLean needs to know everything you know about Margaret Mary. Finding her killer may depend on what you know. I know this is hard for you, but you're not betraying her, you're helping her. Try to think of it that way."

Sister Agatha seemed to consider what Mother Superior had said.

"All right, Mother, I'll try."

She turned to Steve, who had taken a seat at the conference table, turning the chair out to face toward the sofa and chairs.

"You asked about the girl in 1930. Yes, she was one of the girls Sister Theresa helped, but she was also Margaret Mary's first procedure. Sister Theresa had been training her to take her place since Sister was getting older and wanted to make sure there was someone who could take her place when she no longer could do it."

She looked at Mother Superior to see how she reacted to what she had said. But there was no indication that Mother Superior was feeling anything.

"Go on. Agatha," Mother Superior told her.

"Yes, Mother. Sister Theresa felt that Margaret Mary was ready to do it on her own. She was there to watch and assist her, but Margaret Mary was to do the actual work. Something went wrong, and the girl started bleeding heavily. They couldn't stop the bleeding, and they knew they couldn't go for help. Even if they had, it would have come too late to save her. They comforted her as best they could until she passed out.

"Margaret Mary was beside herself with guilt. She told Sister Theresa that she should have given her more instruction. They had a big argument, and Margaret Mary threatened to go to Mother Superior. Sister Theresa told her that if anyone found out, they'd both go to prison, so Margaret Mary felt trapped. It was Sister Theresa who suggested they bury her and tell everyone she had run away. If they did it properly, she said, no one would ever know. Margaret Mary had no choice but to go along with the idea."

She stopped again and closed her eyes. After a moment, she resumed her story.

"Please don't think too badly of Margaret Mary or Sister Theresa either. They were sincerely trying to help the girls. When Sister Theresa first asked Margaret Mary to help her, she said they would be saving the girls from ruining their lives because of that one mistake. What happened with that girl was terrible and what they did to hide it was terrible, but they didn't know what else to do. They truly felt the girls needed them to be here for them."

Mother Superior rose and walked toward her desk. She had much to consider.

How could such behavior be excused? she thought. *How could Agatha have kept silent about it all these years? What secrets might the other sisters be keeping? How could I live with these women for several years and know so little about them?*

She was starting to question whether she was really cut out to be the head of the school and the sisters when another thought crept into her mind. Margaret Mary and Agatha had chosen to keep the secret. She had no way of knowing that something so unimaginable was happening. She couldn't do anything about it while she was unaware of it, but now that she was, it was time for her to take charge and see this to its conclusion. The shock of so many revelations had worn off, and it was time to be the leader she was expected to be.

She returned to the sofa and sat, a new strength showing in her posture and her manner. She addressed Sister Agatha in a formal tone, no longer the patient and comforting presence but the woman in charge.

"I understand that your closeness to Margaret Mary has made you feel a need to defend what she did, but it was clearly against everything we believe. Feeling sorry for a girl who makes her own bed is no excuse to go against the laws of God. However compassionate she and Sister Theresa may have felt, it was not for them to make the choice they did. There have been too many secrets at this school, and Detective McLean and I need to know all of them if we are to prevent any more tragedy."

She turned to Steve.

"What other questions do you have, Steve?"

It took Steve a few seconds to adjust to Mother Superior's new attitude. He stood and began his next line of questioning, circling the conference table as he did.

"I think we've learned everything we needed to know about the girl in the grave. It seems unlikely that what happened here last night could be connected to what happened then. But Sister Margaret Mary's activities continued past that time and even into the present day. There could be a connection to any one of the girls she helped over the years."

He stopped by Sister Agatha's chair.

"We've learned that Sister Margaret Mary had been asked to help the girl who hung herself in the church."

He could tell that Sister Agatha hadn't been ready to hear that.

"What can you tell us about that, Sister?"

She looked to Mother Superior for help, but she found none there. Mother Superior had turned the matter over to the detective, and Sister Agatha had no choice but to answer him.

"Yes, she did go to Margaret Mary, but it was too late."

"Too late?"

"She was overweight and didn't show, and she apparently hadn't been told about those kinds of things. She didn't realize what it meant when she missed her menstrual cycles. Had it been in the early days of the school, she would have been found out and sent away. They checked those things back then."

Mother Superior was curious about what she had just said. Somewhat reluctantly she interrupted.

"Steve, I'm sorry to interrupt, but I'm wondering what Agatha meant by that."

"That's quite all right, Mother. After all, I am your guest here. And I'm a little curious about it myself."

Mother Superior turned to Sister Agatha.

"What do you mean, 'they checked'? How do you know that?"

"You know how interested I am in history, Mother. In my early years here, I found a storeroom in the basement that contained boxes of old school records. They went back to the first years of the school. I found a record book where the girls' menstrual cycles had been recorded."

Mother Superior broke in.

"How would they do that? How could they keep track of every girl?'

"From what I could gather, the girls were required to provide evidence of blood once a month, an undergarment, a bedsheet. It would be recorded in the book after the girl's name with the date and type of evidence."

"Sounds like an invasion of privacy to me," Steve observed.

"Things were different then, Detective. Maintaining order and discipline overrode personal privacy. That's why I like history as much as I do. You can compare the way things were to the way they are now. There is much that can be learned from the past if people choose to do so. Perhaps what you consider draconian measures might solve much of the teenage pregnancy problems if they were in use today. Perhaps they could have saved that girl's life."

"Perhaps. But I like to think we're a little more humane today."

"Humane, Detective? And how do you classify humane? Is it inhumane to invade, as you call it, a girl's privacy in the hope of curtailing her sexual activity until the proper time, yet humane to give her the freedom to conceive an unwanted child which is then destroyed?"

"I don't have an answer to that, Sister, but it sounds very much like you don't approve of what Sister Margaret Mary was doing. If that's the case, why did you keep her secret?"

"No, I didn't approve of it, and I told her so. But as I said, she was sincere in her belief that she was doing the right thing for the girls. I couldn't argue with that, but as much as I didn't approve, I couldn't betray her. She was my friend, and she entrusted her secret to me."

She put her hands to her face and began to cry.

Mother Superior's resolve had softened a bit. She felt sorry for Sister Agatha.

"Agatha, you protected your friend. I'm sure it was a heavy load to carry."

"I'm so ashamed, Mother. I let my friendship blind me to my duty. God will never forgive me."

"God understands more than we know. If you pray for forgiveness, I'm sure you'll receive it."

"I will, Mother. But if I'm to be forgiven, I have to tell the rest of the secret."

Steve had returned to his chair to sit, trying to be as unobtrusive as possible while Mother Superior comforted Sister Agatha. He had been trying to piece what little he knew together in some way that he hoped could point him in the right direction. He turned his attention back to Sister Agatha when he heard what she had just said.

"What else is there to tell, Sister?"

"The girl who hung herself…as I said, when she went to Margaret Mary it was too late. The baby was past the time when an abortion could be done. As she wasn't showing, Margaret Mary told her she would have to carry the baby until it was born. She told the girl she would help her deliver it and find a family for it. She promised her that no one would know anything about it.

"Everything went well. Her weight kept her from showing more than a little extra weight, which no one found unusual. The girl had a few friends who she trusted, and Margaret Mary enlisted them to help when the time grew near. When the girl showed signs of labor, one of the girls was to find Margaret Mary to let her know. Sister Theresa had also passed on more of her nursing knowledge to Margaret Mary, so she had become the one who helped take care of minor medical issues. Thankfully it happened at night when most everyone was asleep. A girl came and told Margaret Mary it was time. She went to the dormitory and was able to get the girl to the discipline room without anyone noticing.

"Everything went well until after the baby was born. Margaret Mary took the child out into the hall between the two doors. The girl told her she wanted to hold her baby, but Margaret Mary said no. She told her it would be easier for her to give the baby up if she didn't see it. The girl kept insisting and began to get upset. Margaret Mary gave her a sedative to put her to sleep and brought the child out to me. She had told me to wait by the door in the garden wall. A man was waiting outside, and I gave the baby to him. She returned to the room and waited for the girl to wake up. When she did, she told Margaret Mary she had changed her mind and she wanted to keep the baby. She was ready, she said, to accept the consequences. She insisted on seeing the child. Margaret Mary knew that wasn't possible, and when the girl kept insisting, she told the girl the baby had died."

She stopped. Telling the story had obviously been difficult, and she leaned back in the chair and closed her eyes.

Steve knew immediately that she had just told him the most important information he would find. If the child was alive, that child, or someone connected to it, could know what happened that night. He felt he had learned almost everything he needed to learn from Sister Agatha, and she clearly needed to rest for a while, but he had two more things he felt were important enough to keep her just a while longer.

"Sister, I think I should let you return to your room. Before you go, though, I have two more questions. I have to ask once more if you know where this discipline room is."

"No, Detective. I wish I could help you, but that's one secret Margaret Mary kept to herself."

"You said you gave the baby to a man who was waiting outside the wall. Did she tell you who he was, a name perhaps?"

"I think she may have said he was a lawyer. I'm not really sure. Whoever he was, she had contacted him several days before and called him earlier that day and arranged for him to be there that night. That's all I remember. I'm sorry."

"Thank you. Officer Hansen will return to your room with you."

"Actually, I'd prefer to be alone right now. If you want, she can accompany me there. I'll lock my door. No one will get in, I assure you."

"Sister, I'd really feel better if…"

"Detective, please understand. My soul is in God's hands now. Whatever my fate, I'm prepared to accept it."

She turned and went to the door, where she turned and bowed to Mother Superior.

"With your permission, Mother Superior."

"Of course, Agatha. Get some rest."

She walked slowly into the hall and through the large door. Steve went to the door and signaled Hansen to go with her then returned to Mother Superior.

"Well," he said. "We have something to go on. I'm sorry I had to push her that hard."

"I've come to realize, Steve, that you can't always pull secrets out gently. There are times when a hard push is the only way. What will you do now?"

"I'll have to give it some thought. There could be several people who knew then, or found out since then, that the child didn't die. I guess John Miller would be the logical place to start. He's the father.

Maybe he found out and was upset about not being told. I doubt, though, that he would kill because of it. He said the girl had talked about marriage, and that was something he definitely didn't want. I can't see him being unhappy about the child being given away. If she had kept it, he'd have been married long before he wanted to be. He may feel a little guilt about her killing herself, but at the same time, I'm sure he's content to have things turn out the way they have. I don't think it'll lead anywhere, but I'll talk to him anyway. I may try to follow up on that lead about the lawyer, if it was a lawyer. He may still be alive, and if he is, he might know where the child ended up. There are only two law firms in the city. The senior partner at one is old enough to be a possibility. I'll make a few phone calls before I talk to Mr. Miller.

"You can use the phone in the hall. It's on a table near the dining room doors. It's the phone the girls use when they get a call from home. There's a chair by the table."

"Thank you, Mother. I was afraid I'd have to use the phone at Sister Agnes's desk."

Mother Superior smiled understandingly.

"Well, let me know if you find anything else. I've been tied up with this, and necessarily so, but I still have this school to run. Find me if you need me. Sister Agnes will know where I'll be."

"Yes, but will she tell me?"

They both laughed as they went into the hall.

Chapter 10

Marjorie and Sarah were sitting in the recreation room visiting with Officer Gordon, who had told the girls to call her Isabelle. The room was what could best be described as a pleasant room. It was about twenty by twenty feet in size. On the far wall opposite the double door entry was a TV. Two rows of small, low back, but comfortable-looking chairs were lined up facing the TV. To the left of the door, near the corner, was a square table with four chairs. A deck of cards was on the table and when Marjorie saw it, she was surprised to realize that nuns played cards.

To the right of the door were several bookcases filled with books. Scattered about the rest of the room were small sitting areas with groupings of wingback chairs and small side tables. One grouping contained a sofa with two chairs positioned to face the sofa. The girls had chosen to sit there, they on the sofa and Officer Gordon in one of the chairs.

The girls had asked Isabelle what it was like to be a police officer. They were sure it had to be exciting.

"Oh, it's not really all that exciting," Isabelle said. "We're really mostly office clerks. We stay there and process reports and file papers. I'm really only here now because Steve wanted women to search the sisters' rooms. If you haven't noticed, I don't even carry a gun. Maybe someday, men will finally realize we women can do a lot more than they give us credit for. Steve's actually ahead of his time. He lets us do things like this. Some of the older guys at the station don't like it when he does."

"Yeah," Marjorie agreed, "he sure surprised me when he asked me to help him. I never thought a detective would think someone my age, especially a girl, could be good at something like that."

"Like I said, he's ahead of his time. He's a really great guy."

"Do you like him?"

"Of course. I just said so, didn't I?"

"I mean, do you 'like' him?"

Isabelle realized what Marjorie was wanting to know.

"No, not like that. I have a boyfriend."

An idea popped into Isabelle's head.

"Do you 'like' him?"

Marjorie felt her face getting flushed and warm. She wanted to crawl under the sofa to hide.

"You do, don't you?" Isabelle teased.

"No! I don't!"

She could deny it, but her face told the truth.

Sarah was giggling.

"I knew it!" she said. "You love Steve! You love Steve!" she added tauntingly, dragging out his name as Steeeve each time. She continued even as Marjorie tried to protest more strongly.

"No, I don't! He's too old for me! Just shut up!"

Sarah could see that Marjorie was getting upset, so she quit her taunting.

"That's okay," Isabelle told her. "A lot of women have crushes on him. I think Helen, Officer Hansen, has one. She can't admit it, though, and nothing could ever come of it anyway. That kind of thing can't go on at the station. It's called fraternization, and it's not allowed. They could never date or they'd both lose their jobs."

Marjorie had calmed down, but she was still feeling embarrassed.

"Gee," she said. "That sucks. What if they were meant to be together, and their jobs kept them from being able to find each other."

Isabelle laughed.

"You're a real romantic, aren't you?"

"Yes, she is," Sarah answered.

Sister Juliette Marie came into the room and approached them.

"May I join you?" she asked.

"Of course." Isabelle replied.

She sat in the other chair next to Isabelle.

"I heard some laughter as I passed in the hall. It sounded like I could find a little shelter from all the seriousness. What were you talking about?"

"Love, Sister," Sarah answered.

"Oh, who's in love?"

Sarah was about to answer when Marjorie gave her a look that said "Keep your mouth shut." Isabelle saved the day.

"Just love in general. When you talk to teenage girls about love, there's always laughter involved."

"Have you ever been in love, Sister?" Marjorie asked.

Sarah was appalled by the question.

"Marge, you shouldn't ask something like that!"

"Because I'm a nun, you mean? It's all right. We nuns are human too. Yes, I was in love, a long time ago. Ten years actually. I was seventeen. We had dated for two years during high school. I loved him dearly, but it wasn't to be. We broke up the day before graduation."

"That's so sad," Marjorie said. "So did you become a nun because he broke up with you and you lost your love?"

Sister Juliette Marie smiled a sad smile.

"No, that's not what happened. It's a misconception that many people have that we become nuns because we've been rejected by men, that we hide out to forget our losses. I didn't become a nun because he broke up with me. I broke up with him because I had decided to become a nun. I knew that this was the life I was meant to live."

The girls sat on the sofa thinking, confused by what she had just said. Why would a woman give up the love of a man to live a life that meant she could never be with a man ever again in her life?

"I can see you don't understand. Few people do. I think the only ones who ever really do are those of us who hear the call."

"But what about your boyfriend? What about your family? Don't you miss them?" Marjorie asked, struggling to understand.

"As I said, I did love Phillip—that was his name. But I loved God more. It would have been a mistake to continue our relationship any longer because the longer it went on, the more it would have hurt when it ended. And my family, strangely, weren't as difficult to leave. I was adopted, and I learned that I was when I was thirteen. My adoptive parents were good to me, and I cared about them, but it seemed that what I felt before I knew was changed after I knew. It seemed easier to leave them knowing that we weren't connected by blood. That may also be difficult to understand, but I can't really explain it in a way that you could."

Sarah was interested now.

"You were adopted? Did your parents tell you anything about your mother? I mean, did they know who she was or anything like that?"

"The only thing they told me was that she was a young girl who was unmarried and couldn't keep me. That's all I know about her."

"Do you ever think about her now or wonder about what she was like?"

"Yes, I've thought about her from time to time. When I was younger, I used to wonder if any of the women I passed on the street might be her. But I'll never know, and there's no sense thinking about it too much. When I do think about her, I say a prayer for her. That's all I can really do."

She stopped speaking, but the expression on her face said there was a question in her mind.

"Is there a reason you're so interested in my mother?"

She asked the question gently, but Sarah felt her heart in her throat. She thought she had sounded simply inquisitive, but she could tell she had given herself away. Sister Joan already knew, and now, not only would Sister Juliette Marie know, Isabelle would know too. She had accepted the fact that everyone would know sooner or later, but she had wanted it to be later. Yet here she was, having to admit it again.

"Yes, Sister, there is a reason."

She looked apologetically at Isabelle then looked down at the floor.

"I'm pregnant."

She looked up, fighting back tears. It was harder than it had been with Sister Joan. Maybe it was because Isabelle was also there.

"You won't tell anyone?" she said quickly. "I know everyone will know eventually, but I'd rather not have them all looking at me with pity in their eyes. I'll probably be gone before I start to show, so maybe the other girls won't know till after I'm gone."

Sister Juliette Marie got up from her chair and sat next to Sarah on the sofa.

"Your secret is safe with me. I'll pray for you. Things will turn out all right. I know they will."

"You don't have to worry about me." Isabelle added. "I'm used to keeping things I hear at the station secret."

Sister Joan appeared in the doorway.

"Excuse me, Sister. Detective McLean asked me to tell Officer Gordon to take the girls back to the guest room. He feels they'll be safer there."

The girls were thankful for the interruption. The conversation had lost its happy feeling. The chairs in the guest room weren't as comfortable as the sofa, but Sarah especially wanted to get away from Sister Juliette Marie. She didn't feel all that bad about Isabelle knowing, but she wished she hadn't asked the questions that had allowed Sister Juliette Marie to see through her. Now, at least, she and Marjorie could go back to the guest room with Isabelle and hopefully find something more fun to talk about.

Sister Joan offered to accompany them back to the room and Sister Juliette Marie went off down the hall, saying she had enjoyed visiting with them.

The girls returned to the guest room and made themselves as comfortable as was possible. They had come to believe after being in Mother Superior's office that all the sisters' quarters were furnished in the same way. The austerity of the guest room was surprising. It would be almost a shock to the sensitivities of any teenage girl.

Two single metal frame beds, two small dressers, a small square table, and four wooden chairs were the sum total of the furnishings. A large crucifix hanging on the wall above the beds, centered between them, and a picture of the Blessed Virgin on the wall next to the door were the only decoration, leaving the room extremely cheerless in the girls' opinion. The gray walls and gray curtain on the window gave the girls the feeling that they were in what they imagined prison to be like.

As they talked with Isabelle, the door opened and Sister Mary Joseph looked in.

"Oh, there you are. I wasn't sure if you'd be here or the recreation room. Mother Superior has instructed me to have dinner brought to you. She feels it would be best. The dinner bell will ring shortly, so I wanted to find you before it rang so you would know not to go down. There will be a tray for you as well, Officer."

She closed the door and was gone.

"She's very efficient," Isabelle said. "You don't mind having to eat up here with just me?"

"Well," Marjorie replied, "we don't usually have dinner brought to our room, so I guess that makes us special. And you're much better company than the other girls."

"Yeah," added Sarah, "and I'll feel much better not being stared at. I'm sure Paula and Brenda have spread the word about what finks we are by now."

"I feel sorry for Rachel, though," Marjorie said. "Who knows how they'll treat her?"

In their earlier conversations the girls had told Isabelle about what Paula and Brenda had done.

"I don't think those girls will tell the others much about anything," she said. "Would you want everyone else knowing that you had done what they did?"

Marjorie considered what she said.

"Well, if I did something like that, which I never would, I suppose I'd want to keep it to myself. But it'll get out eventually. Everything does."

The dinner bell rang, and almost immediately, there was a knock at the door. Isabelle opened it to find Sister Juliette Marie and two freshmen girls waiting with their trays. They brought them in, put them on the table, and left.

"Well, this looks good," Isabelle said. "This job ain't too bad. Away from the office work all day. Good company. And free dinner included."

The girls laughed as they sat down to eat, forgetting their cares for the moment.

The officers who had come with Steve earlier in the day had finished their search of the grounds and the sisters' rooms, so Steve had sent them back to the station. It was close to dinnertime, and he felt there was no reason to keep them at the school. Since Sister Agatha had said she wanted to be alone, he had also sent Helen back with the others. Only Isabelle remained as he still wanted to have someone with the girls.

He sat at the table in the hall dialing the first law firm on his list. The secretary answered and transferred him to Mr. Harold Carson of Carson & Warner Attorneys at Law. Yes, Mr. Carson Sr. was practicing in 1940. He unfortunately passed away two years ago. Mr. Warner joined the firm in 1956. Mr. Carson Jr. would be glad to check their files and let Steve know if there was any record of an adoption having been handled by the firm in 1940. After cordial goodbyes, Steve hung up and proceeded to dial the number for the firm of Hennessy & Mitchell.

He was transferred to Mr. Mitchell, the senior partner. He informed Steve that he had joined the firm in 1941, and in 1953, Mr. Hennessy had died in a car accident. Mrs. Hennessy had a financial interest in the firm but was not an attorney. The Hennessy name remained on the firm because of her financial interest and out of respect for Mr. Hennessy as the founding member of the firm. It was doubtful that Mrs. Hennessy would know anything concerning any of her husband's business at the firm. Mr. Mitchell said he would also check their files and let Steve know if he found anything.

Steve was preparing to call John Miller's home when the dinner bell rang. As the dining room filled with chattering girls grateful for the chance to finally be out of their rooms, he decided it would be best to wait till after dinner to call. It occurred to him that he hadn't eaten in quite a while and was about to tell Sister Agnes that he was going to get a bite to eat and would be back soon in case anyone asked for him when Sister Mary Joseph approached him.

"Oh, Detective, Mother Superior told me I'd find you here. She wanted me to tell you that she's arranged for dinner to be brought to her office for you."

"Really, Sister, there's no need for that. I was just about to run out to get something."

"Now, Detective, you're not going to refuse Mother Superior's hospitality, are you? We're serving roast beef with mashed potatoes. Sister Felicity, our head cook makes an absolutely delicious gravy. It would be a shame for you to miss out on it. And Mother Superior did make a special effort to make sure you don't go hungry."

Steve knew he was beaten. There was no way Sister Mary Joseph was going to accept anything less than a yes.

"All right, Sister, you win. Any chance there'll be green beans?"

"Oh, yes! Green beans are always served with roast beef, and there will be cherry pie for dessert. I'll have your tray brought in right away."

She turned to go but stopped.

"Oh, I almost forgot. Mother Superior said to be sure you had coffee."

She was off into the kitchen. Steve went to the office and sat at the conference table. In less than a minute, a young girl brought in a tray and set it on the table.

"Everything should be there, sir," she said. "I hope you enjoy your dinner. I'm always glad when we have roast beef. It's my favorite."

As she left the room, closing the door behind her, Steve smiled. Her simple pleasure in having roast beef for dinner was a welcome change from the day's events. He just hoped she'd always be able to keep her innocence.

As he began to eat, he found, to his enjoyment, that Sister Felicity did indeed have a way with gravy. He now understood what his young waitress had meant.

He finished eating and went out into the hall and checked the dining room. Only a few girls were left, and it was quiet enough to make a phone call. He dialed the number for John Miller's home and waited for an answer. A female voice came on the line.

"Hello?"

"Hello. Is this John Miller's residence?"

"Yes, it is. Who's calling please?"

"This is Detective Steven McLean. I'm at St. Christopher's, and I'd like to talk to John."

"I'm sorry, Detective, but John's not home. I expected him a while ago, but he hasn't returned. Isn't he at the school?"

"I saw him earlier, but I assumed he had left for the day. I'll have to see if he's still here."

"I don't know where else he might have gone. What do you want to see him about?"

Steve didn't want to say too much.

"There was an incident at the school last night, and I'm looking into it."

"An incident? What happened?"

"I'm afraid I can't comment on it at this time. By the way, is Jack there?"

"No, he hasn't come home yet either. I've actually been a little worried. They're usually here in time for dinner. I had to put it in the oven to keep warm."

"Well, they may have stayed here in case I needed them. I'll look for them and tell them that you're waiting for them."

"Thank you, Detective. I'd appreciate that."

"All right then. Goodbye."

"Goodbye."

There was a definite sound of concern in her goodbye. Something wasn't right. It was obviously out of the ordinary for them to not be home for dinner. He needed to find John immediately.

It was starting to get dark, and Steve thought it would be a good idea to take a flashlight along. Since he didn't have one with him, he stopped at Sister Agnes's desk and asked her if she had one.

"Of course I do, Detective. The power goes out now and then, and during the winter, I'm here till after dark when the days are short.

I don't fancy bumping my shin on my way through the halls. I doubt I'll need it tonight, so here it is."

She reached in a drawer and handed him the light.

"Just make sure you bring it back," she admonished him.

"Well if I don't, just call the police."

Steve hurried away, feeling certain she probably didn't see the humor in his remark. He went into the school, where there was a door leading out onto the walled-in grounds. The gardener's shed was in the right corner of the property behind the convent. As he crossed the lawn, he noticed that there were only a few windows on the side of the convent that looked out over the area where he was walking. The gardener's shed was actually out of the view from any of the windows. A wall around the back side of a grotto blocked the view even more.

No wonder John and Jack had been able to get away with what they were doing, he thought.

When he reached the shed, it was dark inside, and the door was closed. Steve wondered if John had possibly lain on the bed and fallen asleep. He opened the door and called inside.

"Mr. Miller, are you here?"

There was no answer. He switched on the flashlight and went in. There were tools scattered on the floor. He knew immediately that something wasn't right.

He found a light switch near the door and turned on the light. A single bulb on the wall lit up that part of the shed. The tool rack that hid the door to the room with the bed was pushed aside and he shined his light into the room. As he moved the light around the room, it fell on the end of the bed, illuminating John's legs. He moved the light along the bed until it shone on the head of the bed. The light nearly fell from his hand.

He was a trained police detective, but what he saw shocked even him. John lay there with a grass shears plunged into his throat, his face screwed up with a look of agony. He must have lived for a few seconds at least, knowing he was going to die, unable to cry out for help, which wouldn't have arrived in time anyway.

Steve's mind went quickly into detective mode. There was no doubt he was dead. Going further into the room to check might damage any evidence, especially in the dark. After looking around outside to make sure no one was hiding nearby, he ran back to the school and headed to Sister Agnes's desk.

"Well, praise the Lord. I won't have to call the police," she said when she saw him. When he got close enough to see his face, she realized that something was obviously terribly wrong.

"Detective, what happened?"

Steve was out of breath and could only speak a few words at a time.

"I need to call…the station…could I use…the phone?"

"Certainly. Should I call Mother Superior?"

She handed him the phone.

"Not…yet."

He stopped a minute to catch his breath before dialing. Sister Agnes stood by silently, waiting to hear what he would tell the station. He dialed and waited.

"Thompson, this is McLean. I need a team out here at the school, and we need the coroner. Yes, again. Have them bring some lights with them. Tell them to have the sister at the desk let me know when they get here."

As he hung up the phone sister Agnes was already starting to ask her question.

"I heard you tell them to bring the coroner. What's going on, Detective? He was here earlier for Sister Margaret Mary, and that was bad enough. Then he came back when you called for him, but Mother Superior won't tell anyone what that was about. Now he's coming again? We're all getting a little nervous about this."

"I can't tell you anything right now, Sister. I understand that the sisters are nervous, but I don't believe any of you are in any danger."

"What about Agatha? You've talked to her twice, and both times, she came out of the office looking very distraught. If you think she killed Margaret Mary, I think we should know that so we can keep an eye on her."

"One thing I can tell you is that I don't believe Sister Agatha is a killer. She was close to Sister Margaret Mary, and my interviews with her have been aimed at learning as much as possible about Sister Margaret Mary. It's understandable that talking about her friend would upset her."

"Well, there are things going on around here that shouldn't be kept from us. I think we have a right to know if we're in danger, and I don't care what you say, when the coroner comes here three times in one day, there's danger somewhere."

"I see what you mean, Sister. Unfortunately, at this point in my investigation, there are things that must remain in confidence. Could you let Mother Superior know I'd like to see her now?"

Sister Agnes was clearly not happy with his answer, but she knew there was nothing she could do about it. She dialed the phone and informed Mother Superior that Steve wanted to see her. She hung up and told Steve to go in.

At the office door, Steve paused before knocking. Mother Superior was already shaken by the day's events. How much more could she take before the weight became too much to carry? Still, she had to know. He knocked and went in. Mother Superior was waiting for him near the end of the conference table.

"Sit down, Steve," she said, indicating the chair to the right of the sofa. She then took a seat in the opposite chair.

"I'm assuming you'll want me to be sitting down for whatever it is you've come to tell me. There was an ominous sound in Agnes's voice. I can always tell when she feels someone is bringing me bad news. I think she does it purposely to warn me. She's very protective."

"Yes. I've noticed."

"So what is it?"

"Since you're prepared for bad news, I'll tell you. I found John Miller… He's dead."

Mother Superior made a sign of the cross and whispered a prayer.

"May God have mercy on his soul."

She turned back to Steve.

"I don't think I have to ask. He was murdered."

"Yes."

"Where?"

"In the gardener's shed. It looks like there was a struggle. I have a team on their way to examine the scene. I'll be glad to have some men back out here. We're going to have to look for Jack. When I called their house, his mother told me neither he nor John had come home for dinner. It has me wondering. This could be the result of a father-son argument. It concerns me that I don't know where he is."

The phone rang. Mother Superior went to the desk to answer.

"Steve, there's a call for you. I'll have it transferred in here."

She gave Sister Agnes instructions and hung up. A few seconds later, the phone rang and Mother Superior answered.

"Yes. He's here."

Steve went to the desk and took the phone.

"Mr. Mitchell. Thank you for getting back to me… A letter? Yes. Are you there now? I'll have someone pick it up. Thank you very much."

He hung up, a thoughtful look on his face.

"What is it, Steve?" Mother Superior asked.

Steve was obviously uncertain about what he had just been told. He related the call slowly, as if he was trying to figure out its meaning as he did.

"That was Mr. Mitchell from the Hennessy and Mitchell law firm. When I spoke with him earlier, he told me that Mr. Hennessy, who was killed in a car accident fourteen years ago, might possibly have handled an adoption in 1940. He offered to look through their old files to see if there might be anything in them. He told me just now that in Hennessy's files from 1940, he found a letter addressed to the school. There was a date of October 5th, 1953, on the envelope, but it was filed in the 1940s files. Why would he have done that?"

"It does seem strange. And he died that same year? You did say fourteen years, didn't you?"

Steve hadn't thought about that.

"You're right. In a car accident… I need to make a call, Mother. May I do it on your phone?"

"Of course. I'll have Agnes connect you to the outside line."

She dialed the phone and gave Sister Agnes instructions.

"What number do you want to call, Steve?"

"555-4040. It's the station."

Mother Superior gave Sister Agnes the number and handed the phone to Steve.

"Thompson, it's McLean again. I need something else. See if someone there can find an accident report from 1953, possibly October or November. It would involve Richard Hennessy. And I need someone to stop at Hennessy and Mitchell to pick up a letter… Oh, yeah. I wasn't watching the time. So Pete's the only other one there? Well, hopefully, he can find that report. I'll have to figure something else out… Okay. Do what you can."

He hung up.

"I didn't realize how late it's gotten. The night shift is pretty much a skeleton crew. With the two who are coming here with the coroner, there's only one car patrolling in the city. I need to get that letter, but I can't leave right now."

"Is there anyone still here who you could send?"

"Only Isabelle, but she's with the girls. With Jack missing, I don't like the idea of leaving them alone."

"If they lock the door and stay in the room, they should be safe. The sisters are in their rooms, and no one could break down that door without attracting a lot of attention."

"I don't like it, but it's probably my only option. Could you have them brought down here?"

Mother Superior went to the phone and told Sister Agnes to have the girls brought down. A few minutes later, there was a knock on the door, and Sister Juliette Marie showed the girls and Isabelle into the office. Mother Superior asked her to wait in the hall and she went out, closing the door as she did.

Steve took Isabelle aside and gave her instructions about picking up the letter. The girls waited near the door, wondering what was going on. Isabelle confirmed that she understood the instructions and went out, saying goodbye to the girls as she did. Steve then turned his attention to the girls.

"I had to send Officer Gordon into town to get something for me. Sister Juliette Marie will bring you back to the guest room. I want you to go in and lock the door. Don't let anyone else in. I don't want to alarm you, but I think you need to know this to understand how serious the situation is. There's been another murder, and whoever committed it is still unknown."

"Who was killed?" Marjorie asked. "Was it one of the other sisters?"

"No, it wasn't."

Marjorie and Sarah looked at each other, a horrified look on both their faces.

"Then it must have been one of the girls!" Sarah exclaimed.

"It wasn't one of the girls either," Steve assured them.

Marjorie's eyes squinted, and her face tightened into an expression of deep concentration as she tried to think of who else it could be. Watching her, Steve was trying hard not to laugh at her expression.

"Don't think so hard," he told her. "You'll get a headache."

"Well, tell us then so I won't have to."

Steve thought it over.

"Well, since you're going to be locked in the guest room, I guess I can tell you. But you can't breathe a word of this to anyone, including Sister Juliette Marie. Do you understand?"

The girls looked at each other and nodded.

"All right. It was Mr. Miller, the gardener."

Sarah drew in a sharp breath.

"Jack's dad?" she asked. "Did Jack kill him?"

"We don't know. In fact, we don't know where Jack is. That's why I want you to get back to the room and keep the door locked."

Sarah was noticeably disturbed by what she had just heard.

"I'm scared, Marge. What if he comes after me?"

Steve tried to reassure her.

"With the sisters nearby in their rooms, you'll be safe."

"How was he killed?" Marjorie asked.

Steve shook his head.

"I think that's your favorite question. However, I don't think I should tell you. It's pretty gruesome."

Marjorie had remembered what Sarah had told her about his threat to her.

"Was he stabbed in the throat with a grass shears?"

That took Steve completely by surprise.

"Why did you ask that?"

"Because that's what Jack told Sarah he would do to her if she told anyone that he was the father."

This clearly made Jack the number one suspect. It very likely also answered the question of what kind of weapon killed Sister Margaret Mary.

The phone rang. Mother Superior answered and told Steve that his team had arrived. He spoke to the girls as they went out into the hall.

"I have to take care of things with the coroner. Sister Juliette Marie will take you back to the room. Remember to lock the door."

He called Sister Juliette Marie over and instructed her to make sure she heard the door lock before she left them.

"I'd stay with them, but Sister Agnes is nervous with all this going on, she's asked me to stay with her until we lock up."

"That's fine, Sister," Steve told her. "As long as they lock the door, they'll be safe."

The girls and Sister Juliette Marie went to the convent door and on into the hall inside. Steve met with the coroner and the officers who had come with him. He instructed one of the officers to begin a search of the grounds for Jack, while he and the other officer went to the shed with the coroner.

The officers had brought work lights with them as Steve had asked. After the lights were set up, the coroner was able to examine the body. Once a number of photographs were taken the grass shears was removed. When the examination was complete, the coroner gave his initial findings to Steve.

"Looks like he was attacked from behind first. There's a wound on the right side of his lower back. Probably wouldn't have killed him if he'd been able to get medical attention right away. He must have turned around to face his attacker after the first cut. There's another wound on the left side of his stomach. From what I can see, that must have made it hard to fight back. He got pushed or fell onto the bed, and the killer gave the final blow. Pretty gruesome touch if you ask me. Whoever did this must have had a real grudge against the guy. I've never seen anything like it."

"He must have known the person," Steve conjectured. "If he felt threatened, he wouldn't have turned his back. Right now, our best suspect is his kid. Seems like someone he wouldn't expect to attack him."

"That does seem logical. You think he's still on the grounds?"

"I don't know. He could have taken off. I don't think he has a vehicle unless he took his old man's car."

Steve sent the officer to look on the road to see if a car was parked by the door in the wall. John came and went through that door, so it was likely that he'd park near it. The officer returned to tell Steve the door was locked. A search of the shed found the key hanging on a nail on the frame of the door.

With the door locked and the key still in its place, it seemed logical to assume that Jack hadn't gone out that way. All the same, Steve thought, it had been mentioned that years ago boys had scaled the wall to meet the girls. Jack might have done the same. He gave the key to the officer to check for the car. A few minutes later, the officer returned to report that there was a car parked across the road from the gate.

Steve suggested to the coroner that it might be a good idea to bring his station wagon around to the door in the wall and take the body out that way. It would be better than going across the lawn and through the school. The coroner agreed, and John's body was removed and taken to the hospital.

After the coroner had gone, Steve and the officer met with the officer who had been searching for Jack. He of course hadn't gone into the nun's part of the complex or the girls' quarters, but it was unlikely he thought that Jack would be in either place. The rest of the grounds, including the church, showed no sign of him.

Steve considered the possibilities. The convent was definitely unlikely. None of the sisters would have sheltered him, and any who saw him would throw him out. The girls' quarters, though, could be a possibility, albeit remote. Jack had bragged about his conquests of more than one girl. Might one of them hide him in her room?

He'd need Mother Superior's permission and help from some of the sisters if he was going to pursue that possibility. But was it likely enough to merit having the sisters go through all the girls' rooms? And wouldn't it be more likely that if Jack had murdered his father, he'd want to get as far away as possible? The fact was, he couldn't even be sure that Jack had done it. The grass shears in the throat could be nothing more than a coincidence. He could end up looking for Jack while the real killer was covering up their tracks. Besides, if Jack was hiding somewhere on the grounds, he'd have to come out eventually, and he'd have a hard time losing himself in a crowd of nuns and young girls. And as long as he was hiding, he couldn't do any more harm. He decided to go back to Mother Superior's office and think it all over.

He told the officers to patrol outside the grounds. If Jack, or anyone else for that matter, tried to leave they would hopefully be able to stop them. He told them he'd be in Mother Superior's office if they needed him.

As he approached the desk, Sister Agnes stopped him.

"Oh, Detective, there was a call from your station. They want you to call right away."

"Thank you, Sister. I'll use the phone on the table."

"You can use this phone if you'd like."

"No, Sister. I'd rather use the other one, but thank you."

As he turned to go to the table, he could picture Sister Agnes's expression in his mind. It was certain to be one of disappointment. He knew she had been hoping to listen to his call. He sat at the table, dialed, and waited for Sergeant Thompson to answer. After hearing the customary station greeting, he got right to the point. "Thompson, this is Steve. What's up?"

"Hey, Steve, we found the report on that accident. Having the year and months to narrow it down, it didn't take much time to find it."

"So was there anything unusual?"

"Not really. The guy lived a little way out of the city. According to the report, he was on his way home that night after a weekly card game with some other guys. For some reason, he hit the brakes and swerved then ran off the road and was thrown from the car, a Cadillac convertible. The finding was that an animal must have run out in front of him, and when he swerved to miss it, he lost control. The skid marks showed that he was going at a pretty good clip."

"That's all?"

"Yeah."

"What's the date?"

"October eleventh."

"OK. Thanks."

He was about to hang up when he thought of something else.

"Hey, Thompson. Wait. How's Pete doing on that information I gave him about the sisters?"

"I think he's almost done. Wanna talk to him?"

"Yeah, put him on."

He waited for Pete to come on the line.

"Yeah, Steve, what do you want?"

"Have you gone through the information on all the sisters yet?"

"Almost. I've got I think three more to look into."

"You didn't happen to find anything about any of them being adopted, did you?"

"As a matter of fact, there was one. Let me check my notes. Yeah, here it is. It's the one they call Juliette Marie now."

Steve asked the next question and held his breath.

"What year was she adopted?"

"Let's see...1940."

Steve let his breath out. He now had another possibility. And not only a possibility, someone who slept in the room right next to the murder victim. How easy might it have been to tiptoe a short distance down the hall and back again without anyone hearing a thing? Still, he needed more information than what he had before he could make any assumptions.

He thanked Pete and hung up. As he started toward Mother Superior's office, he saw Sister Juliette Marie standing by the desk.

"Sister Juliette Marie, could I talk to you in the office?"

"Certainly, Detective. Will it take very long? I told Sister Agnes I'd cover for her for a while. I think she should lie down. It's been an unusually busy day."

"It should only take a few minutes. You don't mind, do you Sister Agnes?"

"No. It was her idea. I'm used to being here all day. Take your time."

Sister Juliette Marie followed Steve to the door. He knocked and opened it enough to look in and ask Mother Superior if they could come in.

"Of course, Steve. I'm just going over some paperwork. Even in the face of what's happened bills need to be paid and letters answered."

She saw Sister Juliette Marie behind Steve.

"Sister, I didn't see you there."

"I have some questions for Sister, and I thought this was the best place to talk to her. I hope it's all right," Steve explained. "If we're disturbing you, we can go elsewhere."

"No. It's fine. Sit down, Sister."

She indicated the sofa, and Sister Juliette Marie took a seat there. Steve sat in the chair to the right and Mother Superior sat to the left.

"You don't mind if I sit in?" Mother Superior asked.

"No, of course not," Steve replied. He turned to Sister Juliette Marie.

"I've learned that you were adopted. If my information is right, you were born in 1940. Is that correct?"

Sister Juliette Marie was a little confused. What did her being adopted have to do with Sister Margaret Mary's murder?

She answered hesitantly, "Well, yes. That is. Is that important in some way?"

"That's what I'm hoping to find out. Did you grow up here?"

"About a hundred miles from here."

"How did you learn you were adopted?'

"When I was thirteen, my parents told me. I actually asked them because I seemed to be so much different than my siblings. There were similarities in their appearance and my parents' appearance. They were all blonde and round faced. I was dark haired with a thin face. Once I was old enough to know about adoption, I couldn't help but wonder."

"Did they tell you anything about your mother?"

"Only that she was an unwed mother who wasn't able to keep me."

"And that's all you know?"

"Yes, Detective. I'm sorry if I can't be of any more help."

"That's all right. It's just something I had to follow up on. I guess you can go, unless Mother Superior has something."

Mother Superior stood.

"No. Thank you, Sister."

Sister Juliette Marie rose, made a slight bow toward Mother Superior, and left.

"Well, what do you think, Steve?" Mother Superior asked when she was gone.

"It's not much to go on. A hundred miles isn't all that far to bring a baby to be adopted, especially if you want to keep too many questions from being asked. But she really didn't seem to realize why I was asking about it. I didn't see any sign of nervousness, and there was no feeling that she was trying to hide anything. If she's the killer, she's a really good actress."

"I hope she's not who we're looking for. She's a very devout young woman. I'd hate to think it was all an act."

"Well, right now I don't think she is, but I'll see if the guys at the station can dig a little deeper. The problem is, at this time of night, they won't be able to get in touch with any offices that might have the information we need. This second murder makes me feel like tomorrow could be too late. I really wish I knew where Jack is."

"Do you think he could actually have murdered his own father? I understand he has a low sense of morality, but to kill someone, let alone his own father, the way Mr. Miller was killed seems a big step up from seducing young girls."

"I know. That's why I'm concerned. If it's not him, who is it? What piece of information that we don't have could be the key to finding the truth?"

"What secret, you mean. Who in this school is still hiding a secret we have yet to discover?"

Steve circled the table, considering his next move as he walked. He needed to know more than he did, and he needed to know it as soon as possible.

"Mother," he said, "against my better judgment, I'm going to head back to the station. I can't sit and wait here for a phone call. I need to see that letter, and I need to see that accident report myself. If anything happens, there are two officers patrolling outside. I'll be back as soon as I can."

"All right, Steve, but hurry. I won't feel comfortable until you're back."

Steve hurried out into the hall and out through the outside door. As he passed the desk, he said a quick goodbye to Sister Juliette Marie, who had taken Sister Agnes's place at the desk.

He was gone only a minute when Sister Agnes returned and told Sister Juliette Marie that she could go.

"I can't get any rest," she said. "I may as well be here. The doors have got to be locked anyway, and I won't feel comfortable if I don't do it myself. With all that's happened, I don't want any doors left open by mistake."

"Well, I could do it," Sister Juliette Marie assured her.

"No. I want to do it myself. No offense, but I know the routine."

"All right. I'll just go and lie down myself then."

She went into the convent. Sister Agnes took her place in the chair at the desk. She looked at the clock on the wall across from the desk. It was 7:45.

Fifteen minutes more, she thought, *then I can lock up and this day will finally be over. This is no way to run a convent.*

Chapter 11

Marjorie and Sarah had decided to lie down on the beds in the guest room. The wooden chairs had become too much to take any longer. Their dinner trays had been retrieved, and they had pretty much talked themselves out. They felt they now knew each other better than they even knew themselves. In fact, Marjorie was thinking, in their discussions about what they thought about certain things she had learned some things about herself that she hadn't realized before. She didn't know, for instance, that some of the girls looked up to her as someone who had it all together. That's why, Sarah had told her, she came to her for help, and it was most likely why Rachel had too. It was also, Sarah thought, why Paula and Brenda acted the way they did toward her. They were jealous of her because their lives were all screwed up.

As she lay on the bed contemplating all that Sarah had said Marjorie thought about her feelings about Sarah. She had been jealous of Sarah because of her beauty, never knowing that Sarah had been jealous of her because of her confidence. Now she knew that Sarah's uncomfortable reactions to compliments were caused by the way her father had told her for years that she wasn't good enough. He had told her she wasn't pretty and she wasn't smart. She had laughed when Marjorie told her she had been jealous of her.

"Oh, Marge," she said, "if you knew what my life's been like you'd have felt lucky to not be me."

Marjorie had come to realize that she'd been looking at things in her life the wrong way. She had only looked at the surface of other people's lives and made assumptions about them without considering what might be below the surface. She had allowed her assumptions to affect the way she felt about herself and the way she thought about others. She promised herself she was going to change that and feel better about herself from then on.

She looked over and saw that Sarah was sleeping and decided she'd try to do the same. Her attempt was cut short by a knock on the door. Sarah stirred but didn't wake up. Marjorie went to the door carefully, keeping in mind what Steve had said about not letting anyone in.

"Who is it?" she asked softly, trying to not wake Sarah.

"It's Sister Joan. I have a message for you from Detective McLean."

"What is it?"

"Am I talking to Marjorie or Sarah?"

"Marjorie."

"I thought so, but it's hard to tell through the door. He called the desk and told Sister Agnes to tell you that he wants you to meet him in the dormitory right away. Sister Agnes has to stay at the desk, so since I was right there, she sent me to tell you."

"But he told us to lock the door and stay here."

"I understand that, but I was right there when he called. He insisted that he needs you to meet him. I don't know what it's all about, but if he said he needs you, I think you should go."

"Just a minute."

Marjorie was confused. If Steve had told them to stay in the room, why would he want her to go to the dormitory? But if something unexpected came up that he needed her for, she should go, shouldn't she? She decided to wake Sarah.

"Sarah, wake up."

Sarah's eyes opened part way.

"Huh? Marge? What is it?"

"Wake up. I gotta go to meet Steve."

Sarah was only half awake and not understanding what she was being told.

"What? What's going on?"

"I said Steve wants me to meet him in the dormitory."

"But he told us to stay here."

"I know, so I think it must be something important if he sent for me."

Sarah was more awake now.

"I don't know, Marge. He said to stay here. Who told you he wants you to go?"

"Sister Joan. She said he called the desk and told Sister Agnes to tell me to meet him over there."

There was another knock on the door.

"Marjorie, are you coming?"

"Hang on, Sister. I'm talking to Sarah."

"Well, don't wait too long. It sounded important."

Marjorie sat on the bed where Sarah was still lying down.

"What should I do?"

"I guess he wouldn't have sent for you if he thought it wasn't safe."

"I suppose you're right. I just wish he had come himself. I don't know if I should leave you here alone."

"If he wanted us to both come, I'm sure he would have said so. I think you should go."

"All right. Are you sure you'll be okay?"

"I'll lock the door right behind you."

"Well, I'll go then I guess."

She went to the door and opened it.

"Are you really sure, Sister?"

"Yes, I'm sure."

Marjorie hugged Sarah and went out into the hall.

"Okay, Sarah. I want to hear the door lock."

Sarah clicked the lock into place.

"Just be careful, Marge," she called through the door.

"I will."

Sister Joan walked with her down the stairs and to the door to the hall.

"I have to go back to my room now," Sister told her. "Sister Agnes is still at the desk, and she's not in a very good mood. Just go quietly so you don't upset her."

She turned and headed back up the stairs. Marjorie opened the door as quietly as she could. She looked over to the desk and saw that Sister Agnes wasn't there.

As she started through the hall, she saw Sister Agnes in the outer vestibule by the outer doors. She must be taking a break, Marjorie thought. She hurried along and turned into the hall to the dining room. In a few seconds, she was in the dining room, finding her way through with the help of the dim light from the lights outside the windows. In the near darkness, she suddenly felt afraid, wondering if someone could be hiding in the shadows, ready to grab her as she passed. She reached the door into the school and started running through the hall toward the light at the far end.

Sister Agnes finished locking the outer doors and walked down the hall to the dining room doorway. She closed the double doors and turned the key in the lock. Her job done for the day, she turned out the lights in the hall and went to her room to wait until time for evening prayer.

Marjorie was breathing hard when she reached the entrance to the dormitory. "I've gotta work harder in gym," she told herself as she stood catching her breath. She looked back down the dark school hallway. She was glad Steve would be with her when she went back that way.

She looked down the hall toward her room but didn't see Steve.

I wonder if he's waiting for me in my room, she thought.

That made sense. He probably wouldn't just stand around in the hall. She started down the hall, wondering what he might have found that he needed her help with. She opened the door only to find the room empty.

Where else could he be? she wondered. If he had decided to go back to the convent, she would have passed him on her way. Maybe Rachel had seen him.

She knocked on Rachel's door.

"Rachel, it's me, Marjorie."

The door opened.

"What are you doing here, Marge? I thought the detective said you should stay over in the convent."

"I got a message to meet him here."

"What for?"

"I don't know. Sister Joan said he called the desk and told Sister Agnes to have me come over here to help him with something. Did you see him anywhere?"

"No. We've all been in our rooms with the doors closed. We were told we had to keep them closed. Sister Mary Joseph even came around to check. I heard her in the hall a little while ago."

"Are you sure it was her? Maybe it was Steve."

"I'm sure. Haven't you ever noticed how the sisters' rosary beads clink against each other when they walk? Besides, she wears those shoes that sound like tap shoes when she walks. Everybody always knows when she's around."

"I guess you're right. You probably wouldn't have known if he was here unless he talked to you."

A thought occurred to her.

"Wait a minute. I wonder if he's talking to Paula or Brenda. He said he had to talk to them about how they're going to help him catch that guy. That's where he probably is. I'll see you later, Rachel."

She turned and hurried away toward Paula's room.

"Be careful, Marge," Rachel called after her.

"I'll be OK," Marjorie called back.

She arrived at Paula's door and hesitated before knocking. Despite her reply to Rachel, she had to admit to herself that she was a little nervous. She knocked rather timidly but got no reply. After waiting a few seconds she knocked again, this time a little louder. Still no reply. An uneasy feeling came over her.

"Paula, are you in there?" she called.

The door behind her opened.

"Shhh. You trying to get us in more trouble?"

She turned to find Paula standing in the doorway of Brenda's room.

"Get in here," Paula told her.

She entered the room with an almost overwhelming trepidation, causing her heart to feel like it was going to burst out of her chest. Paula closed the door behind her, and she was gripped by a sudden desire to turn and run from the room. She felt trapped, though, with Paula between her and the door.

"What are you doing here?" Paula asked.

Marjorie managed to stammer out her reply.

"I…I'm looking for Detective McLean."

"Why would you think he was here? We already told him everything."

"He sent a message for me to meet him over here, but I can't find him anywhere. I thought maybe he might have come to talk to you about what to do when you go into the city."

"He's supposed to tell us that day," Brenda said. "He's too busy trying to solve the murder now."

Marjorie noticed that Paula was looking at her with a smirk on her face.

"Why are you so buddy-buddy with him anyway?" she asked. "He got the hots for you or something? I know you've got the hots for him. I can tell by the way you look at him."

Marjorie felt her face redden. She regretted having ever knocked on Paula's door.

"He does, doesn't he?" Paula continued. "That's probably why he wants to meet you here. You two can get together in your room and nobody will know."

For a second or two, that suggestion made Marjorie wish it was true, but she knew it wasn't, and she quickly brought her thoughts around to the matter at hand.

"No, he's not like that! He asked me to listen to see if anyone said anything about what happened to Sister Margaret Mary and tell him if they did. That's all."

"I knew it!" Paula shouted. "I knew you were spying on us!"

"I wasn't spying on you. I wasn't spying on anyone. All I was supposed to do was listen to see if anyone seemed like they knew something about the murder. You got yourselves in trouble when you acted suspicious and said you'd have to be careful about talking around us. You acted like you were hiding something. I had to tell Steve about that. He told me to tell him about anything that might be important, and the way you were acting seemed like it could be important."

"Well, it was important. Important to us that nobody else knew. Now everyone's going to know, even our parents. And it turns out it wasn't even anything to do with what you were supposed to be looking out for. But you stuck your nose in where it didn't belong and got us in trouble anyway."

Paula's voice was rising, and the level of Marjorie's uneasy feeling was rising with it. She was searching for something to say that might calm Paula down when Brenda spoke up.

"Cut it out, Paula. She's right. We're the ones who got ourselves in trouble. We did it when we took the first picture. There's no one to blame but us. And when we talked Rachel into doing it, we dug ourselves in even deeper."

She turned her attention to Marjorie.

"We got greedy. We told Rachel he'd pay a hundred dollars for her pictures. We acted like we were trying to help her. But the truth is…"

Paula interrupted.

"Shut up. She doesn't need to know everything."

"Yes, she does. I've been thinking about it, and when they catch the guy, they'll know anyway."

She turned back to Marjorie.

"The truth is, the guy told us he'd pay a hundred and fifty for pictures of other girls, especially the younger ones. We figured if they got a hundred, they'd be happy to make that much, and we could keep fifty for ourselves. We wouldn't really be cheating anyone. We thought nobody would get hurt."

She looked down at the floor.

"But when I saw Rachel in Mother Superior's office, I realized that we were wrong. She looked so scared, and it was our fault. I'm glad we got caught when we did. We could have hurt a lot of other girls, especially if the pictures ended up in magazines all over the country. I just wish I didn't have to tell my parents."

Marjorie looked at Paula. She too was looking at the floor. Marjorie started toward the door, but Paula stopped her.

"Look, Marge, I'm sorry for the way I've been acting. Brenda's right. We got ourselves into this mess. I guess I just wanted to blame someone else instead of having to admit to myself that I only have myself to blame. We may as well all get along for the rest of the time I'm here. I'm pretty sure I'll be on my way home as soon as my parents find out, and they will. Mother Superior said she'd like to keep it quiet for the sake of the school's reputation, but she said she has to do the right thing. Then she said something kinda strange. She said there were already too many secrets. Do you know what she meant?"

"Not really. Maybe it has something to do with Sister Margaret Mary's murder. I mean, someone must have had a reason to do that. Maybe we'll find out when Steve catches the killer."

"Oh yeah, Marge, I guess I shouldn't have teased you about him either."

"It's okay. I guess I haven't done a very good job of hiding it. It's embarrassing, really. I know I'm too young for him to ever notice me other than to help him like he asked me to. I just hope he hasn't noticed. I think I'd die if he did."

"Well he is pretty hot. I'd probably feel the same way you do if I was the one he asked to help him."

Help him! Marjorie suddenly remembered why she had come to the dormitory.

"Oh, gee! Steve! I still have to find him. Maybe he's in one of the other halls. I better get going. I'll see ya."

She was out the door and heading for the end of the hall that led to the other halls in the building.

She looked in every hall on both floors, but he was nowhere to be found. She chided herself for spending so much time in the room with Paula and Brenda. If he had looked for her while she was there, he might have thought she hadn't come, and if he did, he might have gone back to the convent. But then another thought occurred to her. What if he hadn't sent for her? What if someone wanted to get her away from Sarah? Jack could have called pretending to be Steve. On the phone, the sisters might not question if he sounded like Steve or not.

She raced to the doorway into the school but stopped as she looked down the dark hall. What if Jack was waiting for her in there somewhere? What if he wanted to kill her too for telling Steve about him? It didn't matter. She had to get back to Sarah.

She took a deep breath and let it out as she started running through the hall, looking from side to side, her heart skipping every time a shadow seemed to move. At last she was at the dining room. Only that lay between her and safety. In the dark, she didn't see until she got close to them that the doors were closed. She grabbed the handle of one and pulled. Nothing. She jiggled it and pulled again. Still it didn't move. She grabbed both handles and pulled as hard as she could. Finally, she knew. The doors were locked. She banged on them, calling out for someone to come and open them, but no one came.

She looked back into the room, wondering if someone was hiding in one of the corners. The dim light from the lights outside threw shadows of tree branches across the lines of tables. A gust of wind rattled the windows and set the shadows in motion. Her heart jumped, and she stepped back against the doors. She leaned back on the doors, and with tears streaming down her cheeks, she slowly slid down to the floor. Sitting, watching the room for any sign that someone was there, she wondered what Steve would think when they found her body there in the morning.

Chapter 12

Steve arrived at the station just as Isabelle was about to leave to bring the letter to him. He immediately opened the envelope and pulled two sheets of paper out. The first sheet was a letter, and the second was a copy of a birth certificate. Steve read the letter out loud.

"To whom it may concern: The enclosed birth certificate is a copy of one that was completed and recorded by Dr. Michael Grossman at my request. The information was falsified after the birth of a child who was born to a student at St. Christopher's Girls School on February 21, 1940. I am writing this letter and placing it in my files in the hope that it will be found in the event of any questions that may arise in the future concerning the child named on the certificate.

"It has come to my attention that the child may have been involved in the sudden deaths of her parents. As any knowledge of my involvement with the birth of this child and the falsification of the birth record would result in criminal charges, I cannot bring myself to make my concerns known to the authorities at this time.

"Dr. Grossman, who was paid for his assistance, has since died and cannot suffer any repercussions because of it. I, however, have a family who depend on me. If this letter is found, the person who reads it will undoubtedly regard me as a coward, but I cannot at the present time subject my family to the consequences of my past actions. I can only assume that if this letter is found it is because of an event in which the child is involved. In that case, I hope that the finding of this letter will aid in resolving any questions that may arise.

"I make no excuses for the part I played in this matter nor for what some may consider to be my failure to act at this time. It was, at the time, necessary to help a young girl in trouble, and at this time necessary to protect my family."

Steve put the letter down on the desk.

"It's signed by Richard Hennessy."

There was silence in the room as everyone considered the contents of the letter. Finally, Steve broke the silence.

"Quite a letter. I wonder what he meant by the child being involved in the parents' deaths. He doesn't say what happened, and he doesn't say what made him feel she was involved. But at least we know it was a girl. So it could be Sister Juliette Marie."

Pete was still at the table where he was looking through the sisters' information. He remembered what he had found about Sister Juliette Marie.

"Wait a minute, Steve. She was adopted. According to what that letter says, they made up a fake birth certificate. He doesn't say they got her adopted."

"Damn it, that's right. Let's take a look at the certificate."

He picked it up and examined it.

"Okay, it says Mother: June (McCormack) Washington, Father: Frederick Washington. Anybody know any Washingtons around here?"

As they all thought about the question, Isabelle spoke first.

"Well, I didn't grow up here, so I don't know many people yet."

Hank Thompson, the desk sergeant, was thinking there was something familiar about that name but it just wasn't coming to him. Suddenly, he jumped up from his chair.

"Wait a minute. I knew that name sounded familiar. I'd have to check the records to be sure, but I think there was a fire. The husband and wife both died. I think it was in '53!"

"You remember anything else?" Steve asked.

"I don't remember the details, but they might have had a kid. Let me run down and see what I can find in the files. They're all in boxes by year so it shouldn't take that long."

He hurried out to the stairs and went down. Steve read the letter again. He looked at the envelope and noted the date, October 5th. Six days before he died in an accident.

"Hey, Pete, is that Hennessy accident report still around here?"

"Yeah. I think it's on Hank's desk."

Steve went to the desk and looked over the report.

"It says he must have swerved to miss an animal."

"Nothing unusual about that," Isabelle remarked.

"No, I know that. I can't help but wonder, though. He writes the letter on the fifth, and six days later, he runs off the road and dies."

Pete was eyeing him questioningly.

"You don't think the kid had anything to do with that, do you?"

"I don't know. The letter certainly gives the impression that Hennessy thought she had something to do with the parents' deaths. He basically comes out and says it."

He looked the letter over again. Something else caught his attention.

"You know," he said thoughtfully, "he seems to have written this letter thinking it wouldn't be read until after he was dead. He wasn't that old in '53. He shouldn't have had any reason to feel the need to write it unless..."

"Unless he thought his life was in danger," Isabelle added.

"What would make him think that?" Pete asked.

"Well," Steve said, "he seemed convinced that the girl had something to do with the fire. If she did, she must have hated her parents pretty strongly. If she hated her parents that much, she may have also hated the man who put her in that family. How she would know who he was is anybody's guess, but if she did, he might have known she did. If he was right, who knows what she might have been capable of?"

"You're putting a lot on a kid who would have been only thirteen at the time."

"Well, believe me, Pete, if you just spent the day around the teenage girls I've been talking to, you'd realize that they can be capable of doing things you would never imagine. Wait till I tell you about what we're going to be working on in a couple days."

Before Pete could ask what he meant, Hank came running in with a pile of papers in his hand.

"Here it is! They even filed the newspaper story with the report."

He handed the papers to Steve.

"You read it, Steve. You know what to look for better than I do."

Steve sat at the desk and handed the letter and certificate to Isabelle. He first opened the newspaper to the story.

"It says the couple were trapped in the house. It was on their farm a few miles out of town. The girl told the police she was outside in the field and saw the flames. She ran to the neighbors' place for help, but by the time anyone got there, the whole house was in flames. The story says the police determined it was arson."

He put the paper down and picked up the report, looking it over silently. After a while, he put it down on the desk and shook his head.

"They found traces of gasoline in several spots in the house. The bodies were burned beyond recognition. Somebody had a grudge against those people."

"You think the kid did it?" Pete asked.

"Well, she could have. A house far away from any other houses. A farm with probably some gas cans in the barn. There's not much in the report about the kid, though. It doesn't look like anyone questioned her much at all."

He picked up the phone and dialed.

"I wonder if Harry remembers anything about it," he said, talking to himself out loud.

"Harry who?" Isabelle asked.

Pete answered her as Steve listened to the ringing on the line.

"He retired a little while ago. He trained Steve, taught him everything he knows. Harry wasn't just a good detective—he was the best. Steve couldn't have learned from a better guy. He got the job because Harry told..."

"Hey, Harry."

He stopped when he heard Steve talking.

"Yeah, I know it's getting late, but it's not that late. You're not going to bed this early, are you? I've got a couple of tired old men who want to say hello."

He held the receiver up, and Pete and Hank shouted, "Hello!"

"Is that Pete and Hank? Tell them I said it back. And tell them retirement is great. They should try it. So what's so important you have to bother me at this time of night? You calling to tell me you solved the case already?"

"Well, not already, but I may be getting close. I've got an old case I need to ask you about."

"Another one? How many old cases does this new case of yours involve?"

"Well, it seems they're all connected. Do you recall the fire that killed the Washingtons in '53?"

"Do I? It bothered me for years. The thought of those two people being trapped in that house with no way out was tough to think about. What's that got to do with your case now?"

"The girl who hung herself at the school. It turns out she didn't get an abortion. She waited too long before going to the nun and had to carry the baby to term. She was able to hide it because she was overweight so no one noticed. So she had the baby, and the nun arranged for it to be secretly adopted. Turns out, a local lawyer got a fake birth certificate made up and gave the girl to the Washingtons."

"I remember the girl. Really upset about the whole thing. We couldn't get her to say a word. All she said was she saw the flames from the field, then she clammed up. It took her a long time to get over it."

"I read the report. I thought it was unusual that there wasn't any mention of her being questioned."

"Oh yeah. She was so shaken up we couldn't ask her anything. I mean, she watched the place burn with her parents inside. It seemed logical for her to just sit and stare without saying a thing. She was like that for days. It took a while before she said anything, and by the time she did, nobody wanted to bring it up to her and maybe set her back again."

"What would you say if I told you we've found a letter from the lawyer who arranged the adoption and the fake birth certificate where he wrote that he had somehow gotten some information that led him to believe that the girl had something to do with the deaths? The letter sounded like he was afraid of her."

"You mean she might have burned the place down. That's hard to believe. She was only thirteen, I think."

"Well, I'm not sure what the guy might have found out to make him think that, but it's curious that he died in an accident a few days after he wrote the letter."

"Wait a minute. Are you talking about Dick Hennessy?"

"Yeah. Why?"

"I gotta think back a little. As I remember it, he had a Caddy convertible. He had a habit of driving pretty fast. We even had a complaint or two about it not long before the accident. He got thrown from the car. Hit his head pretty hard on a rock or two when he landed. He didn't die right away. There was a guy who found him who told us he said something before he died. We didn't think too much about it at the time. I mean, he was all banged up, and what he said didn't make sense to us. In fact, we thought the guy probably heard it wrong."

"There's nothing about that in the report."

"I know. Like I said, it didn't make sense, so we didn't think anything of it. But if Dick thought the girl had set the fire and he was afraid of her, it could make sense."

"So what did he say?"

"The guy said Dick said, 'I can't believe she did it'."

"You think she could have had something to do with the accident?"

"Let me think about this for a minute."

Steve looked at the others as Harry was thinking. They were close enough to the phone that they had heard what Steve had said and enough of what Harry had said to be putting the pieces together.

The enormity of what it could mean was clearly on all of their minds. Harry started talking again.

"I remember now that the girl went to live with the neighbors after the fire. The house wasn't very far from where the accident happened. With no witnesses, the logical conclusion was that an animal was in the road. Considering everything you've said and what the guy said, it might not have been an animal. Maybe it was a two-legged critter."

They were all trying to comprehend the things they were thinking. Could a thirteen-year-old girl really burn her parents to death and then cause an accident to kill someone else?

Steve's head was reeling.

"Look, Harry, what the hell does all this mean? You didn't prepare me for anything like this. And how exactly does it fit in with what's going on now?"

"You got me, kid. You got yourself a tiger by the tail with this one. Could it be any of the nuns?"

"Well, we thought it could be one, but that didn't fit. Hennessy's letter said he had a fake birth certificate made up. The nun's records show she was adopted, so even though she was born in 1940, that leaves her out."

Pete looked up suddenly from his thoughts.

"What did you say?"

"I said, she was born in 1940, but since she was adopted, that leaves her out."

Pete went to the table where he had been going through the records of the nuns. He fingered through them, frantically looking for something. He pulled a sheet of paper out of the pile and held it up.

"Here it is!" he shouted triumphantly.

"What?" Steve asked.

"You asked if any of the nuns had been adopted. That's all I looked for. But I wasn't looking for any who were born in '40. I didn't know the year was important."

He looked at the paper in his hand and read.

"Born February 21, 1940. Name, Anna Washington. Parents, Frederick and June Washington. It's her."

"Who?" Steve shouted. "Which one is it?"

"The one named Sister Joan."

Steve was out of his chair and heading for the door.

"Hey, Steve," Hank called after him, "what about Harry?"

"Hang up the phone…and tell him thanks. I gotta get back there."

He ran out to the car and sped off, hoping as he drove that nothing had happened in his absence. If things had happened in 1953 the way it looked like they had, there was no way of knowing what Sister Joan might be capable of. She must have killed Sister Margaret Mary and John Miller for some reason, and if she did kill her parents and Richard Hennessy, it seems like it was revenge for something. Did she know about her mother? There didn't seem to be any way that she could. But if she did, did she blame them all for her suicide? Whatever her reason for the murders, one thing was clear. If she was killing everyone who was connected to what happened when she was born, Sister Agatha was in danger. His foot pressed down harder on the gas pedal.

Marjorie sat with her back against the door, her eyes darting back and forth across the room with every movement of the shadows. The wind had gotten stronger, and the tree branches made the shadows move almost constantly. The windows rattled continually, and every sound made her more and more certain that someone was in the room with her.

She had considered making a mad dash back through the school to her room. It was a long way to go, but if she made it, at least she'd be safe in her room where there was light and all the other girls nearby. But her fear of the dark had heightened to a point where all she could do was sit as still as possible and pray that it was only her imagination in the room with her.

Then there was a sound—at least she thought she heard it. It was in the hall, she thought. Then there was nothing, and her heart sank. Wait. There it was again. It sounded like someone walking. She was about to call out, but she changed her mind. What if it was Jack? If it was, she'd give herself away. And if he was on the other side of the doors, she was safe.

She moved away from the doors as quietly as possible. The sound came closer, and she could now hear clearly that there were footsteps coming toward the doors. The footsteps stopped. Suddenly, the door handles began to rattle as whoever was there tried to open the doors. Marjorie held her breath. The footsteps began to move away, but Marjorie heard something she hadn't earlier. It was the sound of rosary beads clinking together. It was a nun!

She shouted and beat on the doors.

"Help! I'm locked out! Help!"

The footsteps hurried back.

"Who's in there?" came Sister Juliette Marie's voice from the other side.

"It's me. Marjorie. Someone locked the doors."

"They're always locked at eight o'clock. We have evening prayer at eight-thirty."

"I didn't know. I came back, and they were locked. I'm really scared."

"I know where the keys are. I'll be right back."

Marjorie heard her walk away from the doors. She turned around and looked at the dining room. It didn't seem as frightening as it did just a few minutes ago.

She heard Sister Juliette Marie returning and stepped back from the doors. The key turned and light burst in through the open door. Marjorie hurried through the doors and into the safety of the hall. She followed Sister Juliette Marie as she returned to the desk and put the keys back in their place.

"You're lucky I came over here," Sister told her. "Everyone is at evening prayer in the church. What were you doing in the school? I thought you were supposed to stay in the guest room."

"I know, Sister, but I got a message that Steve wanted me to meet him in the dormitory."

"Steve?"

Marjorie saw the look on Sister Juliette Marie's face.

"Detective McLean. He asked me to help him with the case and told me to call him that since I was his partner."

"Well, I'm not so sure that was a good idea, but who am I to tell a police detective how to do his job? When did you get the message?"

"I don't know for sure—probably about forty-five minutes ago."

"Marjorie, Detective McLean left here almost an hour ago. Who gave you the message?"

"Sister Joan. She said Sister Agnes told her to tell me."

"Sister Joan? The reason I'm here is because I'm looking for Sister Joan. We gathered for evening prayer, and she was missing. Mother Superior told me to look for her."

A sudden fear washed over Marjorie.

"Sarah! I've gotta check on Sarah!"

Sister Juliette Marie felt the same fear.

"Come with me. Hurry!"

They ran through the convent door and up the steps to the second floor. The guest room was the first room on the right at the top of the stairs. Marjorie knocked on the door.

"Sarah, it's me. Open up."

There was no answer. She tried the door knob. It twisted, and the door opened. Her stomach was in a knot as she entered the room. It was empty.

"Oh, God!" she shouted, almost screaming. "She's gone! It's all my fault! I should have listened to her! It was a trick to get me out of here. I can't believe Sister Joan would help Jack like that!"

Sister Juliette Marie tried to calm her down.

"You don't know that she was helping him. Maybe he called Sister Agnes and pretended to be the detective. Sister Agnes wouldn't have known that he was gone. We can ask her if she gave Sister Joan the message. The best thing to do is to let Mother Superior know what's happened. Come with me."

"No! I have to find Sarah! This is all my fault! I have to find her before he hurts her! If we wait too long, she could be dead!"

"Marjorie, you can't just run around the school looking for her by yourself. If we tell Mother Superior, we can get all the sisters to help."

"I can't wait that long!"

She started for the door and stopped, staring at the floor.

"Sister, look," she said, pointing to a spot near the door. "That's blood! He already hurt her!"

She bolted through the door and down the steps. Sister Juliette Marie tried to keep up, but her habit prevented her from running as fast as Marjorie. After watching Marjorie run out the door that led onto the grounds, she hurried to the church to tell Mother Superior.

Steve pulled up in front of the school and ran to the door. To his surprise, it was locked.

"Oh, you're kidding me!" he exclaimed.

He hurried back to the car and radioed the station. He had another surprise when Isabelle answered his call.

"What are you still hanging around there for?"

"I got to know those girls today. I want to be around to see how it all turns out. Are they okay?"

"Well, that's why I'm calling in. The place is locked. Have Thompson call and tell them I need to get in."

"Okay. I'll tell him. Stay on."

As he was waiting, one of the officers he had left to watch for Jack came around the corner of the convent. Steve called him over to ask where the other one was. The officer told him he was on the other side of the church near the dormitory. Steve told him to get the other officer and wait by the convent door. The officer went off to get his partner just as Isabelle came back on.

"There's no answer, Steve."

"That's just great! What do I do now?"

As Steve looked around, trying to think of another way to get in, he noticed that there were lights on in the rectory.

"Hey, Isabelle, it looks like the priest is still awake. Try calling the church."

"Okay. We will."

A few more minutes passed.

"Steve?"

"Yeah, I'm here."

"The priest said they're all in the church for their evening prayer. If you go to the rectory, he'll let you in."

"Thanks. I'm heading there now."

He turned the radio off and hurried to the rectory. Father Jerome opened the door.

"What's going on, Detective? I told the officer who called I could let the sisters know after they finished evening prayer, but he said you had to get in right away. Has something happened?"

"Well, Father, I don't know if Mother Superior has had time to fill you in, but things have been happening all day. Right now, I'm hoping to keep even more from happening."

"That sounds serious. I'll come with you. It'll be easier than giving you directions through the connecting hallways."

Father Jerome led Steve through the rectory and into a hallway that connected with the sacristy of the church. He could hear the sisters reciting their prayers as they arrived in the sacristy. Father Jerome led him into the church, and Steve followed him to where the sisters were gathered in a section of pews. Mother Superior looked up and saw Steve then bowed her head and continued her prayers.

Father Jerome leaned closer to Steve and whispered.

"I'm afraid you'll have to wait till they're finished. I'll be in the rectory if you need me," he said as he started toward the sacristy.

Steve stepped closer, trying to get to a spot where he could see the faces of the sisters, hoping he could see if Sister Agatha and Sister Joan were there. He stopped when Mother Superior looked up with an expression that told him she was not too pleased with the disruption of their prayers.

From that vantage point, he was able to see most of the faces. With their wimples and veils, he had to look closely to see what was visible of their faces, but he managed to find Sister Agatha in the crowd. He felt a sense of relief knowing that she was safe, but when he realized that he didn't think he saw Sister Joan, his concern grew. As he struggled with the question of whether or not he should just interrupt the prayers, Mother Superior rose and approached him. She motioned for him to follow her as she crossed to the other side of the church. She stopped and turned to him, keeping her voice to a whisper.

"It's evident that you're determined to be a distraction to the sisters. I'm assuming that there's a good reason."

"There is, Mother. It can't wait, or I wouldn't have interrupted. We know who the killer is, and I believe Sister Agatha may be in danger."

"Were we right about Jack then?"

"No. I think you'd better prepare yourself for a shock."

He hesitated. This was something he truly didn't want to tell her.

Mother Superior realized that she was about to hear the one thing she had been dreading all day. She had hoped for a different outcome, but the one fact she couldn't escape was that the murder had taken place in the convent, a place that would have been difficult for anyone but a nun to get into and out of without being noticed. Still, she had told herself that it was possible, and the fact that John Miller and Jack both had access to a key to get onto the grounds had given her hope.

Now that hope was gone.

"Just tell me, Steve. I know what you're going to say."

"We learned, Mother, that Sister Joan is the baby who was born in 1940 to the girl who hung herself."

"What? Are you sure?"

"We found everything we needed to piece it all together. More than that, though, we think she may have been responsible for the deaths of the people who adopted her and even possibly the lawyer who arranged the adoption."

Mother Superior was silent for a moment. She had expected to hear Sister Agatha's name.

"It's unbelievable. I had expected it was going to be one of the sisters, Agatha in fact, but I just can't believe that the Sister Joan I've known for three years could have done that. She's been an exemplary nun. I could understand Agatha reaching a point where she felt she had to stop Margaret Mary, but if what you've told me is true, she must have been planning this for years, even becoming a nun to accomplish it. But why?"

"The only thing we can figure is that she's taking revenge on everyone who was connected to her mother."

"How would she know about her mother? Who could have told her?"

"That I don't know, but it seems to be the only explanation considering who she's killed so far."

"You said you suspect she killed the people who adopted her?"

"They died in a fire, trapped in the house. It was determined to be arson. She was only thirteen, so no one suspected her then, but no other suspect ever came to light. I talked to the detective who was on the case. He said no one questioned her because they thought she was in shock. She sat for days, never saying a word. Pretty good ruse to make sure she didn't slip up when they questioned her."

"What you're saying makes her seem like a monster. To do something like that and to have a scheme to cover her tracks, all when she was only thirteen. And now, to wait all these years acting like a dedicated sister, hiding the fact that she's had murder in her mind all along. If it's true, we've been hiding a monster in our midst."

She walked over to where a kneeler was set in front of a statue of St. Christopher and knelt. Clasping her hands together tightly, she began to pray silently.

Suddenly, Sister Juliette Marie hurried in from the convent hallway. Seeing Steve, she ran over to him. Steve could tell by the look on her face that something had happened, and it wasn't good.

"What's wrong?" he asked, as quietly as he could.

"Sarah's missing!"

"What?"

His outburst caused the sisters to all look over toward him.

Mother Superior's prayers were also interrupted. She rose and returned to where he was standing.

"Has something else happened?" she asked.

"I'm sorry, Mother," Sister Juliette Marie explained, "but Sarah is missing."

Mother Superior managed to catch herself before she too shouted her response.

"How did that happen?" she asked after taking a moment to control herself. "The girls were told to stay in the guest room, weren't they?"

"Yes, Mother, but Sister Joan went there and told Marjorie that Detective McLean had called and asked Sister Agnes to tell her that he wanted her to meet him in the dormitory."

Mother Superior looked at Steve.

"Sister Joan? You don't think…"

"Yes, I do."

He turned to Sister Juliette Marie.

"Marjorie didn't go, did she?"

"Unfortunately, yes. She got locked in the dining room. She didn't know that the doors were locked at eight o'clock. I found her when I was looking for Sister Joan."

A question presented itself in Mother Superior's mind.

"Why would Sister Joan want to take Sarah?"

"At this point, I think she may be capable of anything for any reason," Steve answered. "We need to find them before anything else happens."

He turned to Sister Juliette Marie again.

"Where's Marjorie now?"

"I don't know. When we found Sarah gone, she ran off to look for her. I told her we needed to find Mother Superior, but she wouldn't listen. She ran too fast for me to keep up."

The sisters had finished their prayers and were starting to return to the convent. As Steve hurried toward the convent hallway, he looked for Sister Agatha. Not seeing her, he asked Sister Juliette Marie to find her and stay with her. He and Mother Superior then hurried off to look for Marjorie and Sarah, hoping it wasn't already too late.

Chapter 13

As soon as Sister Joan had left Marjorie, she went back up the stairs and knocked on the guest room door. She asked Sarah if she'd like her to come in and keep her company until Marjorie returned. Looking around the empty room, Sarah thought it would be nice to have some company and she unlocked the door and let her in.

Around 8:15, when footsteps were heard in the hall, Sister Joan explained that the sisters were leaving for evening prayer, but she would stay with Sarah. When the hall was quiet again, she told Sarah she knew of a better place to hide, one that was much safer than the guest room. She tried to convince Sarah that she should go there with her, but Sarah was reluctant to leave. She told Sister Joan that she wanted to wait for Marjorie since if she came back and found them gone, she'd be frightened. Sister Joan assured Sarah that she could take her to the other place and come back and wait for Marjorie. When Sarah insisted on staying in the guest room, Sister Joan became angry and pulled back the long full sleeve of her habit to reveal a grass shears in her hand.

Sarah tried to run past Sister Joan to get to the door, but Sister Joan lashed out with the shears and cut Sarah's hand. The sharp pain and the fierceness of the way Sister Joan had lashed out made Sarah stop trying to get away. By that time, she was certain that Sister Joan was going to kill her right there in the room. But that wasn't what Sister Joan had planned.

She told Sarah to walk in front of her and warned her that if she made even one sound, she'd be dead in a second. They went down the stairs and out through the door onto the grounds. Sister Joan had chosen the time when the sisters were at evening prayer so the convent was deserted and the girls were all in their rooms on the far side of the grounds.

They walked to the St. Christopher shrine. The high, curved wall behind the statue enclosed almost the entire area of the shrine, with just a six-foot opening between it and the wall of the convent. The statue was at least ten feet tall and faced the convent. In the fifteen-foot-wide area between the statue and the convent wall were four concrete benches. A row of tall thick bushes lined the wall of the convent hiding the wall completely.

Sister Joan grabbed Sarah's arm and pushed her through a narrow gap in the bushes. Sarah found herself standing up against the wall with the branches of the bushes almost forcing her against it. Sister Joan pushed her along the wall a few feet to the left to a door hidden completely by the bushes. She was told to open the door and was pushed through it into a dark hallway. Sister Joan flicked a light switch, and a dim light exposed several steps leading down to a hallway about ten feet long with a door at the other end. Sister Joan told her to close the door behind her.

As she closed the door, Sarah had an idea. She slammed the door, giving Sister Joan the impression that it was closed tightly, but she quickly pulled it back just enough to possibly swing a little bit further with a slight passing breeze.

Sarah was pushed to the second door and told to open it. Behind it was nothing but pitch blackness. Sister Joan pushed her into the room. The flick of another switch lit up a single bulb hanging by a cord in the center of the ceiling, exposing a room with gray concrete walls.

In the dim light, Sarah could see a table, almost chest high, in the middle of what appeared to be a twelve-by-twelve-foot room. The table had worn leather straps on either side of both ends. She knew that whatever happened on that table wasn't something good.

To the right was a white three-drawer dresser. Hanging on the wall above it, much to Sarah's horror, were several leather whips.

She turned away quickly, not wanting to see the whips any longer than she had, only to find an even more terrible sight. In the far corner of the room, sitting with his pants around his ankles and his back leaning up against the corner, was Jack. A large pool of blood covered the floor beneath him. She screamed when she saw him and turned away.

"Go ahead and scream," Sister Joan told her. "No one can hear you in here. And he's dead, so he can't either."

"What did you do to him?" Sarah asked, almost afraid to know.

"I did what should have been done long ago. Maybe if it had, you wouldn't be in the fix you're in. I fixed him, though. I made it so he could never do to any other girls what he's been doing to girls like you."

She snapped the blades of the shears back and forth a couple times and laughed a demonic laugh.

"Snip, snip," she said gleefully.

She made a sarcastically sad face and spoke with an overly sad voice.

"Only I couldn't stop the bleeding. Good thing I drugged him. I don't think he felt too much pain."

Sarah's stomach turned. Sister Joan handed her a pail.

"Here," she said. "I think you'll need this."

Sarah held the pail tightly as she vomited. When she finished, Sister Joan took the pail from her, walked over to the corner, and emptied the pail on Jack.

"Just giving him what he deserves," she said.

Sarah choked back a second urge to vomit.

"Why are you doing this?" she screamed.

"Why? I'm trying to help you! I fixed him. Now I can fix you."

"What do you mean? I don't need to be fixed!"

"You have a problem, don't you? I can take care of it for you."

Sarah suddenly understood.

"I should have never told you."

"I knew before you told me. I heard you talking to him."

She pointed at Jack.

"But Sister Margaret Mary can't help you, so I have to now."

"No, I don't want your help. I changed my mind. I want to have this baby."

Sister Joan was getting angry.

"Well, I don't care what you want!" she shouted. "I'm not going to let another child end up living like I did! Your little bastard isn't going to end up like me!"

"What do you mean?"

"I mean, I was born here! In this room! My mother did the same thing you did! Couldn't keep her panties on! Only she was too stupid to know what happened! She wanted to get rid of me, but she waited too long! So I was born, but she obviously couldn't keep me, so they told her I was dead! God help me, I wish I had been! It would have been a better fate than the one they gave me!"

Sarah had an idea. Sister Joan seemed to have more to say. If she could keep her talking long enough, maybe someone would find them. Maybe the door would open enough before it was too late.

"How do you know that?" she asked.

"You want to know how I know that? Good! I'll tell you. I'll tell you what my life has been like, and maybe you'll change your mind about keeping that bastard inside you!"

She started pacing, becoming more and more animated as she told her story.

"When I was five, my so-called father started having me do things to him. I didn't know what it was all about. He just said it made him feel good. But when I was eleven, he decided I was old enough to do more and I didn't like it. He didn't care if it hurt me or that I told him I didn't want to. And that woman who called herself my mother let him do it. I think she was glad he wanted me and not her. He did terrible things to me. I cried every night.

"When I was thirteen, while he was doing one of the despicable things he liked to do, I asked him how he could do something like that to his own daughter. He laughed and told me I wasn't his daughter. He said he had paid for me when I was a baby. I told him I was going to run away and find my real parents. He laughed again and said my mother was dead and I didn't have a father. I called him a liar, so he told me the whole story. I think he enjoyed telling it."

Sarah sat still, trying to be as silent as possible. She didn't want to do anything that might make Sister Joan lose her train of thought and decide to stop talking.

By now, Sister Joan's face was contorted with the hatred she felt for her father. She was breathing harder and pacing even faster.

"He told me how my mother was a student here and how she let some guy get her pregnant. She had to have the baby because she waited too long to tell anyone about it. There was a nun at the school, he said, who helped girls like her. She made arrangements with a lawyer to find someone to take the baby. That lawyer lived down the road from my 'parents', and he knew that the woman couldn't have kids. He asked my 'father' if he wanted a child. Told him how much it would cost. That's all I was, property for sale. The old man said he was glad when he got a girl. That's what he was hoping for.

"Then he told me how my mother died, how she hung herself. He laughed again and said it showed just how stupid she was, killing herself just because she had to give up a kid.

"I knew then that I had to make him pay. I knew I'd make them all pay. So I kept him talking. I wanted to know all about everyone who gave me to that sick bastard. And he told me everything. The way he did it made me think he was enjoying it, thinking he was hurting me with the story. All he did was make me hate him even more.

"He told me about the nun, and he told me the lawyer said there wouldn't be any chance my mother would ever try to find me because the nun had told her that I was dead. When I heard that, I promised myself that I'd find that nun and kill her no matter what I had to do or how long it took."

Sarah thought it seemed like she was getting tired of the story and might decide she'd said enough. She quickly asked another question.

"You waited all these years to do it? That must have been hard."

"Of course it was hard. I had to endure a lot to finally get her. It wasn't as hard as enduring what that man did to me, though. But

I had the memory of what I did to him and that woman to keep me going. I can still hear them screaming. And I got the lawyer too. They were easy."

She appeared to be drifting into her memories, and they seemed to be calming her down. Sarah was afraid she might become too calm, calm enough to bring her back to what she had planned for Sarah. She had to get her going again.

"They were screaming? Why? What did you do?"

She had asked the right question. She could see a change in Sister Joan. Her eyes lit up, and she smiled. It was obvious she was proud of whatever she had done.

"What did I do?" she said gleefully. "I waited for a night when the old pervert was drunk and passed out. The woman was ironing clothes. When she put the iron down to hang up a shirt she had just ironed, I grabbed the iron and hit her on the back of her head. Then I went out to the barn and brought the gas can into the house. I made sure I poured it on both doors and by every window. I lit the front door first then ran through the house, throwing matches at the windows. I went out the back door and threw the last match on the floor just inside and went for a walk in the field. When I came back, I could hear them screaming. It was the best sound in the world to me. I had made sure there was no way for them to get out, so I waited until there were no more screams. I ran—well, not until I got to a place in the road where I knew they could see me—to the neighbors' house for help. But it was too late. By the time the fire department showed up, there was nothing left but ashes. I'm not sure if they were even able to identify the bodies."

Her voice had a self-satisfied sound to it. She paused, enjoying the memory again. When she began again there was definite pride in her voice.

"They knew right away, of course, that it was arson. I used a lot of gas, and there was a smell of it in the air. I knew they'd try to ask me about it, but I was ready for them. I just sat there staring straight ahead and not saying a thing. They thought I was probably in shock, so they left me alone. I played my part beautifully for weeks. Everyone was afraid to say anything about it in front of me.

They were worried about making it even worse for me. None of the fools knew that I was laughing inside. I'd go to my room and close the door and laugh until I cried. Everyone thought I was grieving, but I was celebrating. At the funeral, I had to fight to keep from walking over and spitting on their graves. I hope they're rotting in hell, but even hell is too good for them."

She was into her story completely now, reveling in her revenge.

"The lawyer was easy too. I didn't even have to try to find him. The old man told me he lived down the road. I used to see him driving by every day in his big fancy convertible. I could have done it any time, but I wanted him to know I knew, so I skipped school one day and went to his office. By then I had overcome my grief and I was talking again. I told him I knew he was the one who sold me and I told him what kind of life he sold me into. I told him I'd never forgive him and that someday I'd ruin his life the way he ruined mine. I watched him sitting behind his desk, trying to pretend he wasn't afraid, but I could see him shaking in his boots. The fear was in his eyes, and I knew he was scared. I think I even made him wet his pants.

"The neighbors down the road had taken me in, and the house was near the road, so after that, I stood by the side of the road every day when he was on his way home. He started driving faster and faster, trying to get past me. Some of the neighbors called him and complained about how fast he drove. I didn't wait too long though to put him out of his misery.

"He always drove by around ten o'clock on Sunday night. I don't know where he was coming from but that didn't matter. I crouched down just beyond the shoulder of the road. When I heard him coming, I jumped out into the road. The look on his face was wonderful! He slammed on his brakes and swerved, trying to miss me, but he was going too fast as usual, and as I had hoped, and lost control. He flew off the road and then flew like a wounded bird out of the convertible and into some trees. I ran over to make sure he was dead, but I had to hide in the bushes before I got to him. Some guy drove by right after it happened. He stopped and went over to check on him. He was still alive, and I heard him say, 'I can't believe she did it,' so I knew he knew it was me. I had to bite my lip to keep from shouting. I was so happy! The guy took off to get help, so I went over and the old guy was out cold but still breathing. I found a good-sized rock and bashed him on the head.

"That did the trick, so I ran back to the house through the fields so no one would see me. I snuck in the back door and up the back steps, got in bed, and pretended to be surprised when I heard what happened the next morning."

Sarah was truly frightened now. Sister Joan's story made her realize that she was completely mad and capable of doing anything. She started praying silently, her hands tightly clenched, for someone to find her.

Sister Joan looked at her. She saw her hands.

"You're awful quiet. Let me guess. You're praying. Well, pray all you want, it won't do you any good. I prayed all those years, but God never answered me. If he does exist, he doesn't care. I figured that out when I was thirteen. The only one who was going to help me was me. And now the only one who's going to help you is me."

Sarah searched again for another question she could ask to get her talking again.

"If you don't believe in God, how could you be a nun all these years? How could you pretend to believe?" she blurted out.

Sister Joan snorted out an evil half-laugh sound.

"It wasn't easy. But I just told myself I had to do it if I was going to get that witch. I'm really a good actress, you know."

She was back in her glory again. Sarah kept praying it would continue long enough.

"If I didn't have to waste all these years waiting for my chance, I could have been a professional. I probably could have won an Academy Award."

Her anger started to boil over again.

"I could have, but they took away my chance! They took away all my chances, so I took theirs away. Now I've only got one other person left to punish. I was all set to do it, but you and your nosy little friend had to come along and spoil everything."

She started walking toward Sarah.

"Enough talking. It's time to get this over with, so I can get back to my other work. Let's get you undressed and on the table."

"Don't you touch her!"

The voice came from behind her. She turned to find Marjorie standing in the doorway.

"Marge!" Sarah shouted and tried to make a dash past Sister Joan. She wasn't fast enough and Sister Joan turned and punched her in the stomach. She fell to her knees.

"Sarah!" Marjorie cried out and started into the room to help her.

Sister Joan had put the shears on the table, but she grabbed them and held them out, stopping Marjorie where she stood.

"Back up, you little troublemaker," Sister Joan snarled.

Marjorie's mind was racing, trying to think of a way to get herself and Sarah out of there. She scanned the room quickly, looking for something she might be able to use to fight off Sister Joan. The whips would work, but she was afraid they were too far away to get to before Sister Joan could catch her. Then she saw Jack. The sight was more than she could comprehend.

"Oh my god!" she cried out. "What did you do to him?"

Sister Joan held the shears up and snapped the blades back and forth again. Marjorie swallowed hard. Sister Joan pointed to the pail, which she had put on the table.

"Looks like you might need that. Go ahead. It's been used, but I don't think it'll matter. I'd like to give him another dousing."

Marjorie swallowed again.

"That's okay. I don't need it."

She said it forcefully, in a way she hoped would make Sister Joan think she didn't get rattled that easily. Inside, her stomach was in such a tight knot it almost made her double over. She fought to stand as straight as possible. Her one hope, she felt, was to make Sister Joan think she wasn't afraid of her. She decided to be as cocky as she could make herself sound.

"So I guess they have more than one set of grass shears since you left one in Mr. Miller's throat."

She had hit on another of what Sister Joan apparently considered her masterpieces. Sister Joan's eyes lit up again.

"Yes, that was a stroke of brilliance, I thought. I figured you two might hear about it and tell them that his idiot son killed him. After all, that's what he told your friend he'd do to her."

Sarah was confused. How would she know that Jack had threatened her with the grass shears and what he said he would do?

"What do you mean?" she asked.

"I mean, the grass shears in his throat. I did it just the way he said he'd do it to you."

Sarah's head was spinning. How could she possibly know that he had threatened her that way? She had to know.

"How do you know what he said? We were at the gardener's shed. No one else was around."

Sister Joan smiled such a self-satisfied smile that it was clear she again had something to brag about. She, in fact, looked like she was going to burst with pride.

"How do I know? Why do you think he wouldn't let you come into the shed? Why do you think he kept you outside even after you told him you didn't want anyone to see you talking to him?"

Sarah was still confused.

"How do you know all that?"

Sister Joan stood looking down at her, her smile now a contorted evil grin. She was enjoying playing this game with Sarah, and now she was going to give her the surprise ending.

"I know because I was there, in the back room…on the bed!"

Sarah and Marjorie were both quite clearly shocked. The realization of what she meant was something unimaginable. Sister Joan stood like a triumphant Roman general surveying the army he had just decimated.

"How could you?" Marjorie managed to ask.

"You mean because I'm a nun? Don't let that fool you. I've only pretended to be a nun all these years so I could do what I had to do. Or are you asking because he's my brother? Or was, I guess I should say."

The surprise showed on Marjorie's face. Sister Joan felt another thrill of victory. This was her chance to taunt Marjorie.

"Oh, you didn't know that, did you? I thought that detective boyfriend of yours would have told you everything."

A thought stopped her. She began an almost comedic discussion with herself, talking in two different voices.

"Or maybe he doesn't know… Maybe he's still trying to figure it out… Well, he must know by now… I thought he was a good detective… If he is, he should have figured it out by now… Sister Agatha must have told him… What if she didn't?"

She looked at Marjorie.

"Do you think he knows?"

"I don't know. He doesn't tell me everything. And he's not my boyfriend," Marjorie told her emphatically.

Sister Joan was back to her original train of thought.

"Oh, really? You could have fooled me the way you gawk at him constantly. You'd think he was a rock and roll star. Is he a good kisser?"

"I wouldn't know. I told you, he's not my boyfriend!"

"Oh, but you'd like him to be, wouldn't you? You'd like to know how he kisses, I know you would. You'd probably like to know even more about what else he can do."

Marjorie was trying to control herself. Sister Joan had managed to create a combination of embarrassment and anger in her, causing her to want to scream at her to stop. Her fear held her in check, much to Sister Joan's disappointment. She was hoping to get Marjorie angry enough to attack her so she could kill her without having to chase her. She decided to continue her taunting.

"He'd be better off with me. I could show him a much better time than you could. Or have you had practice like your friend here?"

Marjorie was seething now, but she knew she couldn't lose control. She had to change the subject.

"So was Mr. Miller your father?"

"Well, that shouldn't have been too hard to figure out."

"If he's your father, why didn't Jack know you were his sister?"

"You got just as many questions as this other one has. No wonder you're friends."

She looked down at Sarah and then at Marjorie. Her sardonic smile wasn't comforting to either of them.

"Well, since you two have managed to mess up my plans, which means I'm going to have to kill you so you won't be around to tell anyone else, I guess I'll tell you the rest of the story. I already told her most of it, so I'm not going to go through the whole thing again. All you need to know is that when I was thirteen, I found out that my mother was a student here, and I was sold to a family that wanted a kid. I became a nun to fix the old bag who sold me, but I also wanted to find my father so I could fix him too. I made sure I got close to that hag, Margaret Mary, so I could get her to trust me."

She laughed.

"I did such a good job that she told me she thought I'd be a good replacement for her. She told me about the sister who taught her how to do it and said she'd be too old soon and needed to know there'd be someone to take her place.

"So I asked her questions about how many girls she had helped and if they ever told her about the boys and who they were. She told me about the idiot and that the last two girls said he was the one. There were a couple boys from town who managed to sneak in here too, she said.

"I wanted to find out about my father, but I couldn't ask her directly or she might have figured out who I was, and I didn't want her to know that until just before she died. So I asked some innocent questions about the girls from years ago and how the boys from town got in here. That's when she told me that when the gardener was young, he had been responsible for several of them.

"So I wondered if the idiot could tell me anything about his father. I made friends with him first, then I offered him a thrill he couldn't resist. After that, he was happy to tell me anything I wanted to know. He told me that his father had been the one who told him about Margaret Mary because she had taken care of the girls he'd been with. As soon as he told me I knew."

She stopped and eyed the girls again, her face now set with a look of determination that made them both shiver.

"I took the shears from the shed after I was with the idiot a couple days ago. I was able to get into Margaret Mary's room last night pretty easily. I said I just wanted to talk before lights out. She was always happy to visit with me. She told me she had a girl who needed help and that I would be able to work with her when she did it. Unfortunately, I had already decided last night would be the night, and I had the shears with me. I knocked her onto the bed and covered her mouth, then I stabbed her. I made sure I did it in a way that would let her live for a while. I wanted to be able to tell her who I was and what she did to my life. I held my hand over her mouth as I told her. She tried to say something, but I wouldn't let her. I wasn't going to let her try to make excuses. I would have liked to hear her beg for her life, but if I took my hand away she'd have only yelled for help and I couldn't let that happen. After I made sure she knew everything I wanted her to know, I stabbed her again. Then I waited till everyone was asleep and snuck back to the shed and hid the shears under the mattress. I figured the cops would eventually find it and my 'father' would end up in jail for the rest of his life. But then you two had to send them off after the idiot. They never even found the other room in the shed.

"So when they started looking in the wrong direction, I had to change my plans. I have to admit, though, that I did enjoy getting the chance to tell the old bastard who I was before I stuck the shears in. It was almost as good as when I told the idiot I was his sister. I'll never forget the look on both of their faces. I'll cherish the memory as long as I live."

She stopped to enjoy the memory for a moment with her eyes closed. Sarah made a motion to Marjorie to try to sneak out, but Marjorie shook her head and mouthed *no*. Sarah shouted.

"Marge, go!"

Sister Joan's eyes flew open, and she pointed the shears at Sarah as she shouted to Marjorie.

"You move one step and she'll be dead before you get to the door!"

"Go, Marge!" Sarah shouted. "She said she's going to kill us anyway, so at least you can get away!"

"I'm not going anywhere," Marjorie told her. "I'm not leaving you alone with this nutcase."

Sister Joan's face tightened in anger as she spit the words out through her clenched teeth.

"What did you call me?"

"I called you what you are. Do you think a sane person would do the things you've done?"

"Listen, you little punk! I'm sick of dealing with all you spoiled little bitches. You all should have had to live with what I had to live with. Maybe you'd think a little differently. Maybe you wouldn't all walk around like you're better than everyone else. They used to bring girls like you down here to correct their attitudes. Maybe I should do that to you before I kill you."

She looked around the room.

"Get up on that table and lay down on your stomach."

Marjorie had had enough.

"You go to hell!"

"I've already been there! Now get up on that table, take off your skirt and panties, and lay down or I'll snip a few fingers off your friend's hand!"

Marjorie looked at Sarah and saw the fear in her eyes. She felt trapped. She couldn't let Sister Joan do that to Sarah, but how could she let her do what she was going to do to her? She took a deep breath of resignation and started to unzip her skirt. She was stopped by a voice behind her.

"Keep it on, Marjorie. She's not going to do that to you."

Marjorie knew who it was without having to turn around to look. It was Sister Agatha.

"Sister Joan and I have some business to take care of. You girls go and leave us alone."

Sister Joan was looking Sister Agatha in the eye from across the room.

"They're not going anywhere, and neither are you."

"Your business is with me, Sister."

"Don't call me Sister. I'm not your sister. And don't call me Joan. I hate that name. It's so lifeless and dull. I asked for a different name, but they said no. My name is Anna."

"All right, Anna," Sister Agatha said calmly. "But as I said, your business is with me, and since neither of us is going to leave this place alive, there's no reason to hurt these girls. Let them go."

"No. They know too much. And I disagree with you. You're going to die here, and I'm going to leave, and I'm going to finally have the life I deserve. It's my destiny."

"You're wrong. Both our destinies were sealed in this room twenty-seven years ago. This room is where they end."

Marjorie and Sarah looked at each other questioningly, wondering what to do as the two nuns stood staring each other down.

Steve and Mother Superior had looked everywhere for the girls. Not finding them, they returned to the office. As they passed Sister Agnes's desk, Sister Juliette Marie was waiting for them. She hurried over to them when she saw them.

"I can't find Sister Agatha anywhere," she told them.

"I was afraid of this," Steve said.

"What do we do now?" Mother Superior asked.

"My guess is, Sister Agatha knows where the discipline room is but didn't tell us. If I'm right, that's where Sister Joan took Sarah. She must have gotten Sister Margaret Mary to tell her where it is. I don't know how, but Marjorie must have found it somehow. If she was anywhere else, we'd have found her. There's no other place she could be."

Sister Juliette Marie was confused.

"What are you talking about?"

"There's too much to try to explain now," Mother Superior told her. "Right now, we've got to find the girls. They're in terrible danger."

"From Sister Joan?"

"Yes. But no more questions. We've got to find a secret room, and we don't have any idea where to start."

"Wait a minute," Steve said. "Sister Agatha did say one thing. She said it was in the basement of the convent. How do we get there?"

Mother Superior started for the door.

"Follow me. Sister, you come as well."

They entered the convent, and Mother Superior led them down the hall to a door at the far end just past the recreation room. She pulled a set of keys from her pocket and unlocked the door. She turned on a light, and they descended the stairs. The basement was a series of rooms on either side of a wide hallway. The rooms were all storerooms filled mainly with various records and religious books. Two held stacks of schoolbooks, and another held candles, candle holders, and other things used in the church.

After looking in every room, they had found no sign of an entrance to a hidden room.

"Well, this is a dead end," Steve said, a defeated sound in his voice. "Where else could there be a room?"

Sister Juliette Marie was rummaging through some papers in one of the rooms. Mother Superior called for her to come out as they were leaving.

"Wait," she called from the room. "Come here. This may help."

They joined her in the room. She had a large roll of paper in her hand.

"What's that?" Mother Superior asked.

"Blueprints," Sister Juliette Marie replied triumphantly.

Steve understood immediately.

"What made you think to look for them?" he asked.

"My dad is an architect. I grew up with blueprints around the house. He did a lot of work at home. I saw what looked like they could be and got lucky, I guess."

Steve looked around the room. There were shelves of papers but no flat surface to lay the blueprints out except the floor and only a dim light that would have made them difficult to read, especially since they appeared to be yellowed and faded.

"We need to get back to the office," he said.

He took the blueprints from Sister Juliette Marie, and they headed back up the stairs and down the hall to the office. Once there,

Steve spread the blueprints out on the conference table. There were a number of sheets, one for each floor of the convent and others for the church. As he quickly pulled the unneeded sheets off the pile, he threw them on the floor. There was no time for neatness.

"Here it is!" he said.

The sheet with the basement blueprints was faded quite badly. It was a large sheet, a square about two feet on each side. Steve and Mother Superior examined it from one side of the table, while Sister Juliette Marie leaned across from the other side. They scanned the paper as quickly as possible but found nothing. Steve turned away from the table.

"We're going too fast," he said. "We're missing something, I know we are."

Sister Juliette Marie was continuing to scan, going back and forth across the sheet slowly. Suddenly, she stopped.

"Wait! Look here!" she exclaimed.

Steve and Mother Superior looked where she was pointing. The lines were nearly faded away completely, but there was an outline of something there.

Sister Juliette Marie continued excitedly.

"Next to the stairs there. Can you see it? There's a wall along the hallway. It runs from the stairs to another wall, but there's no door. It's just an empty space."

Steve bent down close to the paper, trying to make out where the faded lines connected.

"You're right," he said. "I can see three adjoining inner walls, but the outer wall is really faded. But there are no doors in any of the three walls."

"Could it just be an empty space that the architect left empty for some reason?" Mother Superior asked.

Steve considered that possibility for a second.

"I doubt it. If there was space there, why not make a room out of it?"

"Maybe it is a room," Sister Juliette Marie suggested. "Maybe the door is in the outside wall."

"There can't be," Mother Superior insisted. "I've walked around the grounds many times and I've never seen a door anywhere on the outside wall."

Sister Juliette Marie was still looking closely at the lines on the paper.

"Whatever is there they didn't want it to fall down."

"What do you mean?" Steve asked.

"Look at the walls. They're much thicker than the others in the rest of the basement."

Steve looked at Mother Superior and knew she was thinking the same thing he was.

"I wish I could see the outer wall more clearly," he said. He felt the paper, which was very thin.

"I wonder if they would show up better if they were lit from underneath."

Sister Juliette Marie started toward the door.

"There's a flashlight in Sister Agnes's desk. I'll get it."

"Just make sure you put it back when we're done," Steve called after her. "I don't want to get on Sister Agnes's bad side."

Mother Superior held back a laugh and tried to sound serious.

"Now, Steve, don't make fun of Sister Agnes. She does an excellent job."

"I know, Mother. I just couldn't resist."

Sister Juliette Marie was back with the light. Steve and Mother Superior pulled the sheet out over the edge of the table and Sister Juliette Marie knelt and shined the light under the area they needed to see. Still faded but a little easier to see were the lines of the outer wall. All three were surprised by what they saw.

Not only was the outer wall of the empty space visible, but a narrow hallway ran along the outer wall behind the room next to the space. What appeared to be stairs were at the other end of the hallway.

Steve pushed the paper back onto the table.

"There must be a door. It must be hidden somehow. Do you know where that part of the wall is, Mother?"

"I think it's near the St. Christopher shrine. There's a section of the wall that's lined with bushes."

Steve wasn't wasting any time. He was already heading for the door.

"Let's go!" he shouted.

As he went through the door, he remembered the officers outside. He stopped long enough to ask Sister Juliette Marie to let them in. Mother Superior led him through the convent door and to the door leading out into the grounds. Sister Juliette Marie quickly unlocked the doors and led the officers in the same direction.

Sister Joan finally broke the silence. Her pent-up anger was there in every word.

"Do you really think you can stop me? I've got the shears, and you've got nothing. You're too old to stop me. You got here too late. Now you're going to have to watch these sweet young things die in front of you. It's their own fault, of course. If they had stayed out of this, it would only be you who had to die."

Sister Agatha kept looking her in the eye.

"They're not going to die. I won't let that happen."

Sister Joan laughed.

"How do you think you're going to do that? And don't tell me you've got God on your side. He give you some special powers? You got some magic that'll just make these two disappear? God's looked the other way for twenty-seven years. Do you really think he's going to start caring now?"

"He's never stopped caring."

Sister Joan flew into a rage.

"What!! You call letting that old man do what he did to me for all those years caring?"

Sister Agatha's expression changed. It had been one of resolve, as if she was confronting a disobedient student. Now it was one of sadness and regret.

"I don't know what he did to you. I don't know what you've suffered. We couldn't know what would happen to you. We were trying to help a girl who had nowhere to turn. We made a mistake—I can see that now—but we didn't know that at the time. Punish me if you must. I don't blame you for that. But let these girls go. They have their whole lives ahead of them."

"So did my mother!"

She was forcing every word through her clenched teeth again.

"You lied to her! You took me away from her! You told her I was dead!"

"To give you a better life than she could have given you."

"A better life?! I'd have gladly suffered any hardship with her than live the life you gave me!"

"Then take my life in retribution, but I will not let you harm these girls!"

"Enough! This one goes first. I'll save her from the life she would have had with that bastard inside her."

She raised the shears above Sarah, who tried to move away but couldn't; her stomach was hurting too badly to move.

"No!" Marjorie shouted as she started to rush toward them.

Sister Joan turned, shears in hand, and lunged toward Marjorie. Suddenly, Marjorie was knocked to the floor as Sister Agatha jumped between her and Sister Joan. They both fell to the ground, groaning in pain.

Marjorie was stunned for a moment, but she collected her thoughts quickly. She was lying on the floor with Sister Agatha next to her. Sister Joan was lying on the other side of Sister Agatha. Both the sisters were breathing short painful breaths.

Marjorie pulled herself to her knees and knelt by Sister Agatha. Her habit was wet where Marjorie put her hand, and as she pulled her hand away, Marjorie saw that it was red with blood.

"Sister," she said excitedly, "I'll get help."

As Marjorie started to stand, Sister Agatha stopped her. She spoke in slow painful phases, broken up by heavy, labored breaths.

"Don't worry about me...help Sarah...take her and leave us... it's too late for me."

"But, Sister, you're bleeding."

"Just go...take Sarah."

Marjorie was conflicted. She didn't want to leave Sarah or Sister Agatha, but she knew she had to get help. Sister Joan wasn't moving, but she might just be knocked out. Marjorie worried that if she left Sister Joan might come to and kill the others. Sister Agatha urged her again.

"Go, girl…take Sarah. She needs you."

Before Marjorie could stand, she heard noises behind her. Voices and hurried footsteps were coming down the hallway. Seconds later, Steve was kneeling next to her. Marjorie could no longer hold back her tears. Through her tears, she cried out frantically.

"She's bleeding! Help her!"

Steve looked over his shoulder toward an officer who had caught up with him.

"Call an ambulance."

He looked around the room.

"Better make it several!" he shouted as the officer hurried back through the hallway.

Mother Superior and Sister Juliette Marie stood near the door, frozen, unable to believe what they were seeing.

Sister Agatha grabbed Steve's arm with her left hand.

"It's too late for us…help the girls."

Steve looked at Marjorie.

"How did you get here?"

"I was looking for Sarah, and I saw a light behind the bushes."

Sarah tried to smile despite the pain she was feeling.

"I left the door open. I hoped someone would see it. And you did," she said weakly.

Steve looked over to where she knelt. He nodded toward her. Marjorie understood and went to her. As she knelt beside Sarah, she noticed blood on the floor under her.

"Sarah, you're bleeding. We've got to get you out of here."

"I know. She cut my hand with those shears."

"No. It's not your hand. Look at the floor."

Sarah looked down toward her legs. The floor and her skirt were soaked with blood. She looked at Marjorie and grabbed her arm tightly. Fear and confusion showed on her face and in her voice.

"Oh, God, Marge. I'm gonna die!"

"No, you're not. The ambulance is on its way. You're gonna be all right, I promise."

"Marge, I'm scared!"

"I know. So am I. But it's gonna be okay."

She put her arms around Sarah, praying that the ambulance would get there soon.

Mother Superior regained her composure and knelt by Sister Agatha next to Steve. She shook her head sadly as she spoke.

"Agatha, Agatha, what have you done?"

Sister Agatha's words were coming slower and with more difficulty.

"I'm sorry, Mother…I had to do it."

"Why didn't you tell us you knew where the door was? We could have stopped this."

"No…this is how it had to be…it was the only way."

"How long have you known?"

"I suspected…when I heard about… Margaret Mary…but I wasn't sure… I didn't know…the girls would be in danger… I thought I…could lure her here…alone…and we could finish it… where it started."

"Oh, Agatha, you should have let us help you."

"There's been no help for me… For many years… I've borne this sin…and it was mine…to atone for… Pray for me, Mother… my soul needs forgiveness."

Steve noticed that Sister Joan hadn't moved. He reached over and felt her neck. "She's dead," he said. "She must have hit her head pretty hard when she fell."

Sister Agatha tried to shift her position.

"No," she said.

She strained to pull her right arm out from under Sister Joan. In it was a bloody carving knife.

"I stopped in the kitchen…before I came here… I knew…I'd need this… These long sleeves…have been an annoyance…but they were useful… She didn't know…I had it… Her pain is ended…and so…is mine."

She took a sudden stuttered breath and fell limp.

The silence that followed was broken by noises in the hallway. Two ambulance drivers hurried in with a stretcher. They stopped short when they saw the room, uncertain what to do.

Steve stood up and took charge.

"The girl over there goes first. There's no hurry for the rest of them."

The drivers brought the stretcher over to Sarah and laid it on the floor beside her. She was barely conscious by now.

"Be careful," Marjorie told them. "She's pregnant."

The drivers looked at the floor beneath her. One of them shook his head.

"Not anymore, I think. We need to get her to the hospital fast."

Marjorie's throat tightened.

"She'll be all right, won't she?"

"I hope so. We'll do the best we can."

They picked up the stretcher and walked as quickly as they could through the hallway. Mother Superior rose and told Sister Juliette Marie to go with them.

"The hospital will need to contact her parents. Hurry and get her parents' information from the file in my office."

Sister Juliette Marie hurried out behind the ambulance drivers. Marjorie watched them go, wondering if she'd ever see Sarah again. Her fear rushed over her, and she ran to Steve and threw her arms around him, holding on as tightly as she could with her face against his chest, her tears staining his tie.

"Oh, Steve," she cried, "what am I gonna do? I'm so scared."

Steve stood helplessly trying to figure out what to do, unsure if he should hold her or try to get her to let go. He looked to Mother Superior to help. She took Marjorie by the shoulders and tried to gently pull her away. Marjorie held on even tighter. Mother Superior pulled harder, admonishing her as she did.

"Marjorie, you must let go."

"No, I want to stay with Steve! Please, Steve, let me stay! Don't send me away! I want to stay with you!"

"Detective McLean has work to do. You have to let him do it."

When Marjorie heard "Detective McLean" and the way Mother Superior emphasized it, she realized that she had allowed her emotions to show. She loosened her hold, and as Mother Superior moved her away from Steve and toward the door, she kept her head down, afraid to look at him and see what she was sure would be a look of horror on his face. Besides, she didn't want him to see hers, which had to be as red as a beet the way her cheeks were burning.

Mother Superior led Marjorie out through the hallway and brought her to her office. As they passed through the hall outside the office, they were met by several sisters who had gathered to see what the commotion was all about. Mother Superior told them she would explain everything shortly and continued into her office. She helped Marjorie onto the sofa and told her to lie down.

"But, Mother," Marjorie argued, "I have to go to the hospital to see Sarah. I don't want her to be alone."

"The doctors will take good care of her. Sister Juliette Marie is with her. And I'm sure you wouldn't be able to see her until tomorrow at least. She needs to rest and you do too."

Marjorie laid her head on a pillow and pulled her feet up onto the sofa. Mother Superior sat in a chair and watched her until she was fast asleep, which took very little time. She then went out into the hall to tell the sisters the sad news.

Father Jerome passed Mother Superior and Marjorie in the hallway, on his way in to see what had happened. The shock showed on his face as he observed the carnage. He had been a chaplain in Korea during the war and had seen many wounded and dead men, bloodied and maimed, but that was during a war. It was a place where sights like that could be expected. To see what he saw in front of him now in what was supposed to be a place of peace and holiness was almost more than he could handle. Steve grabbed his arm to steady him as he began to sway as if he was going to collapse. He regained his balance and composure and raised his hand to bless the bodies.

"Pretty gruesome sight," Steve said.

"It's unimaginable," Father Jerome replied. "How did all this happen?"

"It's a long story. Too long to tell here."

"Well, I'm not sure I'm ready to hear it now anyway. It would appear to be something I need to prepare for before I do."

"Just let me know when you're ready."

"I'll do that, Detective. I'll do that."

He turned and walked into the hallway, a blank look on his face, like a man who was lost and unable to remember who he was or where he was supposed to be. Steve stayed to wait for the coroner. Before long, he heard a familiar voice coming from the hallway.

"Why the hell didn't you just wait till you found them all before you called me? It would have saved me all these extra trips. I heard there's more than one this time. What the hell are they doing out..."

He stopped just inside the door, left speechless by what he saw. Steve gave him a moment before he said anything.

"Quite a sight, hey, Bill."

The coroner collected his thoughts, but he was unable to make sense of the sight that confronted him.

"What the hell happened here, Steve? What kind of madhouse is this? I've had nightmares that didn't shake me up like this. A nun stabbed to death. A girl buried in the backyard. A guy with a grass shears in his throat. Now two more dead nuns..."

He noticed Jack in the corner.

"What in the name of... What happened to him?"

"You'll see when you get over there. I hope you got a strong stomach."

The coroner shook his head.

"I gotta find a new line of work."

Steve tried to give him some positive news.

"Well, at least it's the last time you'll have to come out here."

"You sure?"

"I'm sure."

He pointed to Sister Joan.

"That one's the one who did it all. I'll drop by in a day or two and fill you in. In a way, I kinda understand why she did it. Bad people can make good people go bad."

"You'll have to do a lot of talking to convince me that she had a reason for all this."

He took his camera out of his briefcase.

"I'm going to get started. I want to get this place cleaned up and get outta here."

He went about his work, taking several pictures of the scene. When he got to Jack, he had to stop to regain his composure. After a quick examination of the bodies, hesitating again when he got to Jack, he called in his assistants to remove them. They also were clearly troubled when they put Jack on the stretcher.

As he put his equipment away, the coroner looked around the room at the table and the whips.

"What the hell is this place, Steve? It looks like a torture chamber."

"It was called the discipline room years ago."

"Discipline? Somebody sure had a crazy idea of discipline."

At the door, he turned and looked at the blood that still covered much of the floor.

"Who's going to clean this place up? That's a lot of blood."

"I don't think it's going to be cleaned up. I have a feeling this room will never be seen by anyone ever again. I'm not sure how they'll do it, but I am sure the sisters will see to it somehow."

"Well, I know I never want to see anything like this again. I'll see you later."

He turned and went out. Steve took a final look around the room. He thought back to his arrival early that morning. Of all the possible endings to the day, this was one he could have never imagined. He wondered what Harry and Bernie were going to say when he told them the story. He flicked the light off and closed the door behind him as he went down the hallway.

He closed the outer door and pushed his way through the bushes. Sitting on one of the concrete benches was Father Jerome, still looking dazed and confused.

Steve sat down beside him.

"How are you doing, Father?" he asked.

"I'm not sure, Detective. I just don't understand it. This is supposed to be a place of peacefulness, a place of safety, not a butcher shop. When I got to Korea, I knew I'd see terrible things, and I did. But I thought that was all behind me. I never think about it anymore. This is so unthinkable I don't know if I'll ever be able to get it out of my mind."

"Well, Father, I don't think I ever will either."

He stood up.

"How about I walk with you back to the rectory?"

Father Jerome thought about his offer.

"That would be nice. You know, if you're not too tired, I think I may be ready to hear the story."

Steve was tired, but he could see that Father Jerome needed some company for a while.

"Well, I'm wondering, Father. Any chance you might have a little something to sip on hidden in the rectory?"

Father Jerome gave him a reprimanding look.

"A little something hidden? How could you ask a question like that? There is nothing like that hidden in the rectory. It's right out on the shelf. I am Irish, after all."

The two men laughed as they crossed the lawn to the rectory.

"I hope you like Jameson's. I only drink the best, you know," Father Jerome said as he opened the door and went in. It was going to be a long night, Steve thought.

After giving the sisters only the basic details of what had happened and giving them instructions for what should be done in the morning, Mother Superior had instructed them to go back to their rooms. When they were gone, she looked in the file at Sister Agnes's desk that held the contact information for the parents. She found the phone number for Sarah's parents and prepared herself to make a call she never thought she would ever have to make. As she dialed, she decided it would be best to tell them only that Sarah had been injured and was in the hospital. The details, she felt, would be better discussed later. She finished the call and returned to her office. Opening one of the file cabinet drawers, she took out a small blanket that she kept there to put around her shoulders on chilly winter nights when she worked late. The old buildings were beautiful structures, but they also had old heating systems.

She laid the blanket on Marjorie and sat in the chair next to the sofa. She closed her eyes, and for the first time since she was a young girl, she cried herself to sleep.

Chapter 14

The next morning the girls in the dormitory awoke to discover that the lights hadn't come on at 6:30. Several of them, whose body clocks were in tune with the usual wakeup time, woke up soon after 6:30 and were in the hall wondering what was happening. As 6:45 approached, they began knocking on the doors of the girls who were still in bed. Soon the hall was filled with curious chattering girls.

Rachel noticed that both Marjorie's and Sarah's doors were still closed. She knocked on Marjorie's door but got no reply. After a second knock and still no reply, she opened the door and looked in. When she saw the empty room, she hurried to Sarah's door. Without knocking, she opened the door. She felt an immediate sense of dread.

She hurried up the hall looking for Paula and Brenda. Her fear that something bad had happened overcame her concern about their feelings toward her.

"Paula, have you seen Marge or Sarah?" she asked when she found them.

"Marge was here last night, looking for that detective," Paula told her.

"I know. I talked to her too. I think something happened to them."

"Why?" Brenda asked.

"Both their rooms are empty, and they're not out here in the hall."

Paula looked around the hall.

"You don't think they didn't wake us up because..."

Before she could finish her thought, a series of "shhhs" from a number of girls brought silence to the hall. Sister Mary Joseph was making her way into the crowd. The solemn look on her face gave the silence an ominous feeling. As she began to speak, the ominous feeling grew more intense.

"Something very saddening happened last night. Mother Superior has decided that we will not call another assembly. Rather, a sister has been sent to each hall to inform you of the news. It is my sad duty to tell you that Sister Agatha and Sister Joan died last night."

She waited for the girls' reaction to subside before she continued.

"Regretfully, Mr. Miller, the gardener, and his son also died."

There was another reaction of gasps and murmuring.

"I am not permitted to give any more information about these deaths at this time. I must also tell you that Sarah Collins has been injured and is in the hospital."

She paused again to let the noise die down.

"We have been told she will recover and is not in any danger. Marjorie Johnson is currently under the protection of Mother Superior. She thankfully was not injured, but both girls have been through an unpleasant experience. Keep them in your prayers, as well as the souls of the departed. Mass will begin at seven-thirty and will be followed immediately by breakfast. Please return to your rooms and wait there. The bell will be rung ten minutes before Mass. It would be well to refrain from discussing or speculating as to what has occurred. You will be given any details that are pertinent at a later time."

She turned and made her way through the girls and returned to the convent.

Paula, Brenda, and Rachel waited till she was gone before saying anything.

"Wow," Paula said, "I thought Marge was just trying to act like she was important, but there must have been something really big going on."

"Yeah," Brenda added. "Four people don't all die naturally at the same time. They must have been murdered. It must all have something to do with Sister Margaret Mary."

"Well, I'm more concerned with what happened to Sarah and Marge," Rachel scolded them. "It's too bad about the people who died, but Sarah's in the hospital, and it sounds like something really dangerous happened."

They stood in the middle of the hall considering it all.

"Girls," came a voice from the end of the hall. It was Ginny. "Sister said we should go back to our rooms."

"Oh, stuff it," Paula said under her breath.

The girls giggled, shrugged, and went off to their rooms.

Mother Superior was tired enough to sleep for several hours, even sitting up in the chair. She woke to find Marjorie still asleep on the sofa. She had given instructions last night to cancel classes again and not wake the girls. She knew her instructions would be carried out with Sister Mary Joseph in charge, so she wasn't concerned about the time. She did, however, want to get to her room to freshen up and put on a clean habit. There were spots on hers that she knew were blood.

Despite feeling Marjorie probably needed more sleep, she decided to wake her so she wouldn't wake up in an empty room. She especially didn't want her to wake up alone and decide to go back to her room. It wouldn't be good for her to be exposed to the questions Mother Superior knew would be waiting for her.

She gave Marjorie a gentle shake.

"Wake up, Marjorie."

Marjorie murmured an uncooperative grumble. Mother Superior tried again.

"It's time to get up, Marjorie."

Marjorie lifted her head and looked around the room through half-opened eyes.

"Huh? Where am I?"

"You're in my office, dear. Remember? I brought you here last night."

Marjorie's head was clearing.

"Sarah! I have to see Sarah!"

"You will soon. I'll make arrangements for you to go to the hospital after breakfast.

"No, Mother! I have to go right away! I have to make sure she's okay."

She was on her feet and heading for the door. Mother Superior stopped her with her commanding officer voice.

"Marjorie! Stop!"

Marjorie froze. Mother Superior continued.

"I'll have Sister Agnes call right now and find out how she is. You wait here. I'm going to have breakfast brought in for you. I think at present it would be best if you aren't with the rest of the girls. I have to change."

She saw the puzzled look on Marjorie's face.

"Yes, my dear, we do have more than one of these. You didn't think we wore the same one every day of the year, did you?"

"Well, that makes sense. I guess I never really thought about it."

"Well, now you know. I'll be back shortly. I'll have Sister Agnes tell you what she finds out."

Marjorie's manner got serious.

"You don't think she's…"

She couldn't bring herself to say it.

"No, I'm sure she isn't. They'd have let us know if something like that had happened. Now you just wait here."

She went into the hall and gave Sister Agnes her instructions then went to her room. Marjorie waited as she had been told to do, wandering around the room, unable to sit still until she knew how Sarah was. A few minutes later, Sister Agnes came in to tell her that Sarah would be all right, but she would have to stay in the hospital for a few more days. She would be able to go to see her later in the day.

Steve woke up with a headache. The ringing of the telephone made it even worse. A shot or two of whiskey isn't all that much, but the several he had during the hour and a half he spent filling Father Jerome in starting all the way back with the dead girl in 1930 wanted to be sure he remembered them. He answered the phone more to stop the ringing than because he wanted to talk to whoever was on the other end causing the ringing.

"Yeah, what is it?"

"It's Mike, Steve."

"Oh, Chief. What do you want?"

"Well, it would be nice if someone would fill me in on what the hell went on out at the school last night. I just talked to Bill Martin. He said if he could charge room and board at the morgue, he'd make a fortune off of what you brought in yesterday."

"Oh, yeah. I was going to call you as soon as I woke up."

"Woke up? It's eight-thirty. You still in bed?"

"Um, yeah. It was a long night."

"You sound terrible."

"Well, I'll give you some advice. Never accept an offer of a drink from an Irish priest. Especially if it's Irish whiskey and he's got an extra bottle."

"I'll keep that in mind. Anyway, can you get down here fairly soon? I don't know how soon the papers will get wind of this, but when they do, I need to know what to tell them."

"Sure. I'll take a quick shower and be there in about a half hour. Make sure the coffee pot's full. Thanks."

"Sure, sure. Just get your ass down here."

"Will do, Chief."

He hung up and forced himself out of bed and into the shower. Thirty-three minutes later, he pulled up in front of the station. It took a while to tell the whole story, especially when the Chief kept interjecting *unbelievable* into the narrative.

Around 10:15, as he came out of the Chief's office, Isabelle informed him that Mother Superior had called and said she was hoping he'd be coming by soon to discuss the situation. He asked her to accompany him as he was concerned about Marjorie and felt it would be good to have Isabelle talk to her.

"I think you'd better talk to her too," Isabelle told him.

"Yeah, I know. I hope I didn't make a mistake by asking her to help me."

"It'll be okay. She'll get over it. It's just a crush."

When they arrived at the school, Mother Superior was at the desk, giving Sister Agnes her instructions. She greeted them as soon as they came through the doors.

"Good morning, Steve, and...Officer Gordon, I believe."

Isabelle nodded.

"That's right, but please call me Isabelle."

"Thank you. I will. If you'll excuse me, I need to freshen up. I spent the night in a chair in my office. I didn't think Marjorie should be left alone last night."

Steve cleared his throat.

"Yes, Mother, I have to apologize about how things turned out. I really never expected that she'd be in any danger."

"None of us could have been aware of the evil that was hiding here, Steve. I don't blame you at all. There is another matter that needs to be taken care of though."

"Yes. That's part of the reason I'm here. The other is, of course, to finish my work here and close this out."

"You're lucky enough to be able to close the books on this. We here will never be able to fully put it behind us. Marjorie is in my office. Why don't you take care of that matter while I change? I'll be down shortly."

She turned and went off through the convent door. Steve and Isabelle went into the office, passing Sister Agnes, who watched them pass with her usual disapproving expression. Marjorie was sitting on the sofa when they came in. Seeing Steve, she shifted her body to face away from the door and looked down at the floor. Isabelle came and sat beside her. She put her hand on Marjorie's shoulder.

"You had a pretty rough night," she said.

Marjorie nodded.

"Uh-huh."

"Are you okay?"

"Uh-huh."

"Steve and I would like to talk to you."

As they were talking, Steve moved to the chair to the left of the sofa. Marjorie turned back toward Isabelle, still keeping her head down.

Steve looked to Isabelle for help. She simply nodded.

"Marjorie," he began, "I want you to know I never thought you'd be in any danger. If I had, I never would have asked for your help."

"I know," she said softly. "I'm sorry I caused so much trouble."

"You didn't cause any trouble. Things were going to turn out the way they did. Sister Agatha was the only one who could have changed things, but she felt she had to do it by herself. You and Sarah gave us information Sister Agatha could have given us but she chose not to. You helped, you didn't cause trouble. That was all Sister Joan's doing."

"But I got in the way."

Her eyes had filled with tears that now broke free and ran down her cheeks. Isabelle tried to comfort her.

"From what Steve told me, you saved Sarah's life. That should make you proud."

"But I'm the one who got her into it. She wouldn't have been there if it wasn't for me."

"But you wouldn't have been there if it wasn't for me," Steve told her. "I'm afraid I shouldn't have asked you to help me. I didn't know how much danger it would put you in or how it would affect you."

Marjorie knew what he meant. She knew she had let herself wish for something that could never happen, and she had let everyone see how she felt.

"I know what you're going to say. I feel so stupid."

Isabelle put her arm around her.

"There's no reason to feel stupid. I was your age not so long ago. I had a crush on my older brother's friend. I made a fool of myself trying to get his attention."

Marjorie sniffled and looked a little bit toward Steve, still keeping her head down.

"I'm sorry I embarrassed you."

"You didn't embarrass me. I was flattered, really. But the truth is, I have someone who I may very well marry someday."

Marjorie looked up.

"Really?"

Isabelle started to laugh.

"Yes," she said, "but if he tells you, you have to promise to keep it a secret."

Marjorie remembered their conversation in the recreation room. Her embarrassment was fading. She felt better since they hadn't made too big a thing out of it.

"Is it Officer Hansen?"

Isabelle laughed.

"You remembered what I said yesterday."

She paused a moment then continued.

"Actually, I kinda told a fib about that. I told you I had a boyfriend, but what I didn't tell you—and this is the secret part—it's Steve."

Marjorie looked confused.

"I thought you said that's not allowed."

"I know. That's why it's a secret."

"But it won't be much longer," Steve added. "Isabelle is starting a new job soon, so we'll be able to tell everyone else once she does."

Mother Superior returned from her room.

"I'm not interrupting anything, I hope," she said as she came in.

"No," Steve told her, "everything's taken care of."

"Good," Mother Superior replied. "I have to make arrangements to get Marjorie to the hospital to visit Sarah, and then we can talk."

"Oh, I can take her," Isabelle said. "I came with Steve to keep her company anyway. I'll take her, and you two can take care of what you have to do."

"That sounds like a splendid idea."

She turned to Marjorie.

"Oh dear. You've been in those same clothes since yesterday. I think you should go to your room and change before you go. Isabelle can go with you."

Marjorie and Isabelle started for the door. Mother Superior stopped them.

"I think it would be best if you don't talk to any of the other girls. Isabelle can probably help you with that."

"Don't worry," Isabelle told her. "Mum's the word."

When they were gone, Mother Superior took her seat at the end of the conference table. Steve sat in a chair to her left.

"Well, Steve, how shall we proceed?" she asked.

"The way I see it, the facts of the matter are pretty clear. I don't think there's any reason to bring anyone in for any further investigation. I gave the Chief a rundown of it all and he agrees. I'll get all the records we took to the station back to you this afternoon, and that should close everything out. I will have to be back to go with Paula and Brenda when they go into the city to take care of that other matter. After that, we'll be out of your hair."

"Well, don't put it that way. You haven't really been in our hair. Our wimples actually make that impossible."

She laughed at her own joke and then became serious.

"I'm surprised I can still laugh…much less make a joke anymore. I'm afraid there won't be much to laugh about in the coming days."

She rose and began walking toward the other end of the table.

"You can 'close everything out' as you call it. It won't be like that here. There's a possibility we may never recover from this."

"What do you mean, Mother?"

She continued walking, making her way around the table and back to her chair.

"The secrets of this school, as we discovered, have been hidden for many years. Now they've been brought out into the light. Something like this can't be kept hidden as things were in the past. The reputation of the school is at risk. Sister Agnes informed me when I came down that there have been calls from the newspaper. Unlike years ago, we certainly can't deny that anything happened here last night."

"But you don't necessarily have to give them the whole story."

She turned and went back the way she had come.

"I wish you were right, Steve, but you're not. There can be no more secrets here. And to be honest, a partial story will never make sense to anyone. Questions would linger, and unanswered questions breed speculation and rumors. No, the story must be told, even as far back as 1930. My fear is that this will cause our supporters to back away. I foresee a number of our students being removed by their parents and sent elsewhere."

"They can't blame the school for the actions of one crazy nun."

"If she was crazy, it was because of the things that have been going on here for decades. People will ask how something like that could have gone on for so many years. They'll be uncertain of our ability to care for their daughters the way they've trusted us to do."

"What will you do if that happens?"

"The school is operated as a corporation owned by our order. We have a reserve fund that could keep it going for a while, but if it runs out and losses are expected, I'm afraid there would be only one result."

"It'll be a shame if that happens."

"Yes, it will. Some terrible things have happened here, and they've shaken my faith in a number of ways. But last night, as I looked at the faces of the sisters as I told them what had happened, I saw so much good in them.

"Sister Theresa was guided by a desire to help those in need. Her intentions were initially good, but she lost sight of what was right, and she in turn led Margaret Mary on the same path. Agatha allowed friendship to cloud her vision of right and wrong. Poor Sister Joan had her childhood taken away from her. Can we judge any of them? Can we let their mistakes color our view of the rest of the world? Do we allow the secrets of the past to decide the future?"

She was standing now across the table from Steve with her hands on the top of the back of the chair across from him.

"I believe in this school, and I believe there is still much good here. I intend to do everything I can to keep it going. The old secrets have been brought into the light, and I intend to make certain there will be no more to replace them."

She paused and took a deep breath.

"Now if you'll excuse me, I'll return to my room. I didn't sleep well last night. You may remain here to finish anything you need to finish."

"Thank you, Mother. I do need to talk to Paula and Brenda about how we'll handle their trip into the city. I'll do that and call for a car to pick me up. I doubt that Marjorie and Isabelle will be back that soon."

"Oh, yes. I forgot about them. I had to make an unpleasant phone call last night. It seems I still have others to make. I think it would be best if I have Mary Joseph bring them here to you."

"Thank you. I hope you're able to get some rest."

She started toward the door.

"I do too, Steve," she said as she was going. "I do too."

The door to Sarah's room was open. Marjorie looked in cautiously around the edge of the door frame, afraid of what she might see. To her relief, she saw Sarah on the bed talking to a nurse. She moved a little more into the doorway and cleared her throat.

The nurse had blocked Sarah's view of the door. As she turned and moved out of Sarah's line of sight, Sarah's face lit up.

"Marge!" she said. Her voice was weak, but her joy was still clearly evident.

The nurse motioned for Marjorie to come in.

"So you're the famous Marge," she said. "I've heard all about you. Sarah is lucky to have such a good friend."

The compliment took Marjorie by surprise. She was feeling guilty about leaving Sarah alone last night and didn't see herself as a good friend.

"Thank you," she managed to stammer out.

"Well, I'll leave you two alone. She's very weak, so don't stay long," the nurse said then closed the door as she went out.

Marjorie looked at Sarah. The head of the bed was raised on an angle so that she was partially sitting up. She had an IV in her left arm and her hand was bandaged. Tears started to stream down Marjorie's cheeks as she approached the bed.

"Oh, Sarah," she said tearfully, "I'm so sorry. I should have never made you tell Steve and Mother Superior."

"Don't cry, Marge. We both know it was the right thing to do. It's not your fault."

"But I almost got you killed. I should have never left you alone. It was just a trick to get me out of the way."

"I know. But you didn't know that. I trusted Sister Joan and let her back in the room. I'm the one who screwed up."

She paused, making a quick decision, and continued.

"There's something I've got to tell you, and I don't want you to get upset, so you have to promise me you'll let me say everything I want to say and not stop me."

"Is it bad?"

"Well, it's a little bad, but I think it'll be more good than bad eventually."

Marjorie was curious but a little afraid as well. "Okay. I promise."

Sarah took a deep breath.

"You know how Sister Joan punched me in the stomach? Well, it turns out when she did, it killed the baby."

Marjorie wanted to interrupt but she had promised not to. She let Sarah go on.

"When they told me, I was a little sad at first, but then I realized it was really for the best. So Sister Joan ended up doing what she wanted to do, but if she had done it the way she was going to, I'd probably be dead now."

That was too much for Marjorie.

"Oh, Sarah, don't say that!"

"Well, I'm not, so it's okay."

She got quiet again.

"There is one other thing, though. They told me that I got damaged inside. I can't remember all the medical stuff, but they said because of it, I won't ever be able to have any more babies."

They both cried silently for a while. Finally, Sarah broke the silence.

"That's the bad part. I keep thinking, what if I meet a guy someday who I want to marry? What if he says he wants kids? What am I gonna tell him? I can't tell him about this. He'll think I'm damaged goods."

Marjorie tried to comfort her.

"I don't know. I think if you find the right guy, it won't matter to him. I'm not sure I ever want to have kids, so if a guy says he wants to marry me, he'll have to accept that. I guess it's sort of a love test. If a guy really loves you, he won't care."

"I hope you're right. You really don't want to ever have kids?"

"Yeah. At least right now. Maybe when I get older, I'll change my mind."

The sad look on Sarah's face made Marjorie think she should change the subject.

"Hey, where's Sister Juliette Marie? I thought she came with you last night."

"She was pretty tired, and the doctor said he wanted me to sleep so she went back to the convent. I guess you just missed her. How did you get here? You didn't walk, did you?"

"No. Isabelle brought me. She's in the waiting room down the hall. She didn't think we should both come in. She was with Steve when he came to see Mother Superior, and she offered to bring me."

Before Sarah could say anything more, the nurse returned and told Marjorie that Sarah needed to rest. She told her she could come back later in the afternoon.

The girls reluctantly said goodbye, and Marjorie headed down the hall to the waiting room. As she walked, she thought about what Sarah had said about not being able to have any children and what she had said about not wanting to have any. She hadn't really thought that far into the future until just then. In fact, she realized, she hadn't even thought much about anything beyond graduation.

Maybe it was having actually watched someone die, or maybe it was having experienced the fear of dying herself that now had her thinking about things she had never thought about before. So many things were changed in that room last night. Lives were ended without any warning. People she knew yesterday were now gone forever. Sarah's life was changed forever in less than a second. What would tomorrow bring, or would tomorrow even come at all?

One thing she knew for certain. Her life had also changed in that room. How the changes would affect her in the future was yet to be known.

Epilogue

Marjorie sat on her bed. She was surprised by how familiar it felt after fifteen years. The walls were a different color but the furniture was all the same. So many memories came flooding back, but one, of course, was the strongest. She didn't know that morning when she found Sarah there how it would change the course of her life.

A knock on the door brought her back to the present. She looked up to find Sarah standing in the doorway.

"Sarah!" she said excitedly.

"I figured I'd find you here," Sarah said. "After I got your letter, I told Tom we had to come too. I wanted to surprise you, though."

"Well, it's a wonderful surprise. I just wish it was under better circumstances."

"It is kind of sad. I thought when we were here that this place would be here forever."

"I did too. But things have changed. These places aren't as popular as they once were. And things here have been hard since...well, no sense talking about that now."

"I agree. I'm just concentrating on the good times. Everyone's out on the lawn. Let's get out there and see who else is here. Tom said he'd wait for me out there."

They headed outside, talking as they went.

"Did you bring the kids?" Marjorie asked.

"No, they're with Tom's parents. I've got pictures, though. You're not going to believe how big they've gotten since you saw them last."

"I'm really glad you found Tom. He's a great guy."

"I know. You know he was the one who suggested we adopt. I had thought about it, but I wasn't sure how he'd feel, but one day, he asked me if I wanted to do it. I told him everything when it seemed like he was getting serious and it didn't change anything about the way he felt. He still wanted to marry me. I guess what you said in the hospital that day was right."

"You know I'm always right."

They were laughing as they went through the doors and found Tom waiting nearby.

"Well, I see you found her," he said as he hugged Marjorie. "You know we'd get to see you more often if you didn't keep traipsing around the world."

"I know, but there's just so much to see."

A familiar voice came from behind them.

"Does this young man have permission to be here on the school grounds?"

"Mother!" Marjorie exclaimed. "It's so good to see you!"

"It's good to see you too. It's quite an honor to have such a celebrated author with us, and one of our alumni at that."

She turned to Sarah.

"I'm glad you came. I wasn't sure if you would."

"When Marge wrote that she was coming, I had to come too. Besides, this is my husband, Tom. He knows about everything, and he's helped me to put it behind me."

"It's good to meet you, Tom. It seems Sarah found a very special man. I'm happy for both of you."

"Yes, he is special," Sarah agreed. "I want to show him around. We'll catch up with you both later. I want you to see the pictures of the kids, Mother."

They went off toward the dormitory.

"Walk with me," Mother Superior said. They started across the lawn toward the convent.

"It's a sad day, Mother," Marjorie said.

"Yes, it is. The last graduating class at St. Christopher's. We've done everything we could but there's just no money left. Attendance is only half what it was when you were here. But it's the same at most of the other schools like this. A few will survive, but I think most will be gone sooner than later."

She stopped walking.

"I'm glad you've done as well as you have. Several very successful books. I read your first one. It was a good story. *The Secret of St. Mary's School.* I wonder if St. Christopher wasn't hurt that you changed the name."

"I'm pretty sure he was glad that I did."

"I did feel that you made the Mother Superior seem too nice, though."

"Well, like they say, write what you know. I told it as I saw it."

Marjorie looked around at the buildings.

"What's going to happen to the place?"

"Well, the church will remain. The local congregation will keep supporting it. I understand that a company wants to buy the school and turn it into an apartment building. The dormitory and the convent are most likely going to be torn down."

"That's too bad. The convent is a beautiful building."

"Yes, it is. But it was built for a specific use, and it would be difficult to make it into anything useful without quite a large expense. I hate to say it, but I think it will one day be nothing but a parking lot."

"If they tear it down, they'll find the room, won't they?"

"I imagine they will. No one has been down there since that night. We had the door removed and the doorway walled up so no one could ever go there again. But if they break through the wall, they're bound to find it."

"I wonder what the workmen will think when they do."

"I imagine it will become just one more mystery. One more secret of St. Christopher's Girls School. One that no one will ever be able to explain."

She looked over toward the crowd gathered by the St. Christopher shrine.

"I need to talk to Sister Juliette Marie. I'm sure she'll want to see you too."

"I'll be there in a minute. I just want a little time to myself."

"I understand. You'll be at the banquet tonight, I hope. Steve and Isabelle will be there. I'm sure they'll want to see you as well. You know Steve's the Chief of Police now."

"No, I didn't. It'll be nice to see them again."

"We didn't talk about it back then, but Steve did a good job of limiting the damage afterward. He reported that it was a case of one nun having a breakdown. The reasons were never mentioned. I don't know if the school would have survived for as long as it has without his discretion in the matter. The full story would have been disastrous."

"That sounds like something he'd do."

"You painted a pretty good picture of him in your book."

"Well, he was a really good guy. I really liked him."

"Yes, I know you did."

She winked and went off to find Sister Juliette Marie.

Marjorie looked over to the place where the door had been. Part of her wished the door was still there. She wasn't sure why she was drawn to the room, why she wanted to see it after everything that happened there. She should, she thought, be repulsed by it, but she wasn't.

She had written about that night in the book that had launched her successful writing career. Maybe that was why the room wasn't something to fear.

Her mind went back to the hall in the hospital as she was leaving Sarah's room that morning. She remembered how she had felt that her life had been changed, but she didn't know how the change would affect the future. Now she knew. As terrible as that night had been, as frightening as that room and everything about it had been, it had brought her to where she was now. She had grown up in that room but hadn't understood that until now. Without that room and everything that happened in it, her life would have taken a completely different path.

As she went in search of Sister Juliette Marie, she felt grateful that her life had been touched by the secret of St. Christopher's Girls School.

About the Author

David Crowley resides in Laurium, Michigan, a small town on the Keweenaw Peninsula (known as the Copper Country) in Michigan's Upper Peninsula. He retired from the United States Postal Service in December 2006. At the time of his retirement, he was the postmaster of Lake Linden, Michigan.

He has been writing poetry since sixth grade. Two of his poems have won grand prize awards in national poetry contests. He has published two collections of poetry, *Somewhere Waits an Angel* and *Seasons of a Lifetime.*

He has published three rhyming children's books, *Twinkle Town, This Town Ain't Big Enough*, and *The Town That Lost Christmas.* Each book has a lesson for children, including being helpful to others and not judging others, anti-bullying, and remembering the true meaning of Christmas. He has also written three full-length plays and a one-act play.

In addition to writing, his interests include singing, acting, directing plays and musicals, theatrical lighting design, organizing large community parades, cooking, and baking. He was the play director for the Houghton, Michigan, middle and high schools from 2007 to 2020. In 2020, he was asked to take the position of play director for the Hancock, Michigan, middle and high schools to start a theater program there. He has also directed a play and two musicals for the Calumet Players, a community theater group in his hometown.

David has three children, Megan, Josh, and Mallory, two grandsons, Noah and Samuel, and two granddaughters, Alexis and Marcella. He also has two step grandsons, Aiden and Brantlee.